Detective King

Book I: Magic and Mystery

By:

LionBolt

Special Thanks to my family for their constant support, Kevin for teaching the class that started this journey, and Sir Arthur Conan Doyle, the true Detective King.

Table of Contents

INTRODUCTION — THE STRANGE, SUPERNATURAL, AND FANTASTIC 1

CHAPTER 1 — THE BOY DETECTIVE AND THE ODD GIRL 9

CHAPTER 2 — THE CASE OF THE DETECTIVE'S ASSISTANT 23

CHAPTER 3 — THE REVELATIONS OF THE DETECTIVE'S ASSISTANT.36

CHAPTER 4 — RUN IN WITH THE DARKNESS 42

CHAPTER 5 — OLD MATES AND MURDERERS..46

CHAPTER 6 — THE CHURCHMOUSE...64

CHAPTER 7 — I AM WILLY, OF THE FOUR 74

CHAPTER 8 — THE LABYRINTH..81

CHAPTER 9 — WILLY—THE PROLETARIAT 95

CHAPTER 10 — THE ADVENTURE OF THE WILL PART I 100

CHAPTER 11 — THE ADVENTURE OF THE WILL PART II......................110

CHAPTER 12 — THE ADVENTURE OF THE NECROMANCER.................127

CHAPTER 13 — THE ADVENTURE OF THE NEWSPAPER COLUMNIST PART I 142

CHAPTER 14 — THE ADVENTURE OF THE NEWSPAPER COLUMNIST PART II 154

CHAPTER 15 — HEALING 169

CHAPTER 16 — WILLY — THE OTHER LONDON 172

CHAPTER 17 — CLUES AND CONSPIRACIES...179

CHAPTER 18 — LILY'S DIARY PART I 193

CHAPTER 19 — INTO THE OTHERWORLD 196

CHAPTER 20 — NIGHT BEFORE BATTLE 208

CHAPTER 21 — LILY'S DIARY PART II 212

CHAPTER 22 — LILY'S DIARY PART III: OWEN 217

CHAPTER 23 — WILLY - BATTLE OF THE TREATY PART I 221

CHAPTER 24 — BATTLE OF THE TREATY PART II 227

CHAPTER 25 — BATTLE OF THE TREATY PART III 233

CHAPTER 26 — BATTLE OF THE TREATY PART IV: THE BOY'S LEGEND

.... 239

CHAPTER 27 — WILLY — TIRED OF HATE 247

CHAPTER 28 — THE PAST 250

CHAPTER 29 — ONE LAST BATTLE 261

CHAPTER 30 — RECOVERY AND EPILOGUE 267

INTRODUCTION — THE STRANGE, SUPERNATURAL, AND FANTASTIC

When you've had a gun pointed at your head as many times as I have, you can't help but wonder if you've made a poor career choice. This particular time, my hands and feet were bound to a chair in a dim, cramped room. A smug, greasy looking cockroach of a man doing the gun pointing—square upon my forehead (and messing up my hair in the process). He was the worst sort of criminal, not a conman or a corrupted authority. No, he was an *actor*. I won't bore you with the abuse I suffered in that dressing room, the actor droning on at length as if his perverse tale were the most dramatic to ever unfold in human history. To be honest, I drowned most of it out, wondering to myself what I fancied for supper that evening.

"Ah, the pain which I have suffered! Do you not see? Once that curtain draws and my glorious plot sets into motion—once that spotlight stealing creature of a woman is finally no more, I shall take my rightful place as—"

"My God, would you shut up already?!" I'd settled on steak (I deserved it) and was quite ready to be done with the whole business. "Do you honestly believe killing an officer of the law is a smart move, mister theatre god, or whatever the hell you fashion yourself as?" Waving around one's authority never hurts in situations like these, though it rarely helps much. The pompous waste of space with a gun grinned.

"Arthur Watson. You are nothing but a child—and what's more, I've trapped you like a mouse. Someone like you is insignificant, and best of all—easily disposed of."

He pulled the trigger, laughing like a madman, until he realised (after much too long) that my brains were still very much in my head and not on the floor as intended. Now it was my turn to laugh as he frantically pulled the trigger again and again in futility. Of course I knew the gun was empty the whole time—that's what made the whole thing so tedious, and a little sad on the actor's part (not that I gave much thought to him). The lights flickered, signalling curtain call. The actor spun around toward the door.

"M-my plan will still work; she will still die!"

"No, she won't." I said as I stood up with ease, as if the ropes binding me were mere yarn. A more imaginative person might think they were undone by some invisible force, but there will be time enough to reveal the secrets of our little magic trick. "I must say, you are probably the sloppiest attempted murderer I've ever seen. Would it have killed you to have given me some sort of challenge?"

The actor stared at me with his jaw open, before opening the door and charging out. Curtains rose over the stage—the spotlight cast upon a woman in an elaborate satin dress. The audience applauded and cheered at her entrance. She took the response in with a deep breath, closed her eyes and began to sing. The murderous actor's face contorted with rage, his breath ragged and sharp.

"If I can't kill her by 'accident', then I've no choice...." He pulled a glass vial out of his suit jacket. He raised his arm high, rearing himself to cast it onto the ground in as dramatic a motion as he could muster. Then a mouse crawled out of his shirt sleeve and snatched the vial. The actor yelped in surprise and disgust, tossing the mouse into the air. I sprinted forward and caught the mouse, but the vial came loose from its grip. That's the thing about paws, they aren't very dexterous. Both of us scrambled to recover it, but crash! We could only watch as it smashed onto the floor into countless shining pieces, the dark purple liquid that it housed spilling onto the floor in a glowing puddle. I flicked the mouse on the back of the head.

"So much for an easy job." He responded by rapidly squeaking at me and waving his arms back and forth in a fury. At least, that's what it would've looked like to an onlooker such as yourself, but once again, all revelations have a time and place, and I'd rather you didn't think I'd lost my mind before I had a chance to properly explain myself. It's not that I care what you think, or that I think anyone will even read these notes, but should one of my sisters get hold of these papers and fancy to publish them to the world, I would prefer to come across as the competent detective I am.

My disagreement with my rodent friend came to a halt as a strong chemical smell began to waft up from the puddle, as it made a sizzling sound. The purple liquid rose off the floor and take on a more solid shape. Muted, echoed sounds of the song on stage and the various gasps of awe and occasional cheers and applause of the sold-out audience were distorted and drowned out by a deep, low, piercing growl. The liquid became a hulking, hairy creature, spouting wings, a spiked tail, and a set of sharp looking teeth. It opened its eyes—a burning red colour—and set its sights on the actress on stage. It took an enormous step, its claws leaving behind large scratch marks on the floor. The smell was making me dizzy- it smelled like the sort of chemicals a mortician would use- an overpowering unnatural scent that wrapped around everything and warned of death. The actor gawked at the creature in awe.

"Yes, yes, it wasn't a scam! Go, kill her!" His glee turned to a pale white terror as the creature arched its massive neck to stare directly at its summoner. The actor backed away before breaking into a run. I sighed as he rushed past me. All I wanted was a quick, straightforward job for once, so I could get back to important work, but alas, this idiot was determined to make me work. I whistled, and the actor was bowled over by a jolly blond fellow who was far larger and stronger than I. Sam grinned and tipped his hat as he settled in on top of the criminal, pinning him to the ground. He waved to me in the obliviously cheerful way he always did, and I returned an admittedly unenthused thumbs up. Sam is a reliable chap, but I often lack the energy to entertain him. With Sam having dealt with the cretin that started this mess, I set the mouse onto the floor.

"Find a window. It should be night by now." I said. The mouse nodded and scurried away. I know, I know, I look mad, but I promise, it will make sense eventually (at least that's what I tell myself).

Now it was time to set my sights on the monster that was slowly making its way toward the stage. How many times have I encountered something like this? Something unbelievable, unscientific, in short—not of this world. I fashion myself as a man of reason and science, evidence and fact. Yet time after time, I'm caught in every matter of magic and the occult. I think you can imagine how great of an annoyance it is for a professional sort of fellow like myself when the illogical forces its way into my business. I called out to the creature, trying to sound as loud and intimidating as I could, though I doubtless announced myself as a snack for the beast rather than a threat. It turned in an instant and bore its beady, blood-red eyes upon me. It stepped, one claw at a time, heat emanating from it, getting more intense with each tremendous step. Little by little it came away from the stage, stalking a new prey... me. I trembled uncontrollably, my

Detective King

breath short—I backed away, careful and slow. Surely anyone would quiver at a sight like this monstrosity. It didn't matter how many beasts of myth and fantasy I witnessed and came to blows with, nor did it matter how many malicious criminals and killers I faced- I'm still human, and the idea of being killed before turning 17 by something as grotesque as the thing that moved ever closer to me, it's breath overwhelming me with a toxic feeling in my stomach, it was enough to make me want to run. More than if it were some thief or murderer, this was something... unknown.

Thus, I bolted down the corridor, past dressing rooms and racks of costumes. The creature followed with the speed of a lion on a hunt. I stopped in front of Sam and the actor and tossed a small dagger onto the floor.

Please work. I thought, as the creature bared down on us, its massive jaws opened wide. I have little faith in these sorts of smoke and mirrors sorcery, but when your life's in danger, you do what you have to and hope for the best. A red glow emitted from the floor beneath the creature, and it was soon frozen in place by lightning-like tendrils. Behind the creature, a girl peeked out and grinned at me. In that sweet, innocent way she does, that makes my face red.

"Th-thanks for the save, Gwen." She trotted over to me and grabbed my wrist. *This case wasn't so bad after all,* I thought as my head danced.

"We need to dismiss it all together." She said as she guided my hand onto the beast's rough, crackling fur. It snarled as it was touched, but it could not move. A scream sounded from a dressing room and a boy stumbled out, yanking a pair of costume trousers on as various objects were hurled in his direction from within the room.

"Owen, it took you long enough." I chuckled. He blushed and pulled on a costume vest that made him look as if he'd appeared out of a lamp and was offering three wishes. The pentacle burned into his chest, denoting his curse easily visible.

LionBolt

"There was a cloud blocking the moon! Anyway, I placed my dagger while I was a mouse. Does that mean I..." Gwen took Owen's hand and placed it on the creature as well. I looked toward the final dagger of the circle. I know next to nothing about magic, only what Gwen teaches us for practical use, but one principle that comes up without fail is how important the magic circle is in casting spells. It's all fanciful nonsense to me. Surely there is some scientific explanation for everything I've witnessed up to now, but who am I to argue with results? Gwen had placed two daggers—I placed one, Owen another, and the final... A young girl stepped into view from behind a costume rack, and strolled up to our group. The idea of going out to the theatre must've excited Elaine. Her raven hair well-brushed, she wore a pale blue dress that was probably an old one of my sister's and her face was that of childlike excitement.

"Miss Veronica's voice is so beautiful!" She said, referring to the actress whose song was reaching its climax, to the silent awe of the crowd. Elaine bounced up and down like, well, a kid. One would never know she was something else.

"A little pitchy for my taste." I said. She stuck out her tongue at me in that faux bratty fashion of hers. She placed her hand on the beast and it began to dissipate into twinkling fractals of light. A scream more monstrous and hateful than anything the magical creature could have uttered poured out of the deranged actor, still in Sam's grip.

"If I can't kill her, I can at least kill you!" He bit down hard on Sam's hand. Sam howled in pain, leaving a large enough opening for the actor to break free and hurl a knife in my direction before being tackled to the ground once more. The knife missed me and my associates, but landed between the creature's eyes. A crackling sound welled up from it, as the creature began to glow blindingly.

"Run." Gwen said as she grabbed Owen and Elaine by the hand and sprinted toward the backstage exit. Sam got the message and pulled the moronic murderer along with him in

Detective King

their direction. I ran in the opposite direction, toward the stage where the actress that started all this trouble had just finished her song, to deafening applause and a shower of rose bouquets. It was the threats to her life that brought me here. My duty as an officer of the law was to protect her and bring the man threatening her life to justice. I'd checked off job number 2, now to finish job 1.

The beast exploded with the force of dynamite and the brightness of a small sun, sending me flying directly into the bowing actress, in full view of the shocked and horrified audience. The room grew dead silent, save for smouldering little flames in the blast's aftermath. My back was thoroughly grilled and blackened, but otherwise I was alright, and aside from the shock of my accidental tackle and a mess being made of her hair, my charge appeared unharmed as well. As I helped her to her feet, the crowd applauded, first slow and quiet, then erupting into an even louder crescendo of noise than before. Miss Veronica fixed her hair the best she could, then leaned in close to me.

"Thank you very much, mister detective, take a bow." I'm not one to shy away from a spotlight, and so I bowed graciously alongside her. It's cases like these, when I get to be the hero I've always strived to be, that remind me why I've entered this often troublesome and thankless profession.

After the actor- Vincent Whatever-his-name-is was safely behind bars, I regaled the renowned actress with my vast powers of deduction, revealing how I came to recognise her co-star as the true culprit. Honestly, it wasn't much of a mystery. It was blatantly obvious by watching him during their rehearsals that he despised the woman and wished for himself to be the centre of attention. That tends to happen when you have someone who's not truly talented, but believes they're incredibly so. When someone who actually possesses that talent comes around and steals their high horse from under them, the green monster of jealousy takes hold, and we get incidents such as this one. What was of vastly greater importance to me and my work was where the cretin got that magic beast. I had the chore of asking him myself in one of Scotland Yard's many interrogation rooms, since who else was going to do it?

"A woman..." He said, looking done with life. "I got that stuff from some woman at the market. She was with a boy about your age, except he looked like the spawn of the devil." I had an idea who he meant. I looked to Elaine, who stood behind him, and she nodded at me- she has a rather fantastic ability to tell if someone was lying. Of course, I can deduce the same easily, but it helps to have a second opinion. "May I ask one thing?" He asked, raising his head just enough to look me in the eye. "I don't understand most of what happened, or how you caught me, but what I don't understand more than anything was... the mouse." I smiled as the same mouse popped out of my pocket.

"Just one of my faithful Detective Knights." Leaving him with a hilariously bewildered expression, I made my exit.

As the brilliant detective I am, I can easily unravel any crime that may come to my attention with ease, but when crime and mystery cross into the realm of the strange, supernatural, and fantastic, my round table of sleuths, each extraordinary in their own unique ways, help me get to the bottom of these dark and unusual cases. The following are the notes that detail the grand mystery that threatened to swallow the whole of London. My knights and I journeyed forth in search of the truth, and uncovered a great deal more. If you have, through whatever means, happened upon this legend of mine, know that everything I've written is the whole and honest truth (I can't say the same for the bits written by the others, but you can trust them for the most part). This is the story of how I came to deserve the title of Detective King.

—Arthur James Watson

CHAPTER 1 — THE BOY DETECTIVE AND THE ODD GIRL

Death. I've always hated and feared death more than anything. It's all-consuming, and no matter how hard you struggle, it'll get you in end. Yet death seems to follow me everywhere I go. I suppose that's no surprise, given my profession as a detective, well, a detective in training. At 16 years old, I was poised to become the youngest graduate of the detective program in the London Police Academy's history. Generally, a police officer is enrolled in the program after two years in the force, followed by vigorous training, courses, and assisting a Detective Inspector. I, however, am a prodigy. True, some strings were pulled to get me into the program, I was still a minor after all, but my talent was undeniable, and in a record amount of time I stood a single case away from graduating from Trainee Detective Constable, or TDC, into a full officer of the Criminal Investigation Department. The case in question was one of intense alarm to the public and had so far stumped even the best minds of Scotland Yard.

Approaching the crime scene, I tried to make myself look spiffy. I straightened my tie—I went with a light blue one that day, matching my eyes- then I adjusted my bowler hat, strands of brown hair peeking out over my forehead, telling me I needed a trim, finally I made sure my coat was properly buttoned and neat. The street looked much the same as any other in this part of the city—homes stretching down the lane, all attached and crowded. The few trees had all turned to various shades of yellow, red, and orange, and leaves littered the street, crunching beneath my feet as I approached the crowd of officers, the badges atop their hats shining in the fading sunlight. They spoke in low tones, concern on their faces, and fell into hushed silence when I approached. *Typical...* I thought. They all glared and growled at me as I passed, like chained up dogs hungry for a meal. I didn't care. They could curse me all they wanted—it wouldn't change the fact that they were beneath me. One of them thrusted his foot out just as I was passing, tripping me. They laughed as I laid on the pavement, face down. I picked myself up, brushed off my coat and readjusted my hat, then continued on my way without a word.

"Look who's 'ere, the so-called genius detective!" One called. I ignored the brute.

"The kid thinks 'imself a hot shot just 'cause he figured out a case or two." said another.

"Ya 'ear he says he's gonna solve this 'ere case by 'imself?" The first one jeered, glaring at me with viscous malice. I knew him from the academy. He was among the most frequent of my abusers. Of course, I'd never bothered to learn his name.

"This will be the last disappearance." I said, walking through the doors without another glance as the group of officers burst into laughter.

"He'll get out of our way when he gets a taste of reality!" One of them said. I'd show them soon enough. I was the greatest detective this world has seen since Sherlock Holmes, and no one would be able to dispute that. Into the crime scene I stepped without a second thought to them.

Crying parents, stone-faced police officers, you get the

idea. Long story short, this latest disappearance marked the 10th child to disappear in London in a month. Out of the children, some were poor, some were well off, some boys, some girls. None of them knew each other, none of their families had any remote connections to each other. The only connecting thread between these disappearances was they vanished from their bedrooms without a trace. Naturally, the first step in each new disappearance is to interview the family and search the child's room. I entered alone—I was in no mind to have one of the many officers of questionable intellect barging in and making a mess of a crime scene. Yet this room was much the same as the others—no struggle, no footprints, or blood, no evidence of a connection to the other disappearances, nothing.

In the end, I left this latest crime scene with more questions than answers. I had dealt with disappearances before. Generally, they were rather easy—in almost any case, a family member was to blame, and with luck, the missing person would be retrieved, though more likely a body would be uncovered instead. But this case was very different. There was no such thing as a random set of victims. If this were indeed a serial kidnapping incident, there'd be a way to connect the cases, no matter how faint or contrived. I recalled a similar case a few decades earlier in which a religious sect abducted several children, but Scotland Yard was unaware of any kind of sect large enough to pull that off in London, much less get away with it for this long.

After combing over the crime scene for many, many tiring hours, I resigned to head home and think things over, rather than take up more of the grieving family's time. The wind picked up as I walked home, chilling my entire body as if it were blowing right through me. I'd turned into the alley where the stairs leading up to my flat laid, when I stopped and turned my head around. I had a strong feeling I was being followed and stood still, squinting to see what was in the shadows—but all was still. Slowly, I edged toward the stairs

LionBolt

and came up to my door when, to my shock, the door was unlocked and already opened. I could see light coming from within and peered inside to see who the intruder might be. It was a cheap, one-room flat with a small kitchen, a bed, couch, closet, and a water closet. I could tell the light was coming from the kitchen, and I could hear the clanging of pots and dishes and smell something savoury. Slowly, and carefully, I sneaked through the door, keeping my body pressed against the wall. Who knew what maniac may be lurking in there, trying to steal from me (not that I had much to steal). I had reached the edge of the foray and peeked into the room when...

"BOO!" I nearly jumped out of my skin as I was tackled to the ground by the burglar- none other than my younger sister.

"Lily! What are you doing here!?" I was red-faced. I didn't have time to deal with her childish antics.

"Did I scare you?" Lily asked with a devilish smirk.

"N-no, 'course not." It wasn't a lie. Promise. Lily grinned and broke away from me. She trotted over to the kitchen table and pulled out a chair for me.

"You've been working all day. I thought you would like something homemade when you got home." She gestured to a plate of freshly prepared food, still steaming.

"Oh... th-thanks." I was in no mood to eat, but I knew better than to argue with her. Never was there a more stubborn girl on this planet than my sister. The meal largely consisted of playing with my fork and trying my best to avoid Lily's glare and occasional prompts to take another bite. Lily was a slight, delicate girl of twelve years. She was never to be seen without something frilly and respectable on and her auburn hair tied in a neat braid. Her will was such that I struggled to say no to her, which has in the past resulted in a multitude of shopping bags and even more headaches and distractions for her poor brother. The meat was over-cooked and mostly stayed on my plate. My sister's face was illuminated by the kitchen lamp, and I couldn't help but notice how much she'd grown since I last saw her. I lived alone since my flat was a mere walk away from Scotland Yard. It had been at least a year since I moved out.

"Shouldn't you be getting home? It's pretty late." I tried. Lily wasn't about to take that bait.

"Shouldn't you come home every once in a while? Father worries about you." I looked away and uttered a sound of disgust. Silence befell the table. My excuse for living alone was to be close to The Yard for work and my studies, but it was no secret that I could not bear to stay under the same roof as the venerable Doctor John H. Watson. I don't much care to talk about what happened between us. Even Lily doesn't know the full story, but for all her efforts to reconcile us regardless, I stayed away from the old house as much as possible and kept to my work. All alone, just like I wanted, happy as could be...

"Arthur, tell me what's wrong? Is a case worrying you?" She had crossed her arms and stared at me seriously.

"I just can't find any evidence. This makes ten victims gone without a trace." I said.

"Maybe a ghost took them away!" Lily fashioned a napkin into a sort of ghost puppet, patting it up into the air and allowing it to float down back onto her hand.

"This isn't funny! My whole career depends on this."

"And the children, and their families."

"Right, sure. But you know they don't take me seriously. If I don't prove myself, I'll never..." I trailed off, staring into space as I often do. Lily rested her head on her arms.

"I miss you, Arthur. And I know father does too, even if he doesn't say it. I wish... you'd come back to us someday." I snapped back to reality and glanced at Lily.

"Sorry, did you say something?" I didn't really want to have this conversation, but Lily was already at the door, placing a flower adorned hat on her head.

"Nothing. Take care of yourself, Arthur. Stop by the house soon—you don't need to be alone forever." Before I could respond, she was out the door. I leaned back in his chair and groaned.

She's so annoying. Why can't everyone just leave me alone and let me figure things out for myself? I thought, shaking my head and gathering my files. There was no time to be worrying about Lily, or anyone else. I had work to do, and I was going to get it done by myself on my own terms.

After a long night of theorising, I was nowhere near an answer. I headed back to Scotland Yard to look at their records. It's quite often the answer to a question in the present can be found in the past. Scotland Yard was a large redbrick complex on the Thames, swarming with officers and administrative personnel. It was no place for children, or so I was told incessantly any time I got anywhere near the place. As I hurried down the halls, I was subject to dirty glances and malicious jeers—the other trainees calling me names or curses, while the older officials acted as if I didn't exist at all. It was a common belief amongst the whole of the force that my presence was nothing more than a publicity stunt meant to highlight the shortage of men in the aftermath of The Great War, using the son of one of London's most famous inhabitants. Whether a stunt or not, I've proved myself more capable than plenty of seasoned officers and have managed to maintain my place—prompting The Yard to provide me with ever more demanding jobs in an effort to smoke me out.

I tried my very best to avoid talking to or even making eye contact with anyone, dodging into a hallway—when, of course, I was grabbed from behind and pinned against a wall. He was quite older than me, though still young by adult standards— probably early 20s—I could tell he had walked to work, as his clothes still smelled of the earthiness of the rain, and mud still clung to his shoes. He got up late, as evidenced by the shoddy job he did of dressing himself, with some buttons misplaced and a cuff undone. His face was in the shadow of the hat that stood atop his dark hair, which he had dropped at some point, as there was a mud stain along the brim.

"Hello again, little lad." He said with a spiteful sneer. "Having fun playing detective?"

"Clearly not as much fun as you've been having. Who gave you that red mark on your neck?" I asked, causing him to turn red all over. He reared up to punch me when his fist was caught and he was pushed back. My feet returned to their rightful place on the ground as my assaulter stared down at my saviour, Samuel Tristan.

"Gee Tim, didn't know you were so bashful, but it's nothing to get violent over." Sam said with a contemptuous smirk. Tim glared from Sam to me, then shoved his way down the hall in the direction I came from. Mister Tristan looked at me with that overly friendly grin of his. "You Alright, Arty?"

"I'm fine, and don't call me that. Oh, and thanks." I tipped my hat and attempted to scurry off to the archives. The last thing I wanted was to have one of those dreaded things called a conversation.

"Grumpy as always, I see! No worries, Ol' Sam's here to help!" He placed his hands on his hips and took a heroic posture.

"No, thanks." I said, quickening my pace away from him.

"You sure?!" He called after me.

"Yes." I called back.

"Everyone needs help sometimes, y'know!"

"I'm not everyone!"

"So you remind me! Well, good luck. I'll be at the dorms if you need me!" With that, I finally reached the elevator door and lost sight of my troublesome classmate. While I was almost four years younger than him, I was actually his senior at the academy. I was the subject of universal hatred, frustration, or contempt. No one accepted me as an adult or a detective, except Sam, who was friendly to just about everyone, and was my sole supporter in the halls of Scotland Yard. That didn't mean I was interested in being best-mates. I would prefer the term acquaintance, but that would not stop the youngest son of the Tristan estate.

The archives are a large warehouse-like storage space deep below the ground, with row upon dusty row of files dating back to the founding of the Metropolitan Police in 1829. I squatted down and picked out a box of some decades old files and rifled through for insight. I'd spend hours down there, because Sherlock Holmes' words rang true, that genuinely novel acts of crime were rare, and that most things, however unusual, could usually be referenced from an earlier incident somewhere in the world if you dig far enough. And so I dug, but just as I had felt the day before, there was the gnawing suspicion that someone was watching me. I turned my head toward the door. Nothing.

"Tristan? Is that you? I told you I'm fine on my own." Silence. I was the only living soul in that room. So why did I feel so uneasy? Why was it so cold all of the sudden? Why did I have the urge to run? I gathered some files of interest and bolted out of the room. As I got in the elevator, I felt a gust of air hit my face and I shivered. The elevator always made a racket of creaks and mechanical sounds, but this time was different. It was as if a symphony of screeching metal surrounded me from all sides. I began to sweat, and my breath became fast and shallow. I wanted to scream. Then the noise stopped and the hallway on the ground floor of Scotland Yard was before me once again.

I must be sleep deprived... I thought, feeling stupid for getting so worked up over nothing. But I had no time for rest, I still had work to do, and there was still daylight to do it in. That was another peculiar aspect of the missing children's case—it was always during the day when the victims went missing...

Public transportation is a cruel and merciless beast, and I struggle to imagine why anyone would voluntarily use it. Sitting next to strangers is one thing, it's another to be

Detective King

cramped between two dozen of them in a bucking, nausea inducing streetcar.

As much as I hated the means of transport, it was vital that I revisited each disappearance site. Thus, I zig-zagged around the city, first to an upscale mansion, then to the hovel of a seamstress, and on and on, trying to piece together some rhyme or reason, some pattern to make sense of it all, but I saw none. I briefly had the theory that there were numerous kidnappers at work in various parts of the city, but if that were so, why take turns? None of the children disappeared on the same day, and invariably, they disappeared under the same circumstances. The one and only link between any of them I saw, even after digging through the backgrounds of every parent, uncle, aunt, grandparent, estranged sibling, cousin, etc, was that their homes were always within walking distance to a park and a police station. One victim's house was next door to a station in South London, which made the entire affair that much more outrageous, as if it were a challenge. Throughout my journey through the city, I continued to have the same lingering feeling that I was being tailed. When I turned my head, nothing out of the ordinary. When I paused and listened, there was only the sound of passersby, cars, or paperboys. Truth be told, I wanted to be followed, for the only person (or people) who would follow me would be the one I'm searching for- the culprit. By house number 7 the sun was setting, and I was getting impatient, so I headed home, as house 7 wasn't too far a walk to my flat, and I was curious what my pursuer would do. The chilly air set in, leaves crunched underfoot, and shadows grew larger and encompassed much of the street. I turned into an alley, a dark, lonesome place of endless brick, and there—stronger than even in the archive—was the feeling that someone was sneaking up right behind me. Of course, I got a rush of exhilaration. I was ready this time. It wasn't a phantom of the mind—this was a criminal, who was offering himself to me straightaway, cutting out the hard part of finding him and sending me a ticket straight to graduation. I'd finally have recognition, respect, a title, and a badge, and I simply couldn't wait anymore. When the feeling was directly behind me, I sprang and tackled my pursuer hard onto the ground for the arrest. My triumph was quickly replaced by utter horror and embarrassment, as I saw I'd tackled not a dangerous criminal, but a young girl.

"Owww! Get off me!" I quickly sprang up and offered her my hand.

"I'm so sorry! I thought—" The girl batted my hand aside and got up on her own. She looked younger than 10, had long, dark hair, a neat light blue dress on, and a pair of green eyes that looked more worn and tired than a girl her age should.

"Next time look before doing something weird like that!" I didn't understand. I was sure I'd been followed... what if...

"Hey, were you... following me?" I asked in as courteous a manner as I could muster.

The girl looked around, seemingly unsure how to respond, before darting away from me around a corner. I hung my head low in disappointment.

Well, so much for that... I rounded the last corner and could see my flat block. The building was such that an alleyway in the back featured a staircase that led up to my second storey flat. As I ascended the staircase, I turned around to see the young girl standing behind the corner of the building as if she were attempting to hide from me but doing a sorry job of it.

"Does she think I can't see her?" I said to myself, loud enough for her to hear. The girl gasped, ducking back behind the wall. I groaned and buried my face in my hat.

I've no time for this nonsense! Deciding to ignore her, I continued up the stairs, only to turn again to see the girl had emerged once more and was standing at the bottom of the staircase. *Enough of this already.*

"Well? Why are you following me? I don't have any change to hand out if that's what you're after." She looked up at me, looking more serious than I'd ever seen a child stare.

"You're a detective, aren't you?" She said. I was obviously taken aback by this. Who was this girl? I cleared my throat.

"Of course, the name's Arthur. You're lookin' at the youngest detective accepted to-"

"Yeah, okay, I get it." The girl interrupted. "Are you looking for the children that have gone missing?"

At this, I sat down and gazed at her—trying to notice every minuscule detail. This was no ordinary child. Her face was embraced in the orange and red of the sunset light, whilst the long shadows of the buildings all around us enveloped the ground beneath her. Not a speck of dirt on her, nor signs of any mistreatment, skinny but not malnourished. It was just those eyes of hers staring back at me as if an unseen wisdom laid behind them.

"How do you know about that? Who are you?" I asked.

"I... I know one of the missing children. She's my friend." The girl said. She shuffled her feet and looked down as she spoke.

She's probably lying... "Do you have any idea what may have happened to your friend?" I'd try to probe as much information out of her as I could, just to be sure.

"N-not exactly..."

"Where did you last see her?"

"I don't remember."

"Can you point me to any strangers that may have talked to her? Or any other clues?" I was tiring of this strange girl.

"No, but I can still help! I have excellent observation skills." She said. I laughed, rose to my feet and turned to the door, waving her off.

"You should head home. It's too dangerous for you to get involved." I said over my shoulder. At the door, I searched my pockets for my keys, only for the girl to walk up and dangle them in front of me.

"Looking for these?" She unlocked the door and let herself in. "Some detective!" She said over her shoulder. I stared after her in disbelief. Indignant, I strode after her. I wasn't about to be toyed with by a child.

The girl bounced about, taking in every corner of my little flat, and touching just about everything. I stomped in, incredulous at the invasion of my privacy from this trickster of a girl. She noticed my red face and tossed me the keys, which I dropped in a sorry show of incoordination. It's not my fault! I wasn't ready! In any case, she laughed at me and sat on my kitchen table as I picked up the keys.

"You really live here? It's so small."

"Wha- why- y- I... GET OUT!" I had had enough of this brat.

The girl was ignoring me. Her attention turned to a dishevelled mess of newspapers and files on the table beside her.

"Ew, these all have dead bodies on them. Why-" I scooped my papers up and away from her.

"Research material." I said. The girl smirked and hopped off the table and onto my bed, which she jumped on, all whilst keeping her gaze focused on your disgruntled detective. After a few bounces, she stopped and sat, her gaze becoming more serious.

"I want to help you." She said.

"Help me?! You stalked me here, stole my keys and barged into my home uninvited!" I was seething—my fists hurt, they were clenched so tight—but I reminded myself this was a mere child. I was better than this. Deep breath. "Where are your parents, anyway? Isn't it about time you got home?"

The girl fell silent. She looked uncertain how to answer, and elected not to say anything, looking down and away from me. I glimpsed her face—a sad, lonely expression I knew all too well.

"Oh... I see..." A suffocating silence ensnared the room.

I was 12 years old on the worst day of my life. White light

flooded into the room from the window beside her bed as I sat in a chair at her side. The others had cleared out, and it was just me and her one last time. My mother laid there, hardly moving—yet she gazed at me with that same sparkle she always had. Like a magic spell, she always knew how to calm me down, or lift me up with just a glance and smile. With great effort, she lifted her hand and wiped a tear off my cheek. I hadn't realised I was crying.

"Now, now, my little King Arthur can't cry. He's stronger than that, right?" She said in a raspy whisper before entering another coughing fit. I nodded my head and wiped my face with my sleeve. With my other arm, I grasped our favourite book- *The Legend of King Arthur*. "You're going to grow up and become even stronger and show the world how brilliantly you can shine." I nodded again; I couldn't bring myself to speak because I knew I'd lose control of myself.

"Promise me be you'll be a good king and always stand for justice." She held out her pinky finger, and with my trembling hand, I entwined mine with hers. She smiled at me one last time, then she closed eyes, and let go of my hand.

That isn't a fond memory of mine, and it takes something out of the ordinary to draw it back up. This girl was clearly out of the ordinary, and I determined myself to understand why—if she ended up helping me on the disappearance case, that'd be a bonus.

"Alright, I'll give you a chance. You can be my temporary assistant." I said. She nodded her head and her face brightened up a little. "What's your name?" I asked.

"The name's Elaine. You better not disappoint me, Arthur." And with that outrageous remark, she slipped off her shoes and climbed into my bed, turning over to face away from me. I shook my head, too tired to care anymore. I laid on the couch, which was a tad too small to fit me, and endeavoured to get some sleep. A long day awaited me with my new assistant.

Detective King

CHAPTER 2 — THE CASE OF THE DETECTIVE'S ASSISTANT

Elaine skipped along the sidewalk, past people on their errands, shops, and stands, pausing now and then to look at some trinket or sweet looking pastry. I trudged behind her, becoming increasingly suspicious that this girl was putting me through some elaborate con. She insisted she could lead me to some places her supposed friend frequented, but whenever I tried to press her for details, something conveniently interrupted us, or she would run off to browse something or point out some insignificant landmark or curiosity. We'd reached the upper class shops and well-dressed shoppers on Regent Street when I'd finally reached the end of my patience. Elaine was peeking into a store window, without the slightest care in the world, while I had the weight of that world on my shoulders.

"Excuse me, assistant, but I'm getting rather fed up with being led around like this!" I said.

"I know, I know, we're almost there!"

"Not a single place you've led me has helped at all, you know!"

LionBolt

"Like I said, these are the places my friend would always go, don't blame me if you can't figure it out, mister detective!" We glared at each other, then continued on our way in a huff.

"Oh! Arthur, what are you doing here?!" From across the street, we heard Lily calling out to me and, to our horror, she charged forth with cars barely missing her and the sound of honks and horns blaring. She reached us and smiled at me as if nothing extraordinary had happened and come to think of it—Lily did foolhardy things like that all the time, so I suppose it wasn't out of the ordinary, though that didn't change how terrifying it was to watch.

"Sooooo, have you caught the ghost yet?" She asked. Elaine stiffened up and grabbed onto my sleeve. Leave it to my sister to scare a kid like that.

"Are you really still going on about that? There's no such thing." I said, puffing up my chest and taking a confident stance. "It is only through science and reason that we can find truth! Everything can be explained and reasoned through. Look no further than the great Sherlock Holmes—"

"There you go about Mister Holmes again!" Lily said with a sigh. Elaine tugged my coat.

"Now who's getting distracted?"

"Oh, you're right, sorry. We'll see you later Lily!" I waved to her and continued onward. Lily had an odd face as I left, as if she wanted to say something, but I was in the middle of an investigation.

— ⚜ —

After the Lily incident, Elaine led me through a series of shops, restaurants, and various other localities of suspect importance that she claimed her friend (whose existence I still doubted) would often go. It was when we visited the market, however, when something... unusual took place. Elaine happily marched forward past stalls of produce, trinkets, clothing. Anything that could be legally sold on the street was represented. The murmurs of the crowd and the merchants,

Detective King

the smells of spices, grilled cuisine, and a garden's worth of flowers. Elaine was enthralled by it all, stopping at nearly every stand she passed, admiring one thing, or whining for me to buy her something else. I tried to be patient, I really did, but after some time, enough was enough.

"Elaine, you're wasting my time! Either you take me somewhere worthwhile, or I continue to investigate alone!" I crossed my arms and leaned against a wall next to stall.

"Calm down, we've only been here ten minutes!" She said. I flipped open my pocket watch.

"Well, that may be so, but I assure you, I've been to this market countless times. There's no lead to be found here."

"Maybe you should look with a more open mind this time?" She grinned, before heading off toward some other stall selling fake jewellery.

"Open m—What is that supposed to mean?!" I stomped after her, which, for whatever reason, amused her.

"Come on, if you can't catch me, how are you supposed to catch the culprit?" She called. A crowd of people had formed between us and I struggled to push through to her.

"I knew it. You're just toying with me, aren't you?" As I spoke, I lost sight of her in the crowd. I dodged out from the side and judging by her speed and the directions she'd be able to go—I could deduce her most likely point of exit from the crowd. I skirted around the crowd and waited for her there, and who emerged in her place? Two trainee detectives who had a particularly strong dislike of me.

"Why, hey there, Arty!" One of them said, flicking off my hat and ruffling my hair. "Say, the chief's getting impatient. Best hurry, brat!" He pushed me to one side while his friend laughed and trampled on my hat. After they'd gone, Elaine reappeared, standing next to me as I picked up my hat and brushed off the dead leaves and dirt. I didn't look at her. It was too embarrassing.

"Elaine... I appreciate you trying to help... but I need to-" A scream sounded from down the market, and we both turned our heads to see a hooded figure rushing through the crowd in our direction. As he passed, I could see he was clutching a purse. Elaine looked from the thief to me, then back again. Her face became red with frustration.

"Aren't you going to chase after him?"

"Dealing with petty thieves isn't really my problem to deal with. I'm sure someone will..." I stood in shock as Elaine rushed off toward the criminal. And she was gaining on him!

"The hell are you doing!? That's dangerous!" I ran after her, pushing past startled bystanders and knocking over a basket of apples. Reaching an alley, I was confounded by what I saw—Elaine standing over the robber, who sat on the ground as if in a daze. I walked up to him and crouched down to get a good look. He was in complete shock. His eyes were open, but they weren't looking at anything. His limbs were still and if it weren't for his shallow breathing and low mumbling to himself, I would have thought he had died sitting up. I looked up at Elaine.

"H-how did you-"

"I didn't do anything. From the looks of it..." She picked up the purse from where it laid next to the thief. "He would've dropped it anyway." I looked closely at the boy, trying to discern what was wrong with him... why I felt so uneasy about him...

"Drugs perhaps? But that doesn't seem quite right... Wait, are you..." I lifted his hood, revealing a mane of black hair. His face was definitely familiar, but it was in such a strained state, I couldn't be certain. "You can't be..." I rose and turned away. I didn't want to be certain, and he wasn't my concern anyway. I left him behind, with Elaine following closely behind.

"Shouldn't you arrest him or something?"

"That's not really my job, but I will call it in. He may need medical attention after all. More importantly—what on earth were you thinking, going after a criminal like that?!"

"I know, I wasn't thinking. It's just that you weren't going

Detective King

to do anything! What's the point of being a detective if you don't stop bad guys or help people in need?" I paused at the mouth of the alley. Not once in the years that I'd been working toward becoming a detective had I thought about it like that. To me, it was just a job. Detective work's what I was skilled at. There was no other option.

"It's just what I have to do, and if I can't do it, what good am I?" The woman whose purse was snatched caught up with us and I returned it to her. She wore a scarf over her head, so I couldn't get a good look, but there was something familiar about her too. I followed Elaine out of the market, and she marched on just as before, next taking me to my least favourite stop on our tour of central London.

The church was big and bright, with tall stained glass windows and a few quiet parishioners populating the pews. Yet the church was uniquely unpleasant. I had assumed that strange feeling of being watched had been stress and Elaine when she had followed me earlier, but as soon as I entered in the cathedral, I had an overwhelming feeling that I needed to rush as far away as possible from that place. It was a dark, empty feeling, one of dread and fear. I resisted the urge to run, but an anxiety was welling up in me, which Elaine took notice of.

"Are you alright? You're trembling?" I looked down at my hands to see she was right. I couldn't make sense of it. Why was I so scared?

"I'm f-fine. Maybe it's just that I haven't been in a place like this in a while." I spotted a boy sweeping off to the side of the chapel and trotted over to him, in more of a hurry than I'd intended. He was dressed in monk's robes, yet he couldn't have been less than two years younger than me. I could tell he was skinny, and his eyes looked heavy with lack of sleep, but otherwise he seemed well-kept—his light blond, almost silver hair was freshly cut. I did, however, give him a startle when I approached him.

"Hey, you, I need to ask you something!" I said in a hurried, impatient voice. The boy jumped and dropped his broom. He looked up at me, then from side to side.

"I- I'm not supposed to talk to anyone without permission..." He said.

"Nonsense, I'm a Detective Constable." I left out that I was still a *Trainee* Detective Constable, and at the same time reminded myself that I never reported in with my supervisor, I was going to be in a bit of trouble when I got back, but that was an issue for later.

"B-but you're a kid..." He said. Now I was angry.

"Well, so are you! So, little monk, tell me about your congregation. Any of them have children go missing?" The boy looked somewhat relieved, despite my leaning in toward him.

"Oh, that's all you want to know? The police already questioned Father Michael about that. One boy that went missing did come here. He was even friends with some of the orphans we house, but I can't recall seeing someone suspicious or anything... except maybe you."

"Very funny... well, if that's all, why aren't you allowed to speak to people without permission? What are you afraid of me finding?" The boy backed up against the wall.

"Please, it has nothing to do with your investigation."

"What are you hiding?"

"Nothing, now go before I get in trouble." I lost control of myself and thrust my fist into the wall beside him. Elaine grabbed me and dragged me away from the poor monk boy. We came outside and sat on the steps overlooking the street before us.

"What was that all about?" She asked.

"I don't know, I just..." My face was buried in my hands, I felt so embarrassed at my behaviour. "What am I doing? Investigating with a child, intimidating another? I feel so on edge, and I don't know why..." Elaine placed her hand on my back and patted it.

"You're really a piece of work, aren't you? I get you want to solve the case, but do you have to do it with such a sad face all the time? If you're going to find those kids, maybe you should think more like a kid." I looked up and smiled, a spark of ingenuity brewing in my mind.

"You may be right... Let's go." I said, pulling Elaine up with me as I stood.

"Okay... where?" She asked.

"You tell me, where would a kid go?"

The Regent's Park is a large, sprawling green area in northwest inner London. Even in the cloudy, gloom-filled days of autumn the park had a certain life to it, with children playing in the fields, or getting a treat from a stall, while their parents sat quietly and enjoyed the patch of serenity in the old city.

"So, you came here with your friend often?" I asked Elaine, who bounced along merrily beside me.

"Oh, yes, she and I came here all the time, especially in the summer." She attempting to catch a leaf as it flew by.

"I see... you know that monk said it was a boy that went missing from the congregation..." Elaine paused. I was curious how she'd try to spin that.

"Oh, well... was he a boy? Perhaps I just hadn't noticed." She laughed awkwardly as she ran ahead, chasing her leaf.

If she thinks I'm going to buy that... A man pushed against me, nearly knocking me over.

"'Scuse me, lad." He tipped his hat and continued on his way. I chuckled to myself.

"What's so funny?" Elaine asked. I pointed to the man.

"Elaine, reach into that man's left pocket for me." She looked from me to the old man in confusion, then reluctantly caught up to him and placed her hand in his pocket. Her eyes widened as she pulled out my pocket watch. She tossed it back to me, and I returned it to my own pocket where it belonged.

LionBolt

"First rule of detective work: Everyone's suspect!" Elaine flashed a face that said "get over yourself", then grinned in a most evil manner as she grabbed my hand. Before I could ask where she was taking me, she'd plunged me into a massive pile of leaves. My head popped out of the heap, with my hair a mess. No way was I going to let her get away with that! I dragged her in after me and we began pelting each other with leaves. The people around us started giving me strange looks, and I remembered I was supposed to be a professional. I batted down a torrent of leaves Elaine flung in my direction and located my hat.

"Alright, enough fun—we still have a job to do..." I said, pulling Elaine to her feet with me.

"I think your problem is you're too serious! Why are you a detective, anyway?"

"Because it's what I'm good at, so I want to be the best."

"But... you seem so unhappy. Is it really worth it?"

"Of course! Being happy isn't important—This is my job, my duty!" I said, a little too loudly. "I will be the next Holmes, and all the world will know it." Elaine looked at me with an expression that baffled me—it was pity. As if I were a kitten left on the side of a road, she gazed with a sadness beyond her years, then turned away from me.

"I think that's really dumb. Live your own life, you only have one." She said. I was going to respond when I noticed a couple sitting on a bench, feeding some birds.

"I know them..." I said, half to myself. Elaine pulled on my sleeve.

"Let's not bother anyone else today. Come on, buy me a snack over there." She pointing toward a stand in the opposite direction. I pulled away from her.

"What's gotten into you? I'm going to ask them some questions." I tossed her a coin and approached the couple. "Pardon me," I said, tipping my hat. The sorrow in their eyes as they looked up at me was suffocating. "Your child has gone missing recently, yes?"

Detective King

"I recognise you, you're the young detective!" The father said.

"Would your son visit this park often?"

"Oh yes, he loves this park very much, all the neighbourhood children come here." The mother answered.

"I see... when did visit last?"

"The day before he disappeared, about a week ago. But wasn't the park searched?" The father said. "They even added security." He glancing at a passing patrol of officers.

"That's right... I'm beginning to form a hypothesis, I assure you—I have just one more question..."

I returned to Elaine with triumph and swagger.

"Come along, Assistant, I've discovered our culprit!" She looked at me in disbelief.

"But... how?!"

"You'll see soon enough. All we need to do now is collect our evidence and set our trap." I took her hand and led her away from the park. The wind picked up, and the cold gripped me like death. As I walked with her, the voices of the passersby became muffled and distant. The autumn leaves and city streets became blurred, and that anxiety, that feeling of dread and terror returned, worse than ever. I stumbled and fell onto my knee. I could hear whispers all around me... they sounded like children. One rang out particularly loud, calling my name.

"Arthur!" Elaine was shaking me, and I snapped out of my trance. "Arthur! What happened?" I was still dazed as she helped me up. Before I could answer, I felt another rush of cold and everything went dark.

I woke up in my bed, back in my flat. I looked to my side and saw Elaine lying on my bedside. Evidently she'd been at my side for a while, as it was night. I heard a sound from the kitchen and sat up. Sam was walking over to me with a bowl in his hand.

"You're awake! Thank God, I was worried." He said. Elaine stirred and yawned, then sat beside my bed and held my hand.

"Don't scare me like that, I can't lose my detective." She said. Sam placed the bowl of soup on my nightstand and sat in the chair Elaine had previously occupied.

"I found you lying on the sidewalk with a big crowd looking over you. What happened?" He asked.

"I... I don't know, it was so sudden. I just remember feeling real cold."

"You're obviously working yourself too hard. When was the last time you got a good night's sleep, Hm? I'd bet you can't remember. Here's what you're gonna do, take a day or two off, send me out to do your dirty work. You can't do a thing if you don't take care of yourself." He said.

"But..."

"No, you're not arguing, you're listening—stay in bed." He said.

"Fine, mother." I said sarcastically.

"Oho, you must feel better already! Now eat, that's the only recipe I know how to make, so you better like it." It wasn't very good, but I ate the whole bowl anyway. I told Sam about my activities and my theory about the case.

"So I need you to go to as many parks as you can and take note of everything and everyone." I said.

"You were really going to do that by yourself?" He asked. I scratched my head.

"Well, not totally alone, I mean..."

"Imaginary friends don't count, Arty." I tossed my pillow at his face, which he caught with grace. When he tossed it back, it bounced off my head and back to its place on my bed. I rested my head on my hand and looked over at Elaine. She was uncharacteristically quiet, looking down, only occasionally glancing up. Sam headed to the door and saluted.

Detective King

"Remember, no moving until you're all rested!" I waved him away, and he closed the door behind him.

"Elaine, why don't you get some sleep? I feel fine now." I said. In the light of my lamp, she looked up at me with such a sad expression.

"You're sure you're okay?"

"Of course, I'm not going down so easily. Tomorrow we'll start to put an end to this whole business."

"I thought you were going to rest tomorrow!"

"When did I ever agree to that? Trust me, I'm fine—I'll even take an entire week off after this. We can find you a home too, y'know." She got quiet again and shuffled over to the couch. She lied down and close her eyes.

"I'm glad I'm not your sister, or I'd constantly worry." She said with a yawn before drifting to sleep. I turned out the light and passed out as soon as my head hit the pillow.

A week of gallivanting about London, getting info from Sam, and pouring over every detail passed, and I had gathered the force of the Metropolitan Police at Regent's Park. Throughout the investigation, Elaine was a perfect assistant. Well, not perfect, teasing, and snarky remarks were an unavoidable hazard, but that aside she stuck by my side everywhere I went, took notes when I needed her to, even brought me tea while I worked into the night, and reminded me when I was pushing myself too hard. Now, finally, all would be resolved, and I would show everyone who doubted me I truly am the next Holmes.

"I still don't get it!" Elaine said, marching alongside me behind a row of officers. "Who are you going to arrest? Who do you think did it?"

"You're sure you don't know? Where did those 'observational skills' go?" She turned red and stomped her foot.

"Fine, don't tell me." She stormed off ahead of me,

disappearing into the flood of officers. The police soon surrounded Quentin Baker, the man who attempted to pick-pocket me earlier. As the officers took out their handcuffs, Baker made a futile try at running. While the constables restrained him, he squirmed and yelled and cursed.

"I haven't done anything! Let me go!"

"Enough, you're under arrest for the crime of serial kidnapping-" The inspector couldn't finish reading the charges as Baker spotted me and lunged forward, snarling.

"You! I'll kill you! I ain't done nothin' an' you know it! I'll make sure they-" Sam appeared between us and punched him in the jaw, knocking him unconscious and dislodging a tooth or two. Sam dusted off his hands and turned to me with a thumbs up.

"That shut him up." He said. I nodded and smiled, a little shaken up. The Chief Inspector approached me and patted me on the back. He was a stout man with a thick moustache and top-hat that looked to me like relics of the previous century.

"Brilliant work, Watson!" He said with an artificial extra dose of gusto, like someone congratulating a child who had just beaten them at some game. I'm sure there was relief a suspect had finally been taken in, but my success meant headache for the department at large. "There is still the matter of finding the missing children, but that won't be an issue for you, I presume..."

"Of course not, sir. I—" The chief leaned in very close to me.

"Life is about to get very difficult for you, being a full detective, you know that, right?"

"Y-yes, sir, but I think I've proven—"

"It doesn't matter if you've proven anything—this isn't an easy job. I expect you to produce the bodies within the week." With that, he trotted away, taking his suffocating air of self-importance with him.

"You'll see just what I can prove." I said under my breath.

Detective King

Sam grabbed me and lifted me up with a cheer.

"Hooray for the greatest detective in London!" He cried, while the other detectives stared daggers at us and I squirmed and protested to be let down. I admit that I milked the glory of the moment. Once I was back on the ground, I stepped onto a bench, spread out my arms in a wide, grand gesture, and shouted:

"I AM the greatest detective in this city! Ha ha! The world shall know the name of Arthur Watson!" Sam laughed, while the other officers had mostly scattered and ignored me, so my voice almost echoed in the empty park. Only the lonely howl of the wind and the light crunching of leaves broke the silence. Something was missing. What was it? Who...

"Elaine?" I called. No answer. I looked around—it was just me and Sam. I'd expected some sarcastic applause and a witty remark from my young assistant, mocking my grandstanding, but she was nowhere to be seen. Surely she wasn't that cross with me?

"You alright, Arty?" Sam asked. "Maybe we should get you out of this cold." While I nodded absentmindedly, I hadn't really heard him as I trudged past the trees, hedges, and ponds of the park, looking in every direction for Elaine.

I can't be wrong... I have my culprit, she's not... That dark feeling of dread crept in and took hold of my heart once again. I stumbled and gasped for breath. Sam rushed over to me, but I had already risen to my feet and continued on my search without a word, as if in a trance. He was probably shouting at me, but I didn't hear a word. I halted, frozen in place. It wasn't the cold that froze me—it was a coin. The shilling that I'd given Elaine laid on the grass. I was certain it was the same one. I remember the distinctive scratch mark that gave Queen Victoria a moustache. My fingers ran through every groove, looked at every angle, but my mind stayed blank and utterly useless. She had vanished without a trace in broad daylight, just like the missing children.

LionBolt

CHAPTER 3 — THE REVELATIONS OF THE DETECTIVE'S ASSISTANT

I returned to my flat in a daze. I'd retraced our steps from the past week, looking for even the slightest sign of Elaine. Did I scare her away? Or was it more sinister? It was probably both, but the coin was the only piece of evidence proving her existence that I could produce. Even Holmes needed data to apply his deductive process. With no evidence or clues, a detective is mostly useless, working on mere theory and speculation. I laid on my bed and looked up at the old, cracked ceiling. Was is always so quiet in here? And musty?

Maybe they're all right... I thought to myself. *Maybe I'm just a kid who doesn't know what he's doing.* I sank my face in my pillow. It was late, and I knew Elaine would tell me to rest if she were there. Then a loud banging at my door caused me to shoot up out of my bed. A voice called my name from beyond the door, frantic and with desperation. I opened the door to see the face of my father, flushed of colour and looking more exhausted than I'd ever seen a living human being look in my life. On a normal day, I might've slammed the door in his face, but clearly this was important.

Detective King

"Arthur..." My father wavered and fell into me, embracing me tightly. "Your sister... please, I can't lose anyone else, I can't..." I pushed him off me and took a good look at him. If I didn't know better, I'd have thought he'd spent a night in a gutter and was dying of some awful disease, he was so ragged. On top of that, he was hysterical and his words were barely understandable.

"Dad, get a hold of yourself. What are you talking about?" John Watson, once fearless and strong, knelt in defeat before me.

"Your sister has disappeared. I've searched everywhere, I've contacted Scotland Yard, The Irregulars, no one has seen her. I fear she might've..." He began to sob, and my own hands trembled.

First Elaine, and now Lily... but that makes no sense unless...

"Dad, when did she disappear? Tell me every detail."

"She was reading a book in her room, then about an hour later, I went to check on her and she was gone. It doesn't make sense! If only Sherlock were still active, he could..." I stomped my foot, shutting him up.

"You don't need Sherlock, you have me. I'll find her and prove it to you." I grabbed my coat and my hat and rushed past him out the door.

"Arthur!" my father called after me. I paused and looked back at him, in his sorry state. "I'm coming with you, I can protect you."

"You're in no state to go anywhere! Wait at the house... I'll get her back, okay?" We may have our issues, but seeing my father so distraught was difficult, and I wasn't about to let him rush into something he wasn't ready to face. Dad hung his head and nodded.

"Please be careful, then. Even Holmes knew when to pull out of a danger." I ran down the stairs without another word, electing not to answer his concern. Of course he was right, but this was too critical to be cautious.

LionBolt

I ran as fast as I could. Streetlights raced past as streaks of light in an otherwise dark, all-encompassing void. My hat flew off, but I didn't dare go back for it. I stumbled and fell, scraping my hands and knees, only to rush to my feet and keep running. I was going to find them—I knew it, I could feel it. My mind went back to Elaine, to the things she said, and didn't say.

Think like a kid, right Elaine? I thought. *Where do you go to play?* As if in answer- a park appeared before me. It was a smaller one than Regent's with a quaint little duck pond and a big ancient tree which had shed most of its leaves. A fog had taken hold of the landscape, obscuring the city around me, so that the tree's giant limbs were only barely visible in the darkness. As soon as I crossed into the park, I felt an intense stab of pain in my chest, and I jumped back onto the sidewalk. The pain eased once I did, then returned when I crossed back into the park. I forced myself forward, struggling to breathe more and more with every step. That anxiety, the dark feeling that took the place of every other emotion, consumed me, as if I were lost in an endless nightmare.

"I didn't want it to be you!" I croaked out, "and I didn't want to see the truth. But this needs to stop! Show yourself!" The whispers of children got louder and louder until it was deafening. Then it stopped. The fog fell away in a big gust, and countless stars appeared overhead, shining like the tears of a giant or a god.

All around me stood children of various ages, staring at me with curiosity. I recognised all ten of them as the missing children. By the pond sat my sister, looking rather serene. She was the only one who wasn't staring at me, and she only looked in my direction when I approached her.

"Hello, Arthur. Isn't it nice here?" Her voice felt distant, as if she were talking to herself, rather than me.

"Lily, are you alright? We were worried you'd-"

"I'm alright now. After all, I have nothing to fear here. I'll never be alone again, so long as I stay right here." She spoke in such a matter-of-fact way, like she was reciting a lesson from school.

"Lily, this isn't right—you and these other children need to come home!"

"No! We can't!" She stood up, with tears welling her eyes. The other children began to cry out as well, some of the older ones hugging the youngest among them. "We'll never leave here..." Lily said.

"Yes you will, I'll make sure of it, let me talk to-"

"They're right, Mister Detective, there's nothing any of us can do..." Elaine appeared from behind the tree, with a sad, pained look. "I didn't mean to do anything, or hurt anyone, I just..." My fears were confirmed—my culprit was indeed none other than my assistant through this entire investigation.

"Why, Elaine? All these kids, even Lily..."

"I couldn't stand being alone anymore—I was so empty!" She said through tears.

"Have you really... been dead for over three years?" I asked. She froze like she'd been shot.

"How did you know that?"

"Did you think I wouldn't realise no one else could see you? That you couldn't speak to anyone else?" I tossed the coin back to her. She caught it and looked down at it with a look of shame. "Not to mention what you did to... that thief. All I needed was confirmation..."

I told her that when we first went to the park, and I questioned those parents—I asked about her.

"May I ask you one more thing? Do you know of a young girl named Elaine?" I asked the couple.

"Oh! Elaine, that poor girl!" The mother responded. "There was a girl from around here named Elaine who passed away from the Spanish Flu... but that was years ago, wasn't it?"

"Her mother's put up in the sanatorium now, right?" The father added. I tipped my hat to them as I left.

LionBolt

"That's all I needed to know, thank you."

I gazed at my culprit in disdain.

"I thought you'd come clean when I put away that pick-pocketer for the crime, but you didn't take the bait." Elaine looked so defeated. I looked around and saw the other children stare at her with sadness and pity. Lily had a similar expression, but she seemed to be looking at me. Elaine slowly, painfully, looked up at me.

"I've... been alone for so long..." As she said this, the surrounding scenery shifted and we found ourselves on a quiet residential street at night. An infant's cry sounded from a doorstep and the street was illuminated by light as the door was opened. A man carrying a candle opened the door and a woman beside him picked up the child and took her inside. As soon as they shut the door, the world shifted once more, transforming into the brightly lit sitting room of the house. Sunlight filtered into the colourful room—the man held a young girl that now resembled Elaine in his arms, as his wife, daughter and son looked on. The family laughed and looked very comfortable. Elaine stood beside me and looked away from them. The scenery shifted once again and the happy family had disappeared. Colour drained from the room, and everything turned grey. The patter of rain echoed throughout the otherwise silent house. Elaine's foster mother knelt down with a picture of her husband in her arms. From down the hall, the younger Elaine coughed and called out for help in a weak, raspy voice. The woman didn't show any signs of having heard. I looked at Elaine, who was shaking so much she looked ready to topple over. The scene around us shifted once more to the street in front of the house. Rain poured as Elaine's foster siblings were ushered into a car by an elderly couple who drove off with them. Elaine stood on the street, watching them drive off. The scenery shifted back to the starry skied park. Elaine sat on the grass and curled into a ball,

Detective King

sobbing.

"I've been invisible for all this time. Then I met you, and I started to think I could put an end to this, but I got scared you would end up leaving me..." Her story was about what I'd figured, considering how she died, but actually seeing it was... intense. I debated in my mind how to respond to her. The first priority, of course, was to get myself and the children out of this... wherever we were. But despite my better nature... it pained me to see Elaine in that state. I'd run around London with her for over a week and had scarcely paused to consider who she really was or what she was going through. I tried to tell myself that wasn't my problem—I should smack her over the head, curse her out, force her to set us free. Lily continued to stare at me with an expectant gaze, as if she were trying to tell me something. I sighed and crouched in front of Elaine, lightly placing my hand on her head.

"It's alright, I won't leave you. Let's end this together, okay?" I said.

"But I don't know how! You'll be trapped here forever because of me... all I did was lie to you, and hurt people. Now you must hate me..."

"I can't hate my assistant. We'll set things right together. Then we can go home." She embraced me tightly, and I hugged her back. As she cried in my arms, the stars faded and the sun began to rise. Beyond the park we could see the city all around us, and the children cheered as they knew they could finally return home. I helped Elaine rise to her feet, and she wiped her tears. Lily picked herself up and looked at me with a satisfied grin.

"I won't leave you either, y'know. Not again." I said.

"I know. You're hopeless on your own, Arthur." She brushed off some dirt on her dress and smiled. We followed the other children toward home and I looked down at Elaine, who was holding my hand.

"Shall we follow their lead?" She nodded and cracked a smile.

LionBolt

CHAPTER 4 — RUN IN WITH THE DARKNESS

As Elaine and I followed the others out, the relief of the moment began to fade, and my distrust of my wayward assistant crept in once more. Was she the one that made me faint earlier? Did she cause all those weird attacks of anxiety? Or was that all in my head? Or maybe I was completely mad—I was calling a ghost my assistant after all. No self-respecting detective, or any man of science or education, would believe in something so preposterous, and yet, I struggled to find any other explanation besides her truly being a ghost or my suffering from a very complex series of hallucinations. In either case, I had plenty of questions for Elaine. Unfortunately, those questions would have to wait, as strange forces were not done playing with me. As we crossed the threshold out of the park, the ground before us disappeared. Instead of stepping on solid concrete, we found ourselves falling. It took me a moment to realise what had happened. I was staring up at the park, floating in the air like an island in an unnervingly empty black sky. It was dark all around us, but below... while I couldn't see anything, I could hear a low slithering, scraping sound, like something (or many somethings) was anxiously awaiting our fall into its slimy jaws. My breathing became quick as I started to panic. Elaine grabbed onto me and, just as the maddening noises of whatever creatures were beneath us reached a deafening pitch, we stopped.

We floated in that void, with the insect-like noises surrounding us. Then I heard a female voice whisper in my ear. Calm yet unsettling, it came from everywhere and nowhere.

"My, what interesting spirits you two are…" It echoed unnaturally through my head. "The revolution will be well served by your sacrifice."

I attempted to speak, but all that came out was a frightened squeak. I couldn't move a muscle and could hardly think I was so terrified. It seemed my companion was much less so.

"Who might you be?" Elaine asked casually. "My detective can be pretty sensitive, so would you mind letting us go?" The grinding noises around us intensified.

"Elaine…" The name rang out over and over again all around us. "ElaineElaineElaine! I mean you no harm… I am salvation. I saw what happened to you, my poor dear. Wouldn't you like to live again? Wouldn't you like to fix this cruel world? I can do that for you…"

"Hmmm… I don't know if it's a problem with your presentation, but I can't say I trust you." Elaine said. "Thanks, but no thanks." A hissing sound enveloped us.

"Then I'll just have to take you by force…" Elaine grabbed my arm and lunged forward as a massive body came after us. The indescribably inhuman screeching from behind us and the heat of breath proved that, despite the utter darkness, there was indeed a set of jaws mere inches from devouring us. I was slowly regaining my sense as we half ran, half flew from the creature.

"Wha- what is that, why…" We dodged upwards as the

creature lunged at us.

"Arthur, think of something to get us out of here!" Elaine said.

"Me? How would I know what to do..." Then I had an idea. "The park! Get back up to the park!" We raced for our lives. The soil of the park's underside appeared in the distance and we ran toward it faster and faster as the creature bit at us, getting closer and closer with every lunge. As we got closer, the light of the park shone brighter, until finally we reached the park and scrambled onto the grass. A massive serpentine creature with the legs of an insect, a massive head with huge rows of sharp teeth, and an enormous set of wings flew past us into the void above the park. As it swooped down, Elaine and I got to our feet and ran once more, but we were too slow—the creature's massive body cut off any escape from the park and it moved in to finish us off. Just as it was going to swallow us whole, Elaine grabbed me by my shirt and we plunged into the pond together.

I emerged out of the pool screaming, wide-eyed, and very wet. Lily gawked at me like I was a rainbow-striped elephant.

"What on earth are you doing? It's a tad early to go for a swim, Arthur." I looked around in bewilderment. Dawn was filling the park with warm colours. The sky was various shades of violet, pink, and orange. The city stretched in every direction, just like it was supposed to, as if it had been a strange dream.

"Wha—Where's... Elaine?" I glanced around for her until I felt a force underneath me, tossing me to the side. Elaine emerged at the spot I had previously occupied.

"Jeez, if I weren't already dead, you would have killed me." With a splash and a shiver, I returned to dry land. I was so on edge, I took five minutes testing the ground outside the park before fully stepping out.

"What happened to you?" Lily asked.

Detective King

"That's what I'd like to know." I said, looking to Elaine. She shrugged.

"Some spirit took us into their world, like I did to you and Lily." Lily stared at Elaine with a puzzled look.

"I... know you from somewhere..."

"So you can see her now?" I asked.

"Of course, she's right there, isn't she?" I couldn't help but to chuckle at that.

"If only it were that simple. If only any of this were at all simple." I lived my life in pursuit of logic and reason. Now, here comes the illogical and unreasonable barging into my life. This was only the beginning of the strange, supernatural occurrences that would shape my career, but at least the case of the detective's assistant was finally resolved.

LionBolt

CHAPTER 5 — OLD MATES AND MURDERERS

At last, the moment I'd been waiting for—the moment I had devoted so much towards sacrificing my youth and putting myself in danger multiple times over—it was finally here. With the children all returned to their families safe, I'd surpassed even the grandest expectations of my superiors, assuring that I'd graduate from the academy and be made a full Detective Constable of the Metropolitan Police. Baker was cleared of the kidnapping charge, but he stayed behind bars for his thefts (and several other crimes we dug up). My detractors attempted to argue that despite my retrieving the missing children, my false accusation of Baker should disqualify me from serving in the force, but I managed to talk myself out of it, making up a story of the children organising a runaway independently and using Baker's false conviction to lure them out (which wasn't a total lie, though the target was Elaine). No one would believe stories of ghosts or monsters, so I fabricated a hideout in an old storehouse and claimed that was where I found them. Worked well enough.

Here's my favourite newspaper headline about my

promotion: KID SLEUTH NOW DETECTIVE!
SCOTLAND YARD REDUCED TO SCHOOLYARD.
Whoever wrote that probably got a raise. They could say what they wanted. I was still a detective—I'd get to prove myself again and again and climb the ranks until they had no choice but to respect me. That was, if they would ever let me off of desk duty.

Two weeks passed, and I'd done nothing worthwhile, instead being relegated to mindless paperwork and office night shifts. There would be plenty of time to complain later, though, as I had my own loose strings to take care of. Elaine scarcely left my side, whether or not I wanted her there—so my long hours at my desk in Scotland Yard were a decent time to talk through everything. The only other officers working then were a few of the women officers that had only recently been added to the force and were mostly relegated to night hours and minor disputes. They were friendly to me, but even they would speak to me as if I were a lost toddler, so Elaine and I were seldom interrupted at my desk.

"Alright, let's start with the basics." I said to her, my notepad at the ready. "What was that other version of the park you trapped us all in?" Elaine sat in a chair on the other side of my desk, her legs dangling off its edge. She had a rather goofy smile on her face.

"Ooh, this feels like an interrogation! I wonder what a real criminal might say?"

"Technically, you are a real criminal."

"Oh, that was, like, days ago! Everyone's fine now, right?"

"Just answer the question." I said with a sigh.

"Fine. Think of it like my personal little world. I don't know where it comes from, but I can go back and forth between here and there whenever I'm in a park."

"Just in a park?"

"Yup. The target can be anywhere so long as I know them, but I have to be in a park." She shrugged. "When that monster attacked us, that was her own world she dragged us into."

"Right… so you've encountered other ghosts with the same abilities, then?" I asked.

"I see other spirits from time to time, but ghosts aren't interested in other ghosts. We try to be close to the living, and I guess I'm no different." I jotted down some notes, reminding myself to research paranormal activity in more professional detail. All things have a valid explanation. Ghosts and whatnot, as they apparently do exist, are simply another field in which study is needed in order to understand them.

"Why can only certain people see you?" I asked.

"I don't know. Lily and the other kids should all be able to see me now because I took them to my world, but I have no idea why you could see me from the beginning. Maybe you had a run-in with a ghost a long time ago and forgot about it? Or you just have a special skill most people don't." That wasn't very satisfying. First, if I'd had a paranormal experience, I think I'd remember it unless I was an infant, but that seemed so far-fetched I couldn't accept it. The only option was to find other people who could see Elaine and figure it out from there. I sighed and leaned over my desk in exasperation. It felt like I was an explorer in some adventure novel who just discovered an unknown land. It was exciting, but also daunting and terrifying knowing that such a large unexplored area would have countless dangers and would likely take a lifetime to understand. After several days of 'interrogation', I'd gotten about all the information out of Elaine that I could.

It was the night of the first snowfall when it happened. I never minded snow—I always thought it was pretty, though in early November it can be unwelcome. Perhaps it was the weather that made me careless…

Elaine looked at me with a quizzical look, like she was pondering something about me as we walked.

Detective King

"What?" I asked. It was annoying when I couldn't read her.

"You're such an odd person, Arthur."

"What makes you say that?!" She shrugged.

"You were looking up at the snow with such a distant look, like you were dreaming."

"I think you're the weird one."

"Am not!" She rushed ahead of me, turning around in circles and gazing up at the snow with a smile. "I told you, I have excellent observation skills." She said, looking at back at me. "I noticed you haven't been keeping your word to Lily, for instance."

"What? What did I promise Lily?"

"You said you wouldn't leave her, but you haven't visited her at all since that day at the park, have you?" She got me there. I shoved my hands in my pockets.

"I'll pencil her in... next week, perhaps?"

"Arthur!"

"Fine! Tomorrow... Y'know, I've thought about moving out of the flat lately. Maybe I'll move somewhere closer to her."

"Really? You surprise me, mister 'I'm a loner. I'll live on my own even though I'm 16'." She said in a mocking tone. As if I sound like that!

"Shut up, the main reason for moving is because you're with me now." I said as we reached the stairs to the flat.

"Why should I make you move? I'm a ghost, I don't take up space!" she asked.

"Then why do I sleep on a couch and spend double on food?" I countered as I approached the door. Elaine just blushed and looked off. I shook my head. How does a ghost even get hungry? As I opened the door, I sensed something was off, just barely, but something...

"Do you... smell something?" I stepped into the flat and was immediately grabbed from behind. Elaine screamed, the door slammed behind me, and an arm fastened tight around my neck.

"It's been a while, Arty, how ya doin'?" The voice of my assailant whispered in my ear.

"W-Willy!" I choked out. Of all the lowlife scum of the earth, William Manders was quite possibly the most dangerous. Not only was he brilliant, but he had nothing to lose and knew me like we were brothers. Elaine started punching Willy in vain, then grabbed his hand and bit his finger, which loosened his grip enough for me to push him away.

"Ow! That hurt, little brat!" He said. Elaine stood in front of me, as if to protect me.

"Who are you?! Why can you see me... wait, you're the thief from the market!" I didn't want to acknowledge it at the time, but I was certain that Willy was the one Elaine stunned at the market. That was one point Elaine couldn't explain. It was frustrating she didn't fully understand her own abilities, but my theory was that it had some connection to her emotions. He was the same age as me (actually 2 months younger)—he had slick, black hair, which he kept long, partly covering his ears. I'd been told his mother was a foreigner, whether from Africa or India, I never learned—but in any case, her blood showed in his tanned skin. But the most striking thing about him was his eyes. He is the only person I had ever seen in my life with violet eyes, which shone like amethyst in the moonlight.

"I figured you'd show up, eventually." I said. "What do you want?" Elaine looked at me in shock.

"You know him?!"

"Let's just say we're old mates." Willy said. "You really shook me up the other day! And to top it off, I saw you mentioned in the papers! You got yerself famous from this last case! I figured I'd stop by and congratulate you." I moved Elaine behind me—I should be the one to protect her. Willy has always been my problem.

"I don't know what you've been up to, or what you're

really after, but if it's Elaine you want, you're not getting anywhere near her! You're not stealing her!" I said.

"Whoa, whoa! Don't go jumping to conclusions, Arty! I'm here to warn you. You're messing with things beyond your control—you might hurt yourself, or..." He looked at Elaine, who stuck her tongue out at him.

"I'm not afraid of you, whoever you are! Just stay away from Arthur!" she said, moving in front of me once more.

"You've got to stop this, Will. It won't change anything that happened." I said. Elaine looked back at me in confusion. Willy tossed his hands in the air with a shrug.

"Don't say I didn't warn you, Arthur. Some things are beyond your understanding." Willy casually strolled (you could even say danced) to the window, jimmying it open with ease. He sat on the windowsill and lit a match. I realised what was about to happen and rushed toward him, but I was too late. He dropped the match, gave a little salute, disappearing into the night. The fire rapidly spread across the floor.

"Dammit! He used gas, didn't he?!" I grabbed Elaine by the hand, and we ran out onto the street. Once we were a safe distance, we looked back to see the building completely enveloped in flames. The snow was turning into rain, but the heat was so intense I didn't realise how soaked I already was. I kicked the ground and yelled into the air in frustration. Once I'd calmed down a bit and heard the fire sirens off in the distance, I looked at Elaine.

"Guess we have no choice but to move now."

When Lily opened the door, she was visible, and quite justifiably confused. Elaine and I stood on the doorstep in a downpour of rain—my clothes were drenched and stained with black soot, and we both looked miserable.

"Ummm... wha—"

"It's a long story." I said. "Would you let us in already?" Lily looked over her shoulder.

LionBolt

"Marianne!" she called out to our maid. There was a time when our house had a small staff, but Marianne was now the only one left. "Could you draw a bath... and then get a guest bedroom ready..."

Our house was larger than most, but its fancy trimmings had dulled with time. The foyer was tiled and included the staircase that led up to the second floor, where the bedrooms were. To the right was the dining room, and beyond that, in the back of the house, was the kitchen. On the other side of the foyer was the sitting room and Dad's study. The ornaments on the walls once shined, and the walls used to have such colour to them, but now it felt so grey and lonely. It wasn't dirty or anything, just dulled, as if the house itself were in a depressed mood. I went up the stairs first—they creaked under my weight, louder than I remembered. I needed that bath desperately.

That was the most refreshing shower in my life (at least up to that point). I came to the room I had slept much of my childhood in. It was bittersweet, but I was too exhausted to dwell on it too much—it was a bed, a soft, warm bed. The room was smaller than I remembered. My bed was against the far wall, a large window beside it, over the nightstand. A wardrobe was against the wall next to the door, and a desk took up much of the remaining space between the window and the door at the side of the room. I did much of my studying as a boy at that desk, and it even had a few of my old papers still on it. I tied my old bathrobe—now a couple sizes too small for me, but it covered what it needed to—and sat on my bed, letting out a deep breath, my whole body shaking as I did. My very soul had bags under its eyes. A knock at my door heralded Lily's arrival. She peeked into my room with a little chuckle.

"Are you decent?"

"Close enough." I said. She ducked in and sat beside me.

Detective King

"So what happened?"

"Willy. He set my place on fire."

"Again?!" Lily leaned forward in disbelief.

"Right?! It's because of him I was living in such a cheap place."

"This means he's planning another heist, right?" I rested my chin on my hands.

"Probably. Knowing him, it'll be something way over his head and he'll end up getting caught or hurting himself." I leaned back and laid on the bed. "But he could see Elaine... Is it because of what happened at the market, or...?" I trailed off. Lily looked at me like she was searching for words to sift through a thorny subject.

"That Elaine girl... I don't remember much of what happened, but... do you really trust her?" I sat up again and looked at Lily seriously.

"A detective never fully trusts anyone, but in the case of my assistant, I think she's learned her lesson." I said. "Isn't that right, Elaine?" I asked, looking over toward the door where Elaine was peeking in. Her face turned red, but she shuffled in. She was wearing one of Lily's robes, which hung down to her feet, her sleeves dangling, being too big for her arms. She looked at Lily like a kitten who had just made a mess.

"I'm so sorry. It was wrong to spirit you, or any of those kids away. I was just so desperate for someone to see me..."

"N-no, it's alright!" Lily said, taking Elaine's hand. "I don't really understand it all, but I'll forgive you. I know what it's like to feel invisible." She said, glancing at me. I wanted to say something. It wasn't my fault Dad was always gone after all, but I kept my mouth shut. Lily doesn't lose arguments, whether she's right or wrong. "Speaking of which..." she said, "I was wondering what you're planning to do now... maybe you could think about staying?"

"Perhaps... I just don't want to put you in danger."

"I can take care of myself! But, I think I understand what

you mean. Just think about it, okay?" She said, rising off my bed. She looked over at Elaine. "Shall I show you to your room?" she asked. Elaine nodded, and they finally left. I groaned.

She should listen to herself for once. I thought. She can take care of herself. She doesn't need me around all the time. It's easier to be alone. Less responsibility, more time to focus. I leaned over to turn out the light when my door creaked open again and Elaine peeked in.

"Oh, did you need something?" I asked.

"W-well... not really, it's just... do you think I could sleep here with you one last night?" She said, red-faced. "Ghosts don't really sleep the same way you do, and nights can be really long all alone, so..."

"Just tonight." It was too late to argue. She smiled and climbed into bed beside me.

I'm getting too soft. I thought as I turned the light off and laid down.

"Thank you, Arthur." Elaine whispered. "I know everyone says you're a phoney and a loser, but you're usually not." I'd never been so cheesed off from a compliment, but I let it go—I was already drifting to sleep and it made me smile just a little to hear her giggle at my expense. Just a little, mind you.

If there is a God, I'll have to thank him for pancakes. Warm, fluffy, buttery goodness, with syrup and maybe some berries if they're in season. Pancakes truly are the one thing that makes mornings bearable, and it had been awhile since I'd had a batch homemade. Lily, Elaine, and I sat at the dining room table, with the morning light streaming in from the windows at the end of the room. I had an admittedly tall stack that I was busy devouring, while Elaine sat next to me and Lily across.

"You were certainly hungry." Lily said, laughing at my gluttony.

Detective King

"Thamfkyoo Lily!" I said with my mouth stuffed. Once I'd swallowed, Elaine tapped me on the arm.

"Hey, tell me about that Willy guy. He said you were friends, is that true?"

"Until certain things got in the way and he made some poor decisions." I took a sip of orange juice. Lily pointed at me with her fork.

"Y'know, you could've been more supportive back then." Rather than respond to that grave mischaracterisation, I put another fork-full of delicious buttermilk paradise in my mouth. Elaine leaned over to Lily.

"Whatever happened was all his fault, wasn't it?" She said, gesturing toward me.

"I knew I'd like you!" Lily nodded with enthusiasm, and they both laughed at me while I pretended to ignore them and focused on my pancakes.

"Anyway," I said after they had satisfied themselves. "He is still responsible for destroying my home, and he still threatened you, Elaine! I... won't lose to him..." The girls glanced at each other and seemed about to say something to me, but instead an awkward and unpleasant event took place— my father stepped into the room. He looked so... old. He carried bags and briefcases, but the bags under his eyes and the sagging of his shoulders was... What? You think I'm concerned about him? I'm a detective—it's my job to observe these kinds of things, that's all. We looked at each other in surprise for a long, uncomfortable moment, until Lily had the mercy to finally speak.

"Oh, g-good morning, father. Y-you see, last night, I didn't want to wake you, but... Arthur..." I'd turned back to my pancakes. Dad put on a makeshift crooked smile.

"Arthur, nice to see you in good health. Please stay as long as you need to." I nodded and flashed a similar fake smile. He turned to Lily. "Well now, I'm off." Lily got up from her chair and hugged him.

"I'll miss you! Good luck in Italy. And... don't mind

Arthur, he doesn't mean it." She glanced at me with a fierce expression that made me choke. Dad looked comforted and waved to us as he departed. We all collectively exhaled when we heard the door close behind him. Lily had informed me earlier that he'd been invited to a medical conference in Rome, where he would doubtless be asked about medical applications to the field of criminal investigation. There wasn't a soul in the western world that didn't know of my father, and so these sorts of trips were a fairly common occurrence. Elaine's face looked bright with interest.

"So that was your fath—" I set down my silverware with a clang and rose to my feet.

"We should be off too." I strode towards the coat rack just outside the dining room in the main foyer.

"It isn't his fault, y'know." Lily said to me, looking dismayed.

"Then why does he look so guilty every time I see him?" I pulled on my coat and headed for the door. Behind me, Elaine looked to Lily for an explanation.

"He just needs time to deal with... certain things that happened between them." She said. Elaine didn't look satisfied but followed me to the door. I paced past her back into the dining room and grabbed one last fork-full of pancake, waved goodbye to Lily, and went on my way. I would get to the bottom of whatever Willy was planning, and I had left something in the flat that I would like to get back.

We took the long way, winding through a side streets and alleys toward our now former home. Elaine kept glancing at me, saying nothing until it got too annoying for me to ignore.

"Elaine, it's fine. What's going on between dad and me isn't something you need to worry about, alright?"

"But if I can help..."

"You can't."

"At least tell me about it!"

Detective King

"I don't want to. Not yet. It's complicated and I just don't want to deal with it right now."

"Arthur..." She crossed her arms. "At least tell me you don't hate him." I halted and looked at her seriously.

"Of course I don't hate him. He's my father, and it's thanks to him the world knows of Sherlock Holmes and his greatness."

"Does it always have to come back to Holmes with you?"

"I am looking to dethrone him as the world's greatest detective after all." I said with a smirk. As I spoke, we emerged out into a plaza and heard the laughter of an angel.

"I'm sure you'll dethrone him soon enough, Detective Watson." With a laugh and a wink, Gwen Adler leaned over the counter of her flower stand, an array of pink and purple flowers adorning her hat and short red hair. Her violet dress was in the modern style and complemented her fair skin and heart-melting smile. Though I've known her for years, having grown up in the same neighbourhood, I can only really call her an acquaintance, as whenever I attempted to talk to her, the result looked something like this:

"H-h-h-hi G-G-G-Gwen!" My voice cracked. "H-h-howww are y-y-" Elaine was trying her hardest not to burst into laughter. I was red all over, fidgeting my hands around different parts of my body because I didn't know what to do with them and became too conscious of them.

"I'm just swell Arthur! And, I hear you got a promotion— I'm so proud of you!" Gwen said, nearly melting me. "But I also heard about what happened to your flat—are you alright?" She asked, leaning in close to me. Is it creepy to say she smells like a goddess?... It is?

"I-I'm j-just Sssssswell! No n-need to worry 'bbout me! Heh, so h-how're you?" *YOU ALREADY ASKED THAT STUPID!!!*

"Well, I'm just glad to hear you're safe! But, I suppose that means you'll be moving back in with your family, right?"

"R-rright! I-I'm sure we'll s-still b-be seeing each oth-th-ther ar-round though.”

“I bet you’d like to see her around!” Elaine called out, laughing at me. Gwen giggled and placed her hand on mine. I couldn’t control my breathing—sure I would pass out.

“I’d like that a lot! You’re a nice guy, Arthur.”

I’m dying... I’m not worthy. I don’t think I really responded to her, just stuttering incoherently and making eye contact for way too long until I finally waved goodbye and hurried away in embarrassment. Elaine followed, still laughing hysterically. She looked back at Gwen, who was waving, presumably at me, but she told me later that she thought for a moment that Gwen had looked in her direction. If she did, it was probably coincidence, but I wouldn’t underestimate my dear for anything.

Once we’d gotten some distance from the stand, Elaine jabbed me in the side.

“WELL, that was smooth. Who is this girl who has stolen my detective’s heart?” I hid my face in my arms, wanting to pull my hair out after that disaster.

“Shut up, she’s just a friend.”

“Well, it looked like you cheered up seeing your ‘friend’.” She nudged me in the side with her elbow again, and I uncovered my face to see Sam waving and approaching us with that over-enthusiastic grin of his. “Speaking of friends...” Elaine said. Sam reached us, panting.

“Hey! Arty... Are you... alright? Heard about... the fire...” He wheezed out. “Can’t believe some bastard attacked you like that! Y’know who it was?” He said, recovering somewhat.

“Yeah, he’s like an old rival. But no need to worry about me, I’ll take care of his straightaway.” I said.

“You sound like some old dapper remembering his mafia days. Well, y’seem okay to me.” He said, patting me on the back.

We strolled forward toward the charred remains of the flat block. My now former landlady stood amongst a group of police and stomped toward me as soon as she caught sight of me with a more fearsome expression than I've seen anyone give me, killers and crooks included.

"You. This is all ye' fault! Shoulda ne'er rented to a bullyhawk like you!" I don't know if it was a Yorkshire thing, or if she simply had a habit of making up words. I adopted a very sorry face, as sincere as I could muster.

"Mrs. Hudson, this *is* all my fault. I'm so very sorry. Here-" I handed her a bag. She swiped it with the same furious look and peered inside at the money within. "This should cover the repair costs, ma'am." I said.

"Fine, jus' don't come back! I don't need any more trouble from the likes of you!" She turned and walked away without another word. Elaine watched her go with a sour expression.

"How dare she talk to you like that! You apologised, right? Hmmpf."

"No, she's justified. Either way, all we can do is focus on bringing Willy to justice." I said.

"I just want to punch his face in!" Sam said, smacking his fist against his palm with an eager look on his face.

We passed the group of officers, and I trudged into the smouldering rubble.

"What are you looking for? Clues, bodies?" Elaine asked.

"What's wrong with you?" I asked, suppressing a laugh. "I'm looking for something."

"What're you looking for?" Sam asked, catching up with me. Circling around a few times, my eyes fixed on the ground, then I found it. I don't know how, but I knew it was there, buried in the ash. I reached down and picked up the locket. It was gold and had a design resembling the sun engraved on it.

"This was my mother's. I'm embarrassed to say that I've lost it like this several times before, but somehow I'm always able to find it again." I wasn't worried, but it was comforting having it back in my grasp. Elaine looked at it with great interest.

"Can I see it?" She asked. I handed it to her, but to our

surprise, it passed right through her hand. She tried to pick it up, but she could not physically touch it. I picked it up and stared at it.

"That's odd." I said. "Maybe ghosts can't touch gold or something?" Sam looked at me like I'd gone mad, which, from his perspective, was understandable.
"What are you going on about? Let's get out of here before you drop it again."

As we trudged out of the rubble, I continued to scan the ground. To Willy, everything in life was a game, so to him, it would be poor sportsmanship not to leave me some clue to lead me toward his next mark. He did something similar the last time I had to track him down, but that's a story for a different time. I was about to give up when Elaine pointed to something on the ground.

"Hey, what are these round things I keep seeing?"

"Round things?" I looked where she was pointing, several small, charred spheres laying in the rubble. My eyes widened with understanding. "Round Things! Come on, I know exactly where to go!" I ran off in triumph, leaving my companions standing in confusion.

All was still in the dark, old chapel. The only light came from the moonlight illuminating the altar and centre aisle through stained glass standing high above the congregational space, shining shades of blue, purple, and white. The dust was thick in the air of the silent stone building when the sound of echoing footsteps heralded Willy's arrival out of the darkness.

"Never thought I'd be back in a place like this..." he said to himself. Crouched in the back of the church, I stayed shrouded by shadow and obscured by the pews in front of me—wearing a black coat and hat as an extra precaution. I strained not to sneeze from the musty air, or the freezing draft that leaked from the ancient bricks. Back at the altar, Willy stood basking in the light of the night.

Detective King

"Y'know," He shouted—for a moment I was afraid I'd been found out. "I went through a lot of trouble just to steal a little old relic from some church! Ya know, I usually hit museums or banks!"

After a moment or two, footsteps echoed from deeper within the church. They grew louder as they approached, and with them, that dark, anxious feeling crept in. I felt suffocated, like I was trapped in a box, despite the chapel being a big, spacious hall. A woman appeared, her face hidden by a hood and veil. Her stride carried authority with it.

"I am well aware of your talents, Mister Manders." She said. "However, I believe you were the only one I could count on for this job."

"Oh? And why might that be."

I decided this was the time to make my move—I'd seen all I needed. I stood up and walked into the light of the stained glass, my steps echoing through the space.

"Because I might get in the way?" I called out. Willy's face lit up when he saw me.

"Well, well, well! Ya didn't die! Not that I expected you to. I'm sure you're dying to explain to us how you figured out where I was headed."

"The scorched rosary beads gave it away. Honestly, you could at least make it a little difficult." I said with a cocky smirk. The woman moved between me and Willy.

"He's not the reason I chose you. I need those talents of yours that most people cannot possess." She said, looking back at him. Willy nodded. She waved her arm as a signal, and Willy moved further into the recesses of the church, looking back at me with a grin and a wave. I grinned too and snapped my fingers. As I did, Sam and Elaine burst out from behind me, rushing toward Willy.

"This is for Arthur, bastard!" Sam said, rearing his fist.

"How childish." The woman said. She then clapped her hands once, and in an instant Willy was gone, as was the church, the light, everything. Sam swung into the

LionBolt

nothingness, not realising what had happened. Elaine ran back to my side.

"It's like before... could she be a ghost?" She said.

"Hey bitch, where are we?" Sam yelled. Obviously, Sam could see her, but he still couldn't seem to see Elaine, so she was probably no ghost. I stepped back and leaned toward Elaine.

"Do you know if humans can make worlds like you can?" She shrugged. In the darkness we heard a creaking sort of noise, like old, rusted machinery attempting to spring to life. Little by little, the void around us began to light up with colours. With each streak of colour that flashed around us, the creaking noise grew louder and more complex. Then the ground beneath us shifted and in the illumination, we could see that we were in fact standing atop a massive gear, surrounded by other pieces of gears, valves, and spindles, like we were in the heart of a grand clock, only the machinery glowed in unnatural colours of pink, blue, and green. Sam grabbed the woman's cloak.

"Hey, answer me, where the hell..." The woman glanced at Sam like he was an insect, and batted his hand away. The ground shifted again, and all around us the sound of a bell pierced the air. It was so loud and long, I could feel it in my bones. Sam and I collapsed onto the ground—it was so painful. We tried to cover our ears, but it was no use, and I started to feel my consciousness fade. Elaine put my arm over her shoulder and tried to help me up as the sound slowly faded. She was saying something to me, but all I could hear was high pitched ringing. Sam laid motionless on the ground at the woman's feet, and she began to walk toward me and Elaine. The ringing faded and I could make out the clockwork sounds and the echo of her footsteps once more. The pain in my chest was unbearable, and I gasped for air, but I managed to look up at her, gritting my teeth.

"Who... are you?"

"Who indeed..." she lifted her veil and hood. To my

shock and horror, I looked upon a familiar face. I couldn't breathe or speak, and tears filled my eyes until I could squeak out a response.

"You look like... my mother!"

CHAPTER 6 — THE CHURCHMOUSE

It felt like the world was spinning—I felt sick, like I could crumple up and die any moment. The woman stood over me—Auburn hair, green eyes, that unmistakable face—it was my mother's, but I knew that was impossible. She knelt down and leaned in close, whispering in my ear.

"The Detective King should be able to figure out the truth. Don't tell me you've gone back on your promise, Arthur." She sounded like her, knew things only she could know, yet I knew this could not be my mother. Her words stung like frostbite in my heart. I rose to my feet, slowly and carefully. I would not lose to this fake.

"Of course I've figured it out—it's nothing but illusion. You're nothing more than a street magician! Can you pull a rabbit out of a hat next?" The woman crossed her arms and shook her head.

"Disappointing." She turned toward Elaine. "What about you, Elaine? What keeps you here, tethered to a world you have already departed? Surely it isn't him?"

"Why not? He obviously needs me." Elaine said with a

smirk. The ground shifted once more, now placing us on a steep slant. I fell over again, and this time felt so weak and dizzy I couldn't get back up. The woman sighed.

"Well, I believe I've bought enough time for my thief. But, while I have you…" She grabbed me by my coat and took the locket out of my pocket. I screamed at myself to fight back, but I couldn't move my body and I felt I might pass out at any moment. Elaine grabbed the woman's arm and tried to take the locket back, but, of course, Elaine's hand passed right through it. The woman batted Elaine away. "Now, now, I'll be back for you when you're ready, soon enough."

"What does that mean?!" Elaine said. "How do you know our names, anyway?" The woman didn't respond, instead placing her hood and veil back on. Once she did, the clockwork world disappeared, returning to the empty church. The woman had disappeared, replaced by a flurry of rose petals and a single rose laying where she had stood a moment before. At least, that's what it looked like to me. At that point I was so woozy I couldn't make sense of what was happening around me, and as soon as the woman had disappeared, so had my consciousness.

You know when you have a lucid dream, and when you wake up from that dream it feels like you've been gone for a long time, like you're returning from a journey to another world and come back feeling disoriented, relieved, and just a little bittersweet. That was how I felt when I woke up on the floor of that church, my head still spinning, trying to make sense of what happened. It was morning—the sun was already up, so I must have been out for several hours. As I sat up, Elaine, who had been sitting beside me with her arms and head resting on her knees, embraced me tightly.

"Thank goodness, you're finally awake." She said.

"Sorry…" I said, still feeling distant. "What happened?"

"You passed out."

LionBolt

"I know that—what happened to that woman, and Willy?" Elaine shook her head.

"Who knows? I didn't see them after she disappeared. I sat here for hours and hours waiting for you to wake up. Oh, Sam's already up, talking to those fellas." She pointed over toward the altar, where Sam stood with several police officers. I looked around and saw that the church was filled with them, with several sitting around me.

"Hey! We're askin' if you're alright! C'mon, kid." I hadn't realised they were trying to talk to me. I stood up, feeling weak and stumbling some. The Chief Inspector watched over the officers inspecting rose petals with magnifying glasses. I hobbled over to him, leaning on a pew to keep myself upright.

"Sir..." I said. I needed explanation on what happened.

"Well, look who woke up!" He said. "You come here, informing no one at The Yard, and allow a horrendous crime to take place undeterred. What do you have to say for yourself?" I didn't know what to say for myself—I had no idea what happened, or what crime took place other than Willy's vague mention of stealing something, and that woman's assault on me and Sam. The chief looked at me with fury as I stood there looking stupid, searching for words.

"What... crime, sir?" I felt so pathetic.

"A murder of a priest to start!" The chief said. I couldn't believe what I'd heard. Willy was a scoundrel, but a killer? In any case, that explained the police's presence. "On top of that, a monk is missing and is feared dead, while a valuable artefact was stolen from the church. Who might have done this, Watson?"

"William Manders, and some woman I don't know, sir." I said quietly.

"I see. A teenager and a woman, and you were incapacitated alongside your friend?"

"I... she was..." How on earth was I supposed to explain what she did to us? Perhaps in situations like this, a little lie is the best solution. "She poisoned us with some drug, sir! We didn't see her needle until it was too late. I promise it won't happen again."

"I should think not. You're to stay as far away from this investigation as possible, you hear?"

"But sir, not only was I witness to the culprits, but I have intimate knowledge of Manders and his techniques!"

"Which makes you vulnerable to him. You may know him, but he knows you too, and can easily set a trap for you like he did just now. You're inexperienced, and a sorry liar. Now get out of my sight." I slunk away, wanting to curl up in bed and never wake up. Then Sam stepped in and made things worse.

"Hey, this wasn't Arthur's fault!" He said to the chief. "That woman, she wasn't normal, she did something to us..."

"Well, I can't say my wife's normal either, but I'd certainly be able to catch her in a robbery." The chief said. Some of the officers snickered.

"She'd be out of breath by the time she reached the door, she's so fa—" The officer making the comment shut up as soon as the chief glared at him. The chief's attention went back to me and Sam.

"You're both to stay out of it, and that's final. You're both part of an adult world. Follow orders and prove you deserve to be part of it." That part stung more than anything. Elaine grabbed my hand, and we walked out of the church.

"You alright?" She asked. As she did, a mouse ran across my feet, causing me to jump and yelp. All the officers laughed at me, and I rushed down the chapel steps to get away.

"Of course I'm not alright—this is a disaster. I feel so worthless."

"There wasn't anything you could've done." She said.

"Right, that's the problem." I sat down on the bottom step of the church and wrapped my face in my arms. "Why did she look like her? Why did she take the locket?" I said to myself. Elaine sat down next to me.

"Why don't we find out? You're a detective, after all."

LionBolt

"You heard my orders, I can't."

"So you're just giving up? What happened to 'I'm the greatest detective in the world, no one can stop me'? That's the Arthur I know."

"Maybe you don't really know me then. It's all just a front. I know I'm not special—I'm just as much a fake as that woman, whoever she was." Elaine smacked me in the back of the head. "Ow, what was that f—" Elaine looked furious, and smacked me again on the cheek. "Stop it!" I yelled.

"No, how could you say I don't know you? I'm only here because you saved me—you pulled me out of those lonely three years. Sure, you talk big, you're kinda selfish, and stubborn, and thick-headed, and—"

"I get it."

"But that stuff doesn't matter. That woman asked me why I'm still here, why I haven't passed on yet. Part of it is, I don't know how to pass on, and I'm scared of what's waiting for me once I do. But I also don't want to leave you yet. I want to see you show everyone that you really are the best detective around, no matter what people say, order you to do, or even what you might think yourself." She stood up and reached out her hand. "Let's figure this out together!"

At first, I wasn't sure what to make of her little speech. I hadn't realised I had such an impact on her, or that she cared about me so much. I was touched and felt a little guilty—I hadn't thought about Elaine's feelings more. She was right—I was selfish and stubborn, but if she was counting on me, the least I could do was prove myself to be worth her trust. Besides, I still had a promise to fulfil to my mother. I took her hand and stood.

"You're some assistant." I said. "Thanks."

"Don't thank me, get your sorry-self moving."

"Alright, no need for that." We both laughed and left for home.

—⚜—

Detective King

As we were walking, Sam called out to me. I stopped in front of an alley and he ran up to us.

"Arty, why'd you run off without me?"

"Sorry, I was just upset. Are you alright?"

"I feel fine now, but I could certainly use a nap and maybe a drink. You look... tired." That was his nice way of saying I looked like I'd spent a night in a trench getting shot at by Germans, minus the mud.

"I'll be alright once we bring them to justice."

"So you're not giving up, huh?"

"Of course not! You're talking to the next Sherlock Holmes here!" Elaine looked at me and shook her head, rolling her eyes. "You haven't found anything out, by any chance?" I asked. Sam put up his hands in defeat.

"Nope, and with us unable to go anywhere near the investigation, I'm scratching my head on where we'll find a lead." Sam said. At that, I heard a little voice coming from the alley.

"I could help, if only they could hear me..." It was a whiny little voice, but I definitely heard it, and so did Elaine.

"Did you hear that?" I asked Sam. He looked around.

"I didn't hear anything. You sure you're alright?"

"Maybe it was another ghost?" Elaine said. I nodded and turned back to Sam.

"Never mind—can you go to the library for me and pick up some books? Our first step should be gathering as much information as possible—illusions, religion, and the occult in particular. They took something from that church—we should find out what and why."

"Right! Cheers!" Sam said, giving a salute, then rushing off. With Sam gone, Elaine and I turned our attention back to the alley.

"I think it came from in there." She said. We slowly approached the pile of trash and debris in the alley, peering into the assorted bags of waste and discarded scraps of wood and metal stacked in a sloppy heap. We fell silent and waited,

LionBolt

listening.

"What are they doing?" The little voice squeaked. "Wait... Hello?!" It raised its voice. "Can you understand me?!"

"Yes, where are you..." As I asked, a light grey mouse scurried out of the trash heap and onto my shoe.

"I'm right here!" The mouse said. I think you can recognise that my reaction, kicking the thing off me as hard as possible with a yell, was not only justified, but natural, but enough defending myself. The mouse was flung back into the trash, only to scurry back out. It sat on its hind legs and shook a little fist at me.

"Hey, what was that for!?" it said.

"You're a talking mouse! What else am I supposed to do?!" While I was arguing with it, Elaine crouched down and stared at the creature with great interest.

"What exactly are you?" She asked it.

"My name's Owen Lot. I'm an exorcist in training... or I was until last night." A wave of recognition took hold of me. I knew that voice was familiar!

"You're the monk boy I questioned a few weeks back, aren't you?" Owen's eyes widened.

"Yeah, I remember you! I think I'm owed a few apologies from you!" He said.

"Later, tell me what happened last night, and what... happened to you." I said, gesturing toward his obviously altered form. He sighed and sat down, his behaviour feeling more like that of a human than a mouse. What he told us was... disturbing.

—— ⚜ ——

"I raced toward the inner sanctum with my master, Father Michael. I held a staff, a big cross, that was still a little too heavy for me, but the rush of fear and anticipation lightened the load. This was my first chance to prove myself and help my master and my God protect something valuable and dangerous. When you tried to question me before, I couldn't tell you anything because the thing we were keeping in the sanctum was so dangerous. A powerful demon, a creature of pure destruction and chaos, was sealed away in a chest, and we were the ones tasked with keeping it out of evil hands. I'm a good Christian—I believe in the word of the bible, but I admit, the idea that a demon was in that little box was a bit much even for me. But it wasn't my place to question any of that, and judging by how frantic Father Michael was, I knew whatever was in that box was very important.

We reached the sanctum to see a boy, around your age, with the box in his hands. He had broken into the cabinet it was usually in (or totally smashed the cabinet more like), and was about to open it.

"Go no farther, thief!" Said Father Michael. "That box contains a power beyond your understanding!"

The boy laughed—he actually laughed at a priest!

"I've no need for your foolish superstitions, old man! I'm just doin' my job!" He said, then he opened the box. At that moment, wind swirled all around us. The boy looked surprised and dropped the box, smashing it into a bunch of pieces. We heard laughter coming from everywhere—at least it sounded like laughter, but it was so deep and inhuman—who could tell? It was then that Father Michael and I raised our crosses together and chanted a really long and complex Latin prayer. Light glowed from our crosses, and the laughing sound turned into a terrifying shriek. I was sure we were going to beat it... until we didn't.

"Your attack is as meaningless as your faith!" The demon's voice said, as if it were in my head. Then the wind stopped, the light snuffed out, and everything around us was completely black. "Would you care to make a deal with me?" The demon said to the boy. He trembled and eyes were wide, but he smiled and nodded. "Pledge yourself to me, and I shall give you the full extent of my power!" Then the boy laughed again—as if he had no fear of anything, neither God nor demon.

LionBolt

"Then give me your strength already!" The laughter was everywhere. I feel like I can still hear it. Light came back into the room, and we pointed our crosses at the boy.

"What have you done, child?" Father Michael said. Then...

Then the boy's eyes glowed yellow, bright, unnatural. He snapped his fingers and... I blinked in the moment it happened. I didn't realise until I looked over and saw his corpse on the floor beside me, covered in blood, almost unrecognisable. I screamed and dropped my cross, but when I tried to run, a woman blocked my way. Her face was covered by a veil, and she smelled like roses, so strong that the smell of blood was almost drowned out.

"Well, what have we got here?" She grabbed my chin and peered at me like a snake looks at a... well, a mouse.

"Should I kill 'im?" I... soiled myself when he said it. I couldn't speak, or breathe, or even think really.

"No, I have a more fitting idea." She said. She put her finger on my forehead and whispered something in a language I didn't recognise. Then everything went dark. When I woke up, I looked like this, and ran out of the church in fear and disgrace."

Elaine and I had listened to his story in shock and horror. He was shaking with fear and his voice caught more than once, but he managed to keep hold of himself.

"My church was attacked, m-my mentor was killed, a-and I-I got cursed by that woman and let them get away." He said. Elaine extended her hands toward him, who backed away at first, but then approached and touched her finger. He hopped into her hands and she held him up, making it much easier for conversation. From up close, I could see how upset he looked. I didn't know that mice could show such emotion, but perhaps it was because he wasn't truly a mouse.

"I failed." He said, crying little mouse tears. "You don't

Detective King

know what evil those two unleashed onto the world! I was powerless."

"Aww, it's okay!" Elaine said. "Y'know, you sound a lot like someone else I know, putting the weight of the world on your shoulders." She looked at me, and I glanced away.

"But it was my duty to protect the church!" Owen said. I bent forward and looked him in the eye.

"Then why don't we bring the culprits to justice?"

"Rather than dwell on your mistakes, we can make them right!" said Elaine. "Will you help us, Owen?" He wiped his face, his whiskers twitching as he did, but he seemed to have brightened up.

"You really want help from a mouse?" He said with a little laugh.

"You said yourself you're a... what was it in training?"

"Exorcist. I'm supposed to do away with restless spirits and demons."

"Oh... well, to tell you the truth..." She looked a little fearful. "I'm a ghost. You won't do away with me, right?" Owen shied away in surprise.

"You're a ghost!? I admit I've never actually seen a real one. I should ask why you want to stay here instead of going to heaven?" Elaine glanced at me.

"Because I want to stay for a while longer. Things have gotten interesting, and I can't leave a certain detective without his assistant." So full of herself. Owen nodded in understanding.

"Then welcome to the team, I guess!" I put out my hand to shake, before I realised that'd be difficult for a mouse. "I'm Arthur, and this is Elaine." As if in response, Owen's stomach growled loudly. "Let's take you home with us." I said with a grin. What happened to Owen was terrible, but he was as good a clue as we could have hoped for. As for how we explain this to Lily, was another question altogether.

CHAPTER 7 — I AM WILLY, OF THE FOUR

Arthur probably told you horrible things about me, and hey, some of them are true, but even bad guys deserve to tell their sides of the story, eh? Allow me to start by saying that everything I've done, and plan to do is in the name of justice. Did I burn down a flat or two? Sure. Maybe I unleashed a demon from hell—you've got me there. But in the end, it will all be worth it for the world I'm trying to build. My mind trailed back to those sunny days, four years earlier, when all was right in a world of chaos and suffering.

The sun beat down onto the field—it had rained not long before, so the grass shined and shimmered—a sea of green, just for him and me. The two of us would race through that field more times than I could count. We were fiercely competitive, and even though Arthur wasn't the athletic type, I could always get him to come out to play with me. I trailed behind him, waiting for the right opportunity, then POUNCE. I tackled Arthur to the ground. We tussled and laughed, and I emerged victorious, pinning Arty to the dirt.

"Willy, get off me!" He said, trying in vain to squirm free.

"Hmm... No, I don't think so, Arty." I promptly sat on his torso.

"Come on, get off! We can go swimming next!" I climbed off my friend and sat beside him in the grass.

"Okay. You know, you've never beaten me at wrestling, Arty?" I said with a play-punch to his arm.

"Hmm, maybe not, but you've never beaten me in a race!"

"You're on!" We got to our feet and readied ourselves.

"Ready, set, GO!"

I opened my eyes to a room that felt unfamiliar no matter how many nights I spent in it. I groaned and sat up on my bed, wiping my face with my arm.

"Why am I thinking about that now?" I asked myself. On the nightstand was a silver locket with a design representing the moon engraved on it. I grabbed it and leaned back— running my fingers through the engraving, then pressing my thumb on the clasp on its side, opening the locket. Inside was a single word, written in an old forgotten language. This amulet was the one and only thing I ever stole from him. It was only much later that I found out its significance. Talk of magic and spells are almost always scams and lies, but on the rare occasions you come across something real, it is truly something to fear, and if you're smart, to take advantage of. I placed the locket's silver chain around my neck, as I did every day, slipped on a coat and headed out of the room. It was show time, my first meeting as the devil I'd sold myself to become. It felt good, like I was invincible. I didn't bother to button up—I wanted them to see the reason I was there, that artefact around my neck that made this entire operation possible. I walked down the extravagant hallway, one that befitted a palace or a luxury cruise ship, and after navigating the lavishly carpeted labyrinth, I found myself faced by a row of windows that looked out onto the city below us. The sun hadn't risen yet, and the lights of London shone bright, while the more residential areas were denoted by their darkness.

You wish to see it all burn? A deep, malicious voice rang out in my head.

"I do, but only so those areas in darkness can shine just as brilliantly as those in light."

Humans are unequal by nature. What makes you believe you can change them? He asked.

"Because that's the thinking of an outdated world. We can transcend humanity."

And become what? I smirked.

"Well, well, for a supposedly all-knowing demon, you sure seem to ask me a lot. Just sit back and enjoy the ride, alright?" What followed was the strangest laughter I had ever heard, ringing in my skull like it was coming from every direction, inside and out.

I think I like you, boy. The demon said when it had calmed itself.

"You shall call me master, slave!" I felt a stab of pain all over my body after I said that.

Don't get cocky.

"Message received, bastard." I turned away from the window to find a young boy leaning against the wall, staring at me with amusement. Ginger hair, green eyes, and a Celtic trinity emblazoned on his suit told me he was our Irish comrade.

"Y'know, if you keep cursin' at yerself like that, people will think yer mad." He said with a chuckle.

"From what I hear, you understand what I'm dealing with better than most, Connor McFinn."

"My spirit is a hero, yers is a devil, totally different! Anyway, we're supposed to call each other by our code names, yeah? Call me 'Ash'."

"Like I'm going to do what that bitch says. Call me 'Red' if you want, but my name is William." I made my way through the hall toward our meeting place. The boy followed me every step of the way, cheerfully chatting about nothing in that sing-song tone of his. At last, we reached a towering set of ornate doors.

"Ready, friend?" Connor said, bouncing up and down.

"I don't know what you're so excited about—this is more of a necessary chore than anything."

"How could I not be excited!? This is the beginning of our revolution. Our dreams will finally come true." He turned his head and pointed out the window at the slowly waking city below us. "And they'll all finally get what's coming to them." His eyes glowed a strange colour, and I felt an overwhelming, sickening emptiness in the pit of my stomach, so dark and depressing I wanted to kick him just to make him stop. Instead, I opened the door, breaking his focus and returning that twisted smile to his face as we entered the meeting room.

It was a large, square room—marble floors and columns, freshly polished—shined from the light coming down from the glass dome above. The only sort of furniture were four chairs, all well distanced from each other. I took my seat and looked over at the others. Connor sat in one, on the far side was a fella in a white suit whose face I couldn't make out, as it was buried under a matching hat. In the last chair was a figure hidden beneath a hood, holding a staff with some kind of jewel on it. With a flash of light and puff of smoke, the witch pulling our strings, Scarlett, appeared in the centre of the room.

"Greetings, thank you for coming, my four horsemen." She bowed to each of us in turn. "Are you ready to unleash Wonderland unto the world?" The man in white raised a hand.

"Miss," He spoke with an American accent and kept hold of his hat as he spoke, as if to ensure his face wasn't revealed. "I know you want to put on theatrics, but some of us have travelled a long way to be here, and I would like to know exactly why." The hooded figure's staff raised and was struck against the ground three times. After a moment, ripples of air cascaded around the room, carrying the whisper of a female voice with each pass.

"Are we to begin our work?... I fear that... I have reservations about our colleagues." She turned toward me and I got a glimpse of her face, which looked painted with colourful patterns. I took hold of the locket's chain and started swinging it back and forth, to draw attention to it.

"What's that supposed to mean?" I leaned back, then forward again, so the chair made a loud thud as it hit the floor. "If anyone's shady here, it's you. And anyway, I have more right to be here than any of you." I wasn't here to make friends. The one person I cared about was in the city below us.

"Red, White, enough. The reason we have convened here is indeed to begin our vengeance." Scarlett said. Now Connor raised his hand.

"What does that mean, exactly? I'm in this for my revolution, not your revenge."

"Fear not—the very nature of this world is to be changed by our work. We shall take vengeance on God and reshape this world with true justice and equality. Shall we begin?"

She's a raving, lunatic bitch, and that's exactly why I'm all in. You'd have to be insane to believe even a fraction of what she said, but even so, it takes someone that crazy to create any real change in the world. After the meeting, we were dispersed, but Scarlett beckoned for me to follow her down a corridor. Ancient limestone overgrown with vines and the smell of rain and dirt. Were we still in this world, or had we crossed into the next?

"Do you believe in God, William?" said Scarlett, breaking the silence.

"If anything, I believe in devils."

"What about Hell?"

Detective King

"If you're asking me if I want to back out, the answer is no. I know I'm in the right, and if I have to burn for it, so be it." After that, we were silent until the tunnel opened into a hollow. A waterfall trickled down boulders into a small pool that glowed and sparkled. Grass and beds of flowers laid before us, and above the cliff faces surrounding the hollow, clouds forming a circular pattern in a blue sky. A swarm of multicoloured butterflies flew through the hollow in a shimmering, fluorescent rainbow. Pretty, but definitely not our world. Scarlett knelt down and picked a pink flower. Within moments, it turned brown and shrivelled away into dust. She stared at me with such a... human expression—Sad, tired, in pain. This woman who had just plotted out a rapture was on the verge of tears.

"Do you think me a devil, William?" She spoke so quietly I scarcely heard her.

"Yes, I do." No sense in lying.

"I suppose you would." She stood and placed a finger on my locket. "Even after we've built our army, you'll still be special. Do you know why?" Her gaze. I couldn't look at her eyes—it felt like they were stabbing into my soul.

"'Cause I'm talented and handsome?"

"Because you have a heart. I can see it burning brilliantly. Your love gives you power, use it, and you'll get what you want." I swatted her hand away.

"What are you going on about?! Sentimentality doesn't suit you." Scarlett looked like I'd socked her.

"Maybe so... maybe humanity is beyond my reach after all." She stared at the waterfall with a glazed expression. Was she trying to tell me something? Tell me her sob story or something? Or was she just losing it?

"Are you really Arthur's mother?" I asked.

"What do you think?" She said after a long silence.

"Arthur's mum is dead. But you're not exactly alive. I'm not certain yet, but I'd like to think Rose didn't become a devil like you."

LionBolt

"Then we'll leave it at that. Go on and fulfil your tasks. We have one year until next Samhain[1]. Who do you think will win? The God of the Christians, or the gods of old?"

"Neither. They both bow before the devil." I said, pointing my thumb at myself. With that, I left her staring at the fall. She certainly had a motive behind the chaos she was planning for the world.

What was that all about? I asked the demon as I walked through the tunnel.

She's a being beyond humanity. The further you stray from humanity yourself, the more you'll understand.

Swell. Explains so much, thanks. A stab of pain in my head told me demons aren't fond of sarcasm.

---

[1] The pagan autumn festival, coinciding with Halloween

Detective King

CHAPTER 8 — THE LABYRINTH

If you'd told me before that day that I'd be strolling down the street with a ghost and a talking mouse riding on her shoulder, I'd have asked you to get some help. Yet there they were, chatting with each other, getting acquainted. Honestly, what do I do to get myself into these situations? After some minutes, Elaine slowed down.

"Why are we going the long way!? I'm getting tired!"

"No you're not, you're a ghost! Anyway, I wanted to check something around here before heading home." I said, moving on with greater speed.

"Are you sure you didn't just go this way to see that girl again?" She said with a smirk that said she was confident she hit at the heart of my reasoning.

"What girl?" Owen asked with interest.

"C-Course not... but while we're in the neighbourhood..." That wasn't the whole reason I went that way... I like the scenery, that's all...

When we reached the plaza, Gwen's stand was empty, and had a placard posted in front reading "Closed for the day.". I tried not to look too disappointed, but I admit I sulked a little. We were about to move on when something caught my eye. I went back to Gwen's stand and took a closer look.

LionBolt

"Arthur, she's not there. I know you like her but this is sad." Elaine said.

"Oh, shush." I walked around to the other side of the stand. There were flowers strewn about on the ground, as if they'd been trampled, very odd considering Gwen always took such care of her flowers. I'd watched her from afar long enough to know how lightly and carefully she stepped (no, that's not creepy at all). Based on how the flowers were crushed, almost to a pulp, it seemed to result from a struggle, and was not Gwen's doing. What was stranger was the scorch marks on the ground and Gwen's stand. They weren't visible from the forward-facing side of the stand and seemed quite deliberate and controlled. The question was the cause. I looked around for further clues and saw a string of petals leading into a side alley.

"Sorry Owen, lunch will have to wait. I think something's happened to Gwen, and we're going to find out what."

We headed down the alley together—carefully, as I didn't want to miss any clue—but at a brisk pace. I held out my hand toward Owen.

"Hey, ride with me for a while—tell me where the smell of flowers leads." Owen climbed up my arm (which felt odd—I had to resist flinging him off). He came to a rest on my shoulder and sniffed.

"Well, I'm no bloodhound, but.." Sniff, sniff. "Turn left over there." He pointing to a fork in the alley—I did as he said. As we ducked past clothes lines and garbage bins, I started to notice more and more signs of a struggle. Many of those bins were tipped over, many of the clotheslines were cut, or had ripped clothing on them, and more of those curious scorch marks kept appearing on the surrounding walls. Then that feeling came back. That inexplicable feeling in my chest that takes my breath away, telling me to run. Elaine grabbed my hand.

Detective King

"I feel it too—there's a ghost nearby." She said.

"So these scorch marks are a ghost's doing?" I said, mostly to myself. "How unscientific." I chuckled. We picked up the pace, as I was worried about what the spirit might do with Gwen. I knew how dangerous spirits could be, and worse, how little I understood them.

The pain in my chest and feeling of fear grew stronger as we moved forward. Owen navigated us further and further down a complex labyrinth of alleys—so far I couldn't tell where we'd come from, or how long we'd chased the scent. Was London really this complicated? The scent led us straight into a dead end brick wall, overgrown with vines.

"Owen!" I tapped my foot, waiting for an explanation.

"I told you, I'm not a dog! The scent led me here, that's all I know."

Elaine walked up to the wall and placed her hand on it. Then she stepped through it. Owen and I were both astonished by it, but I remembered Elaine's a ghost, so I figured perhaps it was just a ghostly thing. She poked her head out from the wall.

"Good news and bad news. Which do you want first?"

"Bad news is always useful news—shoot."

"We're in another ghost's world already. We probably entered it a while ago without noticing—look around." I was surprised to see that around us were walls of plants mixed in with brick, like nature had melded with the man-made. I looked up to see the sky, an unnatural yellow colour, with strange patterns that definitely weren't clouds. The Ghost Sense—as I've termed it—must have distracted me so I didn't notice the lack of clotheslines, or any other sign of humans after a point.

"Well, that's no good. What's the good news?" As an answer, Elaine stepped back onto our side of the wall and handed me a hat. It wasn't just any hat—that was unmistakably Gwen's hat, flower and all.

"She's definitely here, somewhere." Elaine said. I nodded.

LionBolt

Curious, I put my hand on the wall as she did and felt the brick and plant-matter.

"It definitely feels real... Can you take us through the wall with you?"

"We can try..." She took my hand and jumped through the wall. I did not follow, instead I smashed against the wall, with Owen falling off my shoulder. Elaine popped her head out of the wall again. "Didn't work, huh?"

"Does it look like it worked?!" I said from the ground, rubbing my grazed cheek while Owen stumbled to his feet (or paws).

"Hmm, weird, I could take the hat..." she said. "Maybe I can't take living things with me?"

"Go on and see if you can track her down on that side—we'll see if we can catch up with you another way." Elaine nodded and disappeared through the wall. I picked up Owen and put him in my breast pocket. We turned back and reached a three-way fork in the maze. Owen looked up at me.

"Are you okay? Your heart's beating really fast." He said.

"Being in here doesn't affect you?" Think back to the time when you were the most stressed, tired, and scared, and multiply that feeling several times over. That's what being in a ghost's world felt like. Perhaps that dark, painful feeling, the ghost sense, is just death slowly ripping me out of the realm of the living. But Owen looked unfazed—he stared at me with as concerned an expression as a mouse can express.

"I don't think I feel any different." Owen leaned out of the pocket and sniffed with all his might. "Try going forward? I smell something I don't recognise over there." I moved forward onto a path that wounded through several turns. The walls of the maze stretched well above my head, and everything looked the same. If I didn't have Owen to guide me, I might still be wandering the labyrinth.

We rounded a corner, and I stopped dead. Owen gripped my pocket tightly and for a moment I felt frozen, the life sucked out of me. Before us lied a human skeleton slumped against the labyrinth wall. The clothes it wore were of the previous century's fashion, sporting a tall top hat and long coat. I drew a deep breath and continued on my way. I'm a detective—this was part of the job. It wasn't long before we saw another such skeleton, then another, some sitting, some strewn across the ground so that I had to step around them. I stepped on a skull by accident, smashing it into dust. I nearly threw up, but I hurried forward until we reached another fork, a choice between left or right.

"Owen, which way?" I waited for an answer, but my pocket stayed silent. "Owen?" I poked him impatiently, but stopped when I saw how he was trembling. "Hey, are you alright?"

"No, I'm terrified." His voice was shaky and strained. "I don't want you to end up dead like those back there... or like Father Michael." I sighed, as I wasn't much for consoling.

"We're not gonna die, but only if you can help me out."

"I couldn't help Father Michael... I'm just a coward."

"Then it's time to start redeeming yourself. Listen, what happened to your priest is not your fault, and I know you're going through one traumatic incident after another, but we've got to work together to get out of this." I put my hand on his back and petted him—it was the only thing I could think of. "My sister's a great cook, you know—we have to make it out of here so you can try some." He seemed to calm down, his little heart slowed down, and he looked up at me.

"Th-thanks, I'll try my best." We smiled at each other, then I realised I was still petting him and it got awkward. I moved my hand away, and he leaned forward to sniff. We never had a pet at our house, but I always wanted one. Owen's certainly not a pet, but for a moment it felt similar.

"What do you smell? Is Elaine anywhere nearby?"

"Elaine doesn't have a scent, but I do smell flowers again and something else..." He covered his nose with his paws. "Eww... I'm not used to being able to smell this well— something really gross smelling is to the right, mixed in with the flowers."

We hurried down the rightward path—which wound through more twists and turns—The Ghost Sense started getting stronger, which was hard on me, but it told me we were getting close.

I'm coming to rescue you, Gwen. I won't let anything hurt you. Over and over, I repeated it in my head like a mantra to dull the pain stabbing at my heart. Finally, we came out into a huge clearing, and what we saw was beyond my imagination.

An enormous creature with the head of a bull stomped about in the centre of the clearing. Smoke billowed from its nostrils and its tail swished back and forth—at times being a bull's, then it would snap forward as a scorpion tail, before returning to its original form. Battling with this Minotaur creature was none other than Gwen. Her dress was ripped at its edges, and she had a few cuts and bruises, but she stood her ground, and to my awe, she swiped at the creature with a dagger, creating what looked like a streak of light in the air that moved forward and burned the creature when it touched its skin. There were burn marks all around the clearing and on the Minotaur itself, and I could now see that its roaring and stomping had become frantic. The beast was losing to Gwen! It swung its massive fist at her, but she dashed to the side and it missed. The thing's tail lashed at her, but she jumped back just in time. She swiped in the air again, hitting the creature in the eye with that shard of energy. From behind the creature, Elaine darted out. Catching sight of us, she ran across the clearing. The beast noticed and charged at her, fire coming out of its snout, leaving the whole clearing smothered in foul-smelling smoke. Elaine got caught up in the inferno, and barrelled into Gwen, who then barrelled into me. For a second we laid in a confused heap, then Elaine noticed her dress was on fire and we all sprang up while she patted it out. Gwen looked from her to me in bewilderment.

"What are you doing here?! It's dangerous—stay back!" She said.

Detective King

"I should say the same to you! Your stand was in a mess and I thought something happened to you!"

The Minotaur roared loudly, as if reminding us not to ignore it.

"We'll get to you in a moment!" Gwen shouted at it. The creature crossed its arms and turned away, pouting. I was dumbstruck by the whole scene. I'd known Gwen for years but, I guess I didn't know her at all.

"Wh- what is all this?" I asked.

"It's an Otherworld, which you have no business in. Just hang back and we'll get out of here once I've killed that thing." She said, jerking her head in the creature's direction. The Minotaur glared at us with glowing red eyes and opened its mouth. To my surprise, it sounded rather high-pitched and squeaky, despite its hulking appearance.

"I'm getting impatient, girl! You said we'd have a fair fight, and it'd be no fun to kill you with your back turned!"

"Based on those injuries, I won't be the one to die in this fight." She said to it. It snorted smoke and growled.

"I haven't lost in over two thousand years! Not since that Theseus bloke! I certainly won't lose to you, girl!" Gwen swiped at it with her dagger, but this time, it didn't produce any spark.

"Dammit." She cursed, throwing it to the ground and producing another from within her coat. To my horror, she cut her own arm with it, a small stream of blood flowing onto the blade. A circle appeared on its hilt, glowing red. She then bandaged her arm and swiped at the Minotaur again, this time producing an energy slice in the air, burning the beast once more. I tried to talk to her again, but she ran back into battle. Elaine, Owen, and I were left watching in awe from the sidelines as she took the creature on.

"I have so many questions…"

"That's the girl you like, Arthur?" Owen said, climbing onto my shoulder for a better view. "She's pretty amazing." I nodded in absent-minded agreement, still trying to process what was happening. I glanced at Elaine, who was examining a strand of her hair. It had been burned by the creature's breath, leaving a singed split-end. Her dress was discoloured and ragged, too.

"Since becoming a ghost, I haven't felt pain, heat, cold, or anything else... but I felt that thing's fire, it affected me..."

"That thing's a ghost, right?" I asked.

"Definitely. It must be the creator of this world."

Gwen was faster than I thought possible, weaving past attacks, all the while getting closer and closer to the monster. For the Minotaur's part, it was clearly getting increasingly desperate and upset.

"I can't lose! It's not fair! Not after so long! Just die already!" It whined. Gwen dashed behind the Minotaur and jumped on its back, grabbing it by the horns. It tried to hit her with its tail, but she dodged—and into its own chest the stinger-tail stabbed. The beast stood stunned, while Gwen took her dagger and traced a circle in the creature's chest with some strange pattern within. The Minotaur screeched, and out of the creature's chest popped a ball of light that sprang forth in our direction.

"Shoot, catch it!" Gwen yelled at us. It flew by so fast, I hadn't realised it had already passed me. Luckily, Elaine was quicker. She jumped and caught the light in her arms.

"Let me go!" The light said in a little, high-pitched voice. "I promise I won't kill any more humans—just let me go!" Gwen came over and we all crowded around the light. Slowly, it transformed and took the shape of a young boy in ancient Greek clothing.

"I just wanted to be left alone—it wasn't my fault people kept getting lost in my maze." He said. Elaine gently let him go, and he sat on the ground in defeat. Gwen knelt down in front of him.

"You know it was still wrong to leave them to die.".

"Then why did we have to die?" He asked. "When the real Minotaur lived, we were all sacrificed to it and died in this place. I don't remember which of the sacrifices I am, what my name was, but it just wasn't fair."

"You've been stuck in this maze long enough. It's about time you move on." Gwen said. The boy began to glow and dissipate into fractals of light.

"I'm sorry for all the trouble. May Athena bless you with wisdom." The child said, and then he was gone. The walls of the labyrinth crumbled, and in moments we found ourselves in London once more, in someone's backyard garden. After awkward stares and apologies to the startled homeowners, we made our exit and came out onto a residential street not far from home.

We found ourselves staring at Gwen, and after a moment of trying to ignore it, she slumped her shoulders and let out a deep sigh.

"I suppose you'd like an explanation?" We all nodded. She looked around, as if suspicious of onlookers. "Not here, somewhere private."

***

I opened the door as slowly and quietly as I could. The sun was already setting, and I knew Lily was going to be furious with me for not coming home the night before. It was best to approach with caution, just as you would approach a hungry lioness in her den. Of course, just as a lion mustn't be underestimated, neither should Lily Watson. The instant I set foot through the door, I was tackled. Lily embraced me tightly and sobbed.

"I was so worried! You didn't come back, I called everywhere!" I was being crushed under her, and I heard a pitiful wheeze from my pocket where Owen was being squashed between us.

"Okay, okay! Air, Lily, I need air!" I said. She let go of me, took a deep breath, then her expression shifted to a more unpleasant one. She began smacking me on the head in rage.

"You stupid, arrogant, no-good brother! Where were

you!?”

"Ow, stop hitting me! I thought you wanted me alive, not dead!" At that point, Gwen cleared her throat and Lily noticed her and Elaine standing on our porch. Elaine waved at her awkwardly. Lily smiled at them.

"I didn't notice we had company—it's nice to see you again, Gwen."

"It's been too long Lily." Gwen smiled in return. "I see you're lively as ever."

"With *him* to deal with, I have to be." She lifted me to my feet by my collar. At that moment, Owen popped out of my shirt pocket. Lily stared at him in surprised, and Owen stared back.

"She's... pretty..." He said to himself. Lily blushed.

"You've found another strange friend, Arthur, he's very polite." I didn't know mice could turn red like he did.

"She can understand me too..." He covered his face with his paws—probably wishing he were invisible.

We all filed into the dining room and explained to Lily what happened to us.

"She really looked like mum? And she stole her locket?" She said, her voice trembling.

"Yes, now they're both lost. We're going to find her and get it back, I'm sure." I said, hoping to calm Lily, who looked upset about the whole business. For all her confidence, I forget that's she's just a schoolgirl. Our eyes all returned to Gwen, who sat at the head of the table. She stood and looked at each of us. Lily to her right, Elaine and I to her left, and Owen sitting on the table between us.

"Do you all promise never to repeat what I say to anyone?" We all nodded. "Alright, first off, I'm a witch. My family has practised witchcraft for generations." We stared at her, dumbstruck. Did my fair maiden just say she was a witch, of all things? "Ever since I was a child—I'd been taught about magic and the worlds that lie beyond our own. That's why I can see ghosts and hear cursed creatures." She glanced at

Elaine and Owen in turn. "You had wandered into an Otherworld, a place beyond the living realm created by a spirit, or a collection of them. I'm what's called a Guardian Witch—I only use magic for good and I search for otherworlds so I can put those angry spirits to rest and protect the public. You wandered into the midst of my work, but I must say—the spirit would've escaped had Elaine not caught him." Elaine blushed and smiled, looking proud of herself. Gwen looked at me. "I didn't want you to find out because I thought you'd think it was all nonsense."

"N-no! I-I'd nnnever!" Actually, I would. Before that day, I'd think she was mad, though I'd never say such a thing to her. Owen raised his paw, and we all looked at him.

"So, um, if you can use magic..." He said, "Then, could you cure my curse?"

"I'm sorry," she said with a sympathetic expression. "I don't have that kind of power yet. But I can find out what kind of curse it is." She took out her bag and produced a piece of chalk. With it, she drew circles on the table with strange symbols in them. "The first rule of magic is that we need a circle, and the second is that a sacrifice is needed." She took out a sparkling green gemstone and with the same kind of daggers she used in the fight—smashed the stone, grinding it into dust. "That should be enough for this kind of spell. Now, stand in the circle." Owen looked at it with distrust, but shuffled into the chalk circle and sat down in its centre. He looked up at Gwen with his mouse arms crossed.

"Magic... that's what made me like this in the first place. It goes against the will of God. How can I trust you?" A flash of guilt came across her face, as if he'd hurt her feelings.

"Owen! She's only trying to help you!" I said, determined to defend her... even if none of this made sense.

"It's okay, Arthur. I understand how you feel, Owen." She said. "Magic can do great good and help people, but it can also cause great evil and suffering. It all depends on who's using it. I think if you have good intentions, and only use

magic for the benefit of others, then it is a tool you can trust."
Owen took a deep breath and nodded.

"I don't really have a choice, anyway."

Elaine leaned over toward me.

"Do you believe in any of this?"

"Well, I wouldn't normally, but..." I looked over to Gwen and all my doubts melted away. I couldn't help but to smile when she was near—she was so bright and kind. I trusted her. Elaine rolled her eyes and returned to her seat. Lily whispered something to her and they giggled. *They can think what they want. Given what we've seen thus far, I have no reason to doubt her... nor do I want to.*

Gwen whispered some words under her breath, then tossed the three daggers in the air above the circle. Owen cringed and yelled in terror as the daggers hit the edges of the circle, missing him by a whisker. As soon as they landed, a flash of red light emanated from the chalk circle, which was gone as fast as it came.

"I see..." Gwen said, examining the burn marks. "Good job Owen, you were very brave." I think he peed a little, and he was too dazed to say anything for a while, but then again, I probably wouldn't have gotten in that circle. Oh, no, no, I trusted her completely! I swear!

"I've determined this is a fairly low level curse—" Gwen said. "Your mousification is most likely triggered by something, and thus can also be deactivated."

"S-so all we need to do is f-find out what triggers his curse?" I said.

"Exactly! For my next trick..." She seemed to enjoy herself, watching our amazed faces as she cast her spells. She took out a deck of cards and spread them out. "We predict your future." Spells and such were one thing. I had no explanation for them when I saw them, but fortune telling was something entirely different. Even if it was Gwen doing it, that occult nonsense was nothing but a ploy by con-men to bring in suckers. I sat back and allowed my scepticism to show. Gwen smirked at me and began turning over the tarot cards in sequence. At the last card, she clapped her hands.

"The Judgement card, well Arthur, it looks like you will achieve your goals and get that locket back."

I'd be willing to believe, telling me such positive things as that, but it's still a bridge too far.

"But you must defeat that which stands against you, even if it is yourself. Beware the holder of the moon and accept the support of your allies."

"What is the holder of the moon?" Elaine asked. I stood up, having heard enough. Maybe some of that was real, but even in the much more likely even that it wasn't, I'd been given the boost I needed.

"Well, you heard her—I can't stop now. If you're all willing, I'd like your help." Sure, I could do it all myself, but having a house full of assistants doesn't sound so bad. Besides, I get to be around Gwen more!

The others nodded.

"We can get that woman to lift my curse!" Owen said, returned to his senses.

"We can find out who that woman is and how she's connected with our mother." Lily said, her eyes filled with more fire than I'd ever seen in her.

"We can help you out along the way!" Elaine said. "Knowing you, you'll need it." From the other side of the doorway into the foyer, Sam showed himself and leaned against the wall with a look of excitement.

"We can punch that bastard in the face!"

"When did you get here?" I asked.

"A little while ago, your maid dropped those books off in yer room—they were super heavy. Oh, don't worry, Miss Gwen—" He tipped his hat to her. "I won't tell anyone about yer secrets." She nodded. The atmosphere in the room felt like electricity running through us, connecting us through our shared goal. I was going to use them to stop Willy and that woman.

LionBolt

Whatever they're planning, whatever mystery they're setting into motion, I'll solve it first, and fulfil that promise to be a king.

"Then I hereby found The Detective Knights!"

Detective King

CHAPTER 9 — WILLY—THE PROLETARIAT

I stood in an alley, in front of a sheet of dirty glass, trying to inspect my reflection as best as I could.

"Demon, how do I look?" I asked. It was nearly showtime, and I needed to look presentable.

Humans all look much the same to me. You at least appear less... filthy than most around here. The demon responded.

"Do you have friends, or a family, demon?" I knew nothing of the creature that I'd essentially sold myself to—the least it could do was tell me about itself.

Those are mere human concepts, for which I have no need.

"Then where do you come from?"

The origin point of all human fear. Was it trying to scare me? I wouldn't give it any satisfaction.

"Fine, don't tell me. Do you at least have a name?"

Another mortal concept... He was starting to rile me.

"Alright, I'll call you Fred—how's that?" A sting of pain in my stomach was his response. "Jeez, nice way to treat your friend, Fred." Before he could hurt me again, I pushed my way through a set of big heavy doors into the factory. This sweatshop was being used to build machinery for some big corporation. The hours were long, the room was stuffy, loud, and boiling, despite the time of year. Rows of men and boys, some as young as 12, {others wounded from the war}, slaving away for peanuts. I'd seen enough of these scenes of the working class being taken advantage of by those who hold all the power and money. Whether it's the police, the government, or the executives, it's nothing but corrupt, and I was going to speak my mind about it. That was the job I was assigned, after all. I stepped up atop a stack of crates, cleared my throat, and yelled in the loudest voice I could muster:

"Who wants a new job!?" That caught their attention. The sound of work slowed and stopped. "Boys, I've got an offer you can't refuse. Aren't you sick of it? This country preaches justice, fairness, opportunity, but does it live up to those promises? Hell no! The people in power, the rich, the well-connected, they have those things, but for us down here, people who look like us, talk like us, we're nothing but pillars to them, holding up their palaces while we're crushed under their weight. Think about how much you bring home for your families? Is it enough? Can you really say you're happy? Can you really look around and tell me the world is fair, or just? No. That's why we change things. We stand up, raise our voices, and demand change until there's not a shred of that palace remaining, and we're all on equal, equitable ground." Throughout my speech I heard a spattering of cheers, applause, grumbles, emotions. In this factory, and all the other places I made the same pitch, I could feel a power course through me, something telling me what to say and when to get the crowd on my side. I raised my fist. "Who will stand with me for revolution?!" At that, I would usually get somewhere between 40 and 70 percent of the crowd to cheer, depending on the place. "I will help you! I can lead you! Now let's take this world back for the proletariat!" I only added the last part there the first time I gave the speech, as the response was a lot of 'huh? What's that mean?'

"In other words, let's burn shit down!" That did the trick. I set up these little riots and strikes all over the city, and after some time, the effects were felt in supply shortages and violent clashes with the police. I believed every word I said—it was why I fought as I did. The injustice of this world took everything from me- my dad, my childhood, and Arthur. If I had to cause some chaos to fix it, even if I had to destroy the very foundations of society and hurt a lot of people, I believed in my heart that it was worth it, that in the end we'd build a better world, and Arthur would stand by my side as my friend once more.

In any case, now that I'd dealt with the proletariat, it was the Bourgeoisie's turn. Get ready, this is the fun bit!

People crowded the extravagant hall, wearing flourishing dresses and strikingly dapper suits. Glasses of wine or champagne touched the lips of the guests. Haughty laughter, gossip, and outdated chamber music filled the air. Masks concealed the faces of the partygoers. A certain devastatingly handsome devil sat on the railing of the second-storey balcony looking down at the revelry—watching with hungry anticipation.

A rich bastard by the name of Richard Banks, the host of the affair, clinked a glass, grabbing the attention of the crowd.

"I thank you all for attending this celebration!" He said. "Surely we have cause to celebrate such a successful fiscal quarter! In appreciation for all the work you have done, and the money we have all made..." The crowd laughed and some cheered that disgusting display of privilege. "I propose a toast!"

"Show time!" I said and sprang down from the balcony as the glasses were raised. I landed squarely in front of Banks and performed a grandiose bow for the crowd before me.

LionBolt

"Here's to greed and hypocrisy of the highest calibre!" I said, raising my fist. A chorus of haughty, pretentious gasps and scoffs followed from the crowd. Banks was red with anger. He grabbed me by the arm and looked me in the eye.

"Who the devil are you, boy?" I placed a hand on his shoulder and leaned in close.

"Why, your newest business partner, Mister Banks. Pleasure to make your acquaintance. You see, you are going to help me- with all that money you and your friends make." The old man batted me away.

"Obviously, you're either a madman or a fool. I've no reason to help you do anything!" I smiled, quite more politely than I should have—after all, he just insulted me, but I am nothing if not a merciful devil. Still, he required a demonstration of his new benefactor's abilities. At my silent command, the lights in the hall darkened, one of the partygoers collapsed, causing screams, followed by more and more people collapsing to the ground until only myself and my horrified new underling remained.

"Don't worry, they'll be fine as soon as I lift the spell. They won't even remember my presence here. However, should you refuse to offer your assistance..."

Banks fell to his knees, biting his nails with a most deliciously desperate expression on his face. "My assets... Please, I'll cooperate any way you need, but leave my business and my assets out of it."

What a lowlife piece of... The man's wife is supposed to be in that crowd and that's what he's worried about? More than his own life, it's his money he cares for above anything else.

Demon... I called out in my mind. Who gets his precious assets if he's dead? I asked.

I thought you'd ask. According to his will, everything goes to his brother. The demon answered in my head.

Mind changing it for me? I asked, humble as always.

Already done, Ernest William Manders. It said.

You know I don't appreciate that full name. This creature that

Detective King

lived within me found it amusing to tease me, it seemed. I snapped my fingers and at once the party was as it was before. The light returned, the horrid display of wealth on full display, only I stood atop the platform overlooking the crowd, and the precious business associates of the late Richard Banks basked in the glamour of the night by merrily dancing around his corpse that lay in the centre of the ballroom floor.

LionBolt

CHAPTER 10 — THE ADVENTURE OF THE WILL PART I

Lily and Elaine stood outside Owen's new room (right next to mine). I joined them and tapped my foot.

"Is he still moping in there? It's nearly lunchtime."

"Oh, leave him alone." Elaine said. "I'd be embarrassed too."

"I just feel so bad." Lily said, her head down. "It's my fault, I upset him..."

"No, he's just an idiot." I said as I knocked on the door. "Owen, get up—I want some more info out of you before I head in for my night shift." No response. A worry flashed across my mind that he may have gotten trapped in his sheets or something. I opened the door (it was already ajar, since a mouse can't exactly open doors), and I stepped in. Our mouse friend was sitting on the bed, wrapped in a corner of a blanket. When I came in, he dipped under the covers.

"Go away..."

"Come on, it wasn't that bad." His head reappeared, and he gave me a nasty look.

The previous night, we had all been celebrating our

newfound resolve as Detective Knights. Lily and Marianne had prepared a delicious meal—we all had a good laugh as we attempted to introduce Sam to Owen, even though all he saw was a regular mouse. Best of all, I got to sit next to Gwen! It was a merry atmosphere until Lily got up to part the curtains that were covering the window.

"The moon's still nearly full—let's brighten it up in here!" She said as she opened the curtains. As soon as she did and the white light of the moon filtered into the room—a bright glow flashed on the table. Lily turned with surprise to see us all staring at the naked boy sitting on the table. Owen looked around, at first not realising what had happened.

"Well," Gwen chuckled. "I guess we found what deactivates the curse."

Owen looked down, and his face turned red. A blanket was fetched, and we seated him next to Sam. He wrapped his body in the blanket and sat in a pout, still red in the face. We all looked off in other directions, though I couldn't help but notice the black, circular markings on his chest.

"I wasn't ready to see that..." Elaine said, looking like she was in a daze. Owen planted his face on the table in embarrassment.

"N-now that we know about... this..." Gwen said with an awkward smile. "I would keep an eye out in the morning. If moonlight is the deactivator, then my first guess for the trigger would be sunlight." I thought that made sense—so far as any of this made sense. What kind of twisted, perverted person would put a curse like this on him? Sam patted him on the back.

"Don't worry, we'll get that bitch to lift this stupid curse. At least we can communicate with each other now, right?"

"Nice to meet you..." Owen mumbled without looking up. Lily stood up and clapped her hands.

"I know, Arthur's old clothes! I'm sure they'll fit—just give me a minute!" She raced out of the room as if she were running from a raging fire. I looked at Owen, who continued to sulk. So we saw his... yeah, I suppose that'd make me want to sulk too. I decided to change the subject.

"Tell me about what Willy stole." I said, leaning forward and gazing at him seriously. His eyes widened in terror.

"I don't know everything, but this is what I was told..."

"A shadow darted across the full moon. The hooves of horses rushed forward, bringing up dust from the path. A group of knights beckoned the horses forward, their armour gleaming silver in the moonlight. The shadowy figure snarled at its pursuers. It generated a ball of fire and hurled it at the knights, causing the horses to jump and shriek in fear. One knight managed to charge forward, sword drawn, with a fire in his eyes. The shadow dived into a run-down hut. Silence fell, save for the sound of the knight's boots hitting the ground as he dismounted, and the ghostly wailing of the moor. He crept into the structure, alert and on edge. Darkness filled the room. The knight looked around, searching for the spirit—prepared to strike. The knight halted at a rustle. A pair of red eyes glowed directly behind him. The shadow leapt forward, but the knight turned at just the right moment, holding out a box. It wailed as it was drawn into the box, and as the last of the malevolent shadow disappeared into it, and the knight sealed it."

"The box was placed in the church sanctum, and remained there until he stole it." Owen said, looking rather depressed despite delivering such an impassioned retelling of the legend.

"Interesting..." I said. "Not sure about helpful. Do you know of a way to defeat it?" He shook his head.

"Not a clue. This thing hasn't seen the light of day in hundreds of years, so I doubt the priests could've taught me that even if they wanted to." Gwen had been listening intently, leaning forward with her eyes fixed on Owen.

Detective King

"From the sound of it, I'd say the only way to force this thing out is if Willy himself casts it out."

"R-really? Wh-what makes you so s-sure?" *She's so smart...* In response, she shrugged.

"Just a hunch, really, but I figure if Willy willingly took this thing in, as a sort of deal, he can break that deal too, right?"

"So we force him to give the thing up, eh?" Sam said with a grin.

"It probably won't be that easy, but yeah." I said.

"How reassuring." Elaine said with a hefty dose of sarcasm. Owen looked particularly upset. I changed the subject again.

"Owen, do you have clothes, or other belonging we can get for you?"

"Everything's at the church, but... I can't go back there."

"Why not? It's your home, right?" A tear welled in Owen's eye.

"I was supposed to guard the relic and protect my master. But I failed and let everyone down. Now he's dead. That evil is loose on the world. All because of me. It makes sense—I shouldn't have even been born to begin with." I could tell from his eyes that he believed what he said. I was going to say something when a shirt hit Owen in the face, followed by a pair of trousers. Lily stood in the doorway looking furious.

"Don't you ever say that about yourself! No matter what you did, your life is still worth living! So go up to your new room and get some rest, because tomorrow we're going back to that church and getting your things! Okay?" Owen looked about as surprised as the rest of us. He stood up, grasping the blanket and clothes close to him, and rushed past her out of the room. I got up and started after him.

"I'll show him to his room, the empty one next to mine, right?" Lily nodded, looking shaken up. "Are you alright?"

"Yeah, I just... can't stand it when I see someone in pain." She said. I nodded and followed Owen out of the room.

LionBolt

"Well... he seems like a nice lad." Sam said as I left. "If it's any consolation to him, he had a decent set on him."

Owen buried himself under the covers again. Lily and Elaine entered after me and we sat on the side of his bed.

"Hey..." Lily said. "I know a lot was said last night... I'm sorry." Owen poked his head back up.

"I'm sorry. This has all been so much for me... thanks for trying to bring me to my senses." He poked out from the covers some. "All of you, you had no real reason to take me in... if it weren't for all of you, I'd be dying on the street, so thanks." He then bowed his little mouse head.

"Of course! You are one of my Knights now after all." I said.

"Right..." Owen said with a chuckle. "So I've been thinking that I'd rather not go back to my church for now. I think... I need to earn that. Once I've made up for my mistake, and I'm free of this curse, I'll be worthy of that place again." I nodded in understanding. Lily energetically spun around and headed for the door.

"Okay then, everybody head downstairs for breakfast! Afterwards, we'll head over to get Owen's things."

"But the police won't let me near there." I said.

"Hmmm... Well, in that case, Elaine and I will go. I'm sure you two can find some way to be productive." She looked back and forth between the two of us, then burst out the door, being the whirlwind of a girl she was. Owen and I glanced at each other.

"Welcome to the Watson house." I said with a shrug.

Breakfast makes life worth living, never let anyone tell you otherwise. After another brilliant meal courtesy of Marianne, Lily and Elaine bundled up and rushed out the door, leaving me and Owen standing there with just each other. I picked him up from the floor and placed him on my shoulder.

"What do we do now?" He asked.

"Well, I looked over some of the books Sam got..." I yawned. "All night I might add, and I think the new case in the papers has all the markings of something... unnatural, so might as well start there. Did you read it?" Owen shook his head.

"Reading's not a strong point of mine." He said, embarrassed.

"That's alright—it's a grisly business about a well-known investor who was murdered at his own party last night. Apparently his guests kept on as if he weren't laying there, and that even his own wife stepped over his corpse, oblivious." Owen shuddered at the description.

"God bless him. You think a ghost did it?"

"A ghost... or someone who knows his way around the like."

The telephone that sat on a table near the door rang, the sound echoing through the hall, sharp and hard on the ear. I picked up the earpiece and spoke into the candlestick looking device. I won't bore you with a transcript of the call—what's important was that I'd been called into work early to meet with the chief. Apparently, he wanted to speak with me about something. Either I was getting promoted, fired or somewhere in between, but closer to the latter. I opened my breast pocket and beckoned Owen inside.

"Hop in, we're going to Scotland Yard."

"Is it about that murder?"

"Doubtful, but I suppose stranger things have happened." Understatement of the century.

I stood at the secretary's desk, hopping about in place anxiously. She looked down at a newspaper, paying me no mind.

"Um, excuse me, ma'am." I said. No response, not even a

flinch. I cleared my throat. "Excuse me!"

"If you have an emergency, go to your local station—this is no place for children." She said without looking up. I smirked and shook my head. Finally, my first chance to show off had arrived! Out of my coat I produced a shiny police badge.

"I'm here on official business, actually." I said in an authoritative voice, my hat tipped to look neat. Owen chuckled from within my pocket.

"You show off!" The secretary looked up and appeared unimpressed.

"Wow, that almost looks real."

"WHAT?! It is real! I'm Detective Arthur Watson, I have an appointment with Chief Inspector—"

The chief appeared from within his office.

"Watson, quit dawdling and get in here!" I looked from him to the secretary, red-faced. She gestured with her thumb that I could go in and I hurried past her to the chief's office. Owen laughed from my pocket. When I became a full officer I had hoped that sort of thing would stop happening, but evidently the problem would persist until my next growth spurt at least.

I plopped myself in the chair opposite the chief, who peered at me with hands tented. I felt like a schoolboy who'd been called back from break by the teacher.

"Watson... I like you—you remind me of your father. That's why I want you to succeed." He said. I nodded my head.

"Thank you, sir." He isn't yelling at me—so far, so good.

"I'm just not sure you're ready for big cases just yet. So I'll be assigning you cases I feel are within your abilities. Impress me, and perhaps you will be trusted with bigger investigations. Do you understand?" I nodded again, like an obedient little dog, despite the growing fire in my heart.

"Yes sir. I'll do my best." I did my best not to bite my lip, or scream at the man, at least. To think he too, would treat me like a child. I felt a tap on my chest from Owen.

Detective King

"You've got a team behind you—why can't you investigate that witch yourself?" He said. The chief craned his neck and looked puzzled.

"Do you hear a squeaking noise?" I punched Owen to shut him up.

"I don't hear anyth—Oww!" He bit me. He actually bit me! I tried to hit him again, but I was too forceful and he spilled out, right onto the desk. The chief and I stared at Owen in a stunned, awkward silence for what felt like forever.

"Watson... did you... have a mouse in your pocket?" He said finally.

"Ummm... Yes..." My mind was racing to fix this mess. "This is my pet mouse, he... helps me think." The chief looked at me like I had turned into a mouse myself. He must've thought I was mad as I helped Owen back into my pocket.

"Alright... whatever, just don't bring it back here again." He slid a file toward me. "Have this resolved by tomorrow, that'll be all." He waved me away. I stood, red-faced, and nodded.

"Understood, good day, sir." As I turned to go, Owen waved at the man as a farewell. I shoved him back in my pocket with force. "Don't wave!" I growled under my breath. The chief looking exasperated as I left, and I thought I overheard him say— "Why do I always hire the strange ones?"

I laid the file on a ledge running along a path on the Thames. My hand plunged into my pocket and threw Owen next to the file (with perhaps more force than necessary). I leaned onto the ledge and ran my hands over my face.

"Why? What is wrong with you, Owen?" I uncovered my face and glared at him. He wasn't defiant anymore—he looked like a kid who had gotten caught stealing from the biscuit jar.

"I'm sorry..." He said in a small voice. "I got worked up. But you shouldn't have let him talk down to you like that!

LionBolt

You know way more about what's going on than he does."

"How was that supposed to work out? If I'd told him you can talk, but only I can hear you, he'd have put me in an institution rather than a case." The file was a quick read (though I only skimmed it). I slapped it down and let out a bitter, cynical laugh. "They think I'm a joke." Owen trotted over to it and read it aloud, occasionally stuttering over some words as he went.

"'O-Ophelia Thomas, 73, reported hearing strange noises and noticing things around her house being moved around. After repeated requests for police inv-investigation, it has been deemed ne-necessary for an officer to reassure Mrs. Thomas and put a stop to her near daily reports, which have reached a certain level of... t-tedium for the department.'"

"Do you have dyslexia, Owen?"

"What's that?"

"Never mind. In essence, they want me to check in on an old lady just to shut her up."

"It's not... that bad." He was desperately searching for some bright side. "Maybe there really is something to what she's reporting."

"Or she's just senile." I folded the file, making a loud flapping noise. A smirk came across my face. "What do you say we skive off[2] for a while and conduct our own investigation?" I put my hand out for him and he bounced onto it.

"I don't know what 'skive' is, but should you be defying orders like that? Sure, it's rotten, but now that he's given the order..."

"Owen..." I said in an overly friendly fashion and scooping him up, pressing him between my arm and chest in a 'hug' and ruffling his hair/head fur. "We're mates now, right? And you owe me for what you did back there, don't

---

[2] I've heard Americans use the term 'playing hooky'

you, mate?" I squeezed him tighter to get the point across. "We'll check in on the old bag once we've done some looking of our own. Sound good?" I released him into my breast pocket and he coughed for a moment.

"Right, you're the boss. Just make sure we're not out past sunset or else... y'know."

"Of course, now come on, we're going to solve a murder."

CHAPTER 11 — THE ADVENTURE OF THE WILL PART II

R ichard Banks lived in a luxurious estate, standing atop a hill, surrounded by intricate gardens and stone walls around the property. The house was an ornate monstrosity, mashing architectural bits from gargoyles to Greek columns, to towering Gothic windows and battlements upon the roof. The visual horror of the place—including its obvious new paint job—indicated not only a ridiculous amount of wealth for one to waste, but recent wealth, as the building probably hadn't stood before the war. Police were swarming the grounds, as expected, but I had my methods for getting in. At the front gate, there were two constables standing guard. How to rid of them? Pay some kids to lead them away, of course. They chose to throw a rock at one of them, which did the trick nicely.

"That was pretty shady, Arthur." Owen said as I picked the lock of the gate.

"Nonsense, the kids will be fine—I gave them enough to buy a case of chocolates." Snap—the lock was undone and onto the grounds I went. Avoiding the crowd by the entrance,

I went around into the back gardens. We were well hidden by the rows of hedges and fountains.

"According to the newspaper, the ballroom looks out over the garden, so the crime took place... there." I pointed toward a second-story balcony, and the ballroom beyond it. "What's key is whether someone could reach that room from outside, or if the culprit was already inside."

"If what you said about how the party guests acted is true, could they have all known he was gonna die?" asked Owen.

"The thing is—none of them remember him."

"What?" He almost fell out of my pocket, then repositioned himself on my shoulder.

"They've questioned all of them, not even his wife recognises him."

"Are they lying?"

"It'd be some conspiracy if they were. It'd mean everyone he knew plotted to kill him and coordinated together to do it. While not impossible, I think there's something else at work here." After a quick glance around, I sneaked up to the wall and looked up.

"There—you see that platform, with the potted plant?" I've never been the most athletic around, but I fancy myself capable when I need to be. I stepped onto a windowsill, then jumped and pulled myself onto the platform about halfway to the balcony.

"Arthur, don't drop me!" Owen had almost slipped off me. I set him on the platform.

"Can you climb up these vines?" They were growing all over the wall.

"Why are we doing this?" He asked as he shimmied up.

"To prove that someone could get in here without an invitation, unseen." Owen reached the balcony and sat.

"Everywhere is far away when you're small." He said, out of breath. I grabbed onto the vines myself and started to climb (carefully, mind you, heights aren't my friend), when a click and a thud sounded from atop the balcony—someone had come out from inside. Owen scurried behind the stone guardrail. "It's two fellows in suits."

"Well Stanley, what do you make of it?" One of them said.

"Haven't seen anything like it. I'm trying to piece it together, like he would, but what do you do with a murder in a crowded room with apparently no witness? It makes no sense." The smell of smoke wafted from the balcony, and I saw one of their backs from my vantage point below.

"Can't blame you, you're not the young ace detective you once were." The first one said.

"Then let's hear what you've to say about it, Gregson."

"I think I'll hold off until will is read. I'll wager whoever's listed on it had something to do with this mess."

"You say that as if it were some astute observation." Ashes dropped on my head and I struggled not to sneeze. Footsteps meant they were retreating inside. "I'm keen to know whether Mrs. Banks' claim of being nothing more than a housemaid are lies or ravings"

"If anything, it implicates her. Can't be hard to kill a man when you know your way around chemicals, even the ones for cleaning." The thud and click of the door meant we were safe.

"Were they detectives?" Owen asked as I climbed onto the balcony.

"That was Inspectors Stanley Hopkins and George Gregson. If either see me here, I'm dead."

"Should we go?"

"Go inside, sure. That last thing they said was interesting. Why would she claim to be a maid? And the will..." I scooped Owen into my pocket and went inside.

The ballroom was possibly bigger than my house. Chandeliers twinkled from where they hung, while stairs on either side of the colourfully patterned dance floor led up to parlours overlooking the hall. The ceiling was a glass dome, and in the centre of all the splendour, laying in a gruesome pose at the feet of a dozen police—was Richard Banks' body. I couldn't get close to it, but I saw no blood, neither on the floor, nor on him, and no obvious injuries save from signs of trampling. His face looked terrified. That's what was most peculiar, though. He knew death was coming—no poison could replicate that face. Turning my attention to the ceiling, it was conceivable someone could sneak through on the upper floor landings. If I could climb to the second floor, a more athletic person could easily have reached the room.

What we have so far: Banks died with no external injuries, but I was convinced he was murdered by someone who wasn't already present at the party. Someone crashed the party, and either injected him with poison, or scared him so violently that he died on the spot. But why the strange reaction of the guests? I slipped away from the ballroom, and after dodging several officers, reached the first floor. Ducked in a side room, I summoned Owen out of his pocket.

"We're going to split up now, okay?" I said.

"Isn't that dangerous?!"

"It's necessary. Don't worry, you won't be seen, so long as you aren't stupid. The drawing room is down the hall past the stairs we came down. Go in there and wait. They'll be reading the will from there, judging from the number of people going in and out. I need you to remember what the will says and report back—can you do it?" Owen nodded.

"I'll try. Where are you going?"

"The head butler's office. I want to see a guest registry."

"Arthur, shouldn't we let the police handle this?"

"I am a police officer. If I'm right, they're missing the entire context of the murder. If I'm wrong, then we simply get out of here and no one needs to know a thing."

Owen scurried into the drawing room, while I descended another flight of stairs into the servants' quarters. There were more people down there than expected, both police and servants. Almost getting spotted, I ducked into a closet and changed into a servant's uniform. I got into the butler's office and saw the registry right away—the police must have been searching it too. Nearby footsteps caused me to tuck the registry in my shirt and rush out of the office.

"Hey, boy! Where are you going?!" I froze at the unknown voice behind me. I turned to see the butler himself, for any servant who commanded such authority must have been the butler. "Who are you?"

"I'm... the new footman, gov. Name's James." I added a splash of cockney for effect.

"I hired no footman." He looked murderous with anger.

"I was hired by Mr. Banks himself, just before... y'know..." The butler looked exhausted. He pinched the bridge of his nose.

"I don't care anymore. Take the hat off and get to work. We've still a household to maintain, with or without its master."

"Of course, sir." *Dammit.* I removed my hat and got a tray thrust into my hands.

"Erm, do we not have a mistress, sir?" The butler paused like I'd stabbed him.

"Mrs. Banks is not to be disturbed. Only I'm to see her, understand?"

"Yessir!" Got him there. I went up the stairs and ditched the tray as soon as I was clear. I couldn't stay out in the open since I would've been recognised straightaway without my hat on. A loud bang and a scream came from the drawing room. I had a hunch about what caused it.

"Mouse!" Owen sprinted from his pursuers, who shouted and threw various objects at him. As he approached, I took a bowl from the tray and caught him.

"I'll take him outside straightaway!" Before anyone could recognise me, we'd made our escape and were catching our breath back in the garden. "What... happened?"

"I tried my best to stay unseen, but the lawyer spoke so quiet, I had to move closer to hear. You can guess what happened then."

Detective King

"And the will?"

"All his money went to someone named Ernest Garland."

"Willy." I couldn't believe he was involved in this, too.

"What?"

"That name... it's definitely him. So he killed Banks." I took out the registry and examined the list of names. "As I thought. Willy would be able to pull off a farce of this scale alright. I've solved the case well enough. Now we just find our killer."

"But what about the guests, how they all acted?"

"That's the trick—There were never any guests at all."

"You... lost me."

"Richard Banks thought his business associates were all gathered for a party, when really the hall was filled with people Banks had wronged through his dealings. Former employees, partners, lovers, etc. They stomped on his corpse happily after Willy had his name transferred into the will and killed Banks. His 'wife' was truly just a housemaid, though I suspect his actual wife exists somewhere—perhaps she learned of his affairs and took part in the whole charade."

"You figured that out just now?"

"I confirmed my suspicions just now." We started walking toward the front gate. "I'd suspected that the partygoers conspired against him, but found it hard to imagine they were his associates or friends. The big clue was that it was a masquerade party—he couldn't see the faces of anyone. All Willy needed to do was find people to fill the part, and possibly turncoat a few fellow investors for the right price. The best part of Willy's plan was to throw the police off by falsifying the guest registry, sending the police to random names he probably got from the phone book."

"How do you prove—"

"The butler. He let it slip that Mrs. Banks was a fake. I'm confident that once he's brought in, we can prove that a mistress maid was fashioned as a false wife, and the crowd was filled with similarly positioned people." As Owen stared at me in awe, a man stormed out of the manor—the door had banged open and the gentleman stomped through the front garden, ploughing over flowers and shrubs. "Let's follow him." I said. "Something tells me he thought himself entitled to some money, and that he'll be looking to talk with Ernest Garland."

We followed the man in a taxi into a residential area, and to my astonishment—we ended up precisely where I'd been scheduled to go! Ophelia Thomas' house, on a well-worn street that'd seen better days. The man charged in there like he owned the place, because he probably did. What connection did a senile old woman have to this strange plot of Willy's? I peered into a window and saw the man waving his arms in the air—his shouting wasn't audible enough to make out words, but his tone was irate. Opposite him was the old woman, shrinking back at regular intervals. The man's back was toward us, while the old woman spotted us after a time. I ducked into a bush, expecting the man to come after us, but no one came. Mrs. Thomas had not alerted the man of our presence. From my position near the ground, I noticed a hole in the house wall, along the ground. Under normal circumstances, such a hole would be meaningless, but for this detective, a mouse hole was an opportunity.

"Owen…" I pointed out the hole. "Mind gathering some intel for me again?" Owen's ears twitched with annoyance.

"No! Y'know I'm not really a mouse, right?"

"But you can get inside through there, and you can probably communicate with the mice, right?"

"How should I know?!" The window opened and Mrs. Thomas looked down at me.

"Can I help you?" She said. I stood (letting Owen fall to the ground).

"Actually, I'm here to help you!" I pulled out my badge. "Forgive my attire—my name is Detective Arthur Watson. You had requested police assistance, but it didn't seem like a good time…”

“Thank goodness. First this ghost business, now my nephew is calling for someone he says cheated him out of his brother’s money.”

“You mean Richard Banks?”

“Yes, his mother was my sister. I live here with Winston, his brother.”

“May I come in and ask some questions? To both of you?” The old woman looked panicked at the suggestion.

“He’s in his study now, but I’d rather not bother him…”

“No problem, I’ll keep this short.” I glanced at Owen, who flashed me a scowl before heaving a sigh and scampering into the mouse hole.

“Now we’re even!” He called.

As soon as I was let into the house, I knew something was indeed amiss, though it wasn’t a ghost’s doing. Traces of muddy footprints, scuff marks on the walls indicating struggle, a flower vase with a large chip in it along with a mosaic of cracks, as if it’d been shattered and glued back together. It smelled musty—like mothballs and something else… something bitter and dangerous. Winston’s boots laid near the door, and I noticed a residue on them, not dust, or dirt, but the confirmation of my suspicions—gunpowder. Moving into the sitting room the most obvious point of alarm was the bullet holes littered throughout the wall.

“You say a ghost is haunting you?” I asked Mrs. Thomas.

“That’s right! I hear strange voices at night and my things move around. Last night I heard a dreadful noise, like screaming—I was too afraid to check what it was.”

“Did Winston hear this noise?”

“He says he didn’t…” She didn’t trust him. It was obvious from her body language, the constant looking over her shoulder, the look in her eyes.

“Do you have a husband, or…” Her face told me to drop the subject. I approached the wall with the bullet holes, where I found another mouse hole. “Owen?” I whispered near it—no response. *Maybe he went back outside after all.* I rose and ran my fingers over the frayed wallpaper streaked with brown and black stains. "How did these holes get here?"

"Couldn't say." I turned to see Winston Banks glaring at me, his aunt cowering behind him. "Sorry for the trouble, officer. My aunt gets confused in her old age. I assure you nothing's amiss here." He delivered his apology like a threat, his voice deep and menacing. He was the sort who never smiled. A towering figure—his hands were double the size of mine, and his eyes glinted with a distrusting, eternal hate of everything he looked up. As he walked, the ground shook beneath him, and I noticed his fingers and expression twitching with his stride—perhaps a tick, or perhaps he was struggling to keep from unleashing his massive strength on the young intruder before him. The old lady looked timidly at me, with a fear in her expression that signalled my danger.

"I see... has she told you she believes a ghost is haunting her?"

"Oh, think nothing of that! Ever since Uncle's passing, and now with Richard, she's been..."

"Right, my condolences for your brother. Were you close?"

"I thought so..." His fists twitched and a low growl welled up in his throat as he spoke. Murder in his eyes. It was time to leave.

"Then I won't bother you any further—good day Mr. Banks, Mrs. Thomas." As I passed Mrs. Thomas, I flashed her a glance and nodded to her, which she seemed to understand as a sign that I'd be back. Down the hall from the foyer, I saw a study from an open door. Winston came over and blocked my view, so I rushed out the door, tipping a hat I forgot wasn't on my head. He didn't want me to see what was in there, so of course I was going to sneak in. Once I was outside, I dived straight into a hedge, as a certain benefactor of the late Richard Banks was approaching. Willy whistled with a spring in his step. He hopped onto the doorstep and

Detective King

knocked many more times than necessary. The door opened and Willy was dragged in by the collar. Slam! Willy was in for some fun. I poked my head out of the hedge, and to my surprise, I was faced by a bewildered Lily and Elaine. Lily held a large cross, while Elaine had a folded robe—Owen's belongings.

"What are you doing in there?!" Elaine asked. I climbed out of the shrubbery.

"Long story—basically I need to get back into that house, Willy's involved... oh, and I left Owen in there." The girls glared at me. "Which is why we've gotta go in there and get him!"

***

Poor Owen would later recount the horrors he underwent in that house. Here's an abridged rendition—

"The walls were dark and rickety. It smelled foul, like dusty pee, and there were tons of bugs. The faint sounds of mice in the distance sent shivers up my spine. I craned my neck up to see a bunch of boards stretching off into the distance, with light poking through what looked like holes in the wall. A nearby squeak made me jump in fear. I realised I was surrounded by mice coming out from the shadows.

"Ey! Outsider! What'ye doin' 'round 'ere?" The biggest among them stepped forward and squeaked. I could understand them, but they spoke funny. I was too terrified to respond (and I wasn't sure they'd understand me anyhow). The big mouse stared down at me in suspicion. "Eh? Which clan 'ye come from?"

"I-I'm Owen! um... my clan is... Lot clan? I'm uh... lost." It was all I could think of. The mouse peered at me with those beady, soulless eyes.

"Ne'er heard of Lot Clan." He leaned in and sniffed me—it felt so gross. "Ye smell like giant." The mice all nodded in agreement.

"Giant?"

LionBolt

"Ye were fancy mouse, yeh?"

Oh, they mean humans? "Um... sure, right! But I got tired of being a pet, so..." The big mouse moved his massive head, which I took to mean he wanted me to follow. We entered the enormous group of wooden boards where mice milled around, some nursing children, others collected sticks and leaves. I was in the heart of a mouse colony. They scurried about all around me. Some mice came up to a gigantic pile of food to add to it or bring some back to their families. Others worked to maintain the structures of the colony. All the mice glared at me with suspicion.

"Ye wanna join Clan, yeh?" The big mouse squeaked. I really didn't want that.

"I kind of just wanted to know more about this house, like how to get inside, then I'll be on my way." The big mouse moved in close, and so did the other mice around me.

"Outsider Owen! Ye trespass on clan territory! Ye join, or ye..." They all bared their teeth and claws.

"I'll join!"

"Then let initiation begin! We start with spreading of scent!"

"W-we're doing what?" The mice crowded closer to me and I smelled something really, really gross. After that... unpleasant experience—they led me toward a dark corner of the colony.

"Ye stay 'ere, nightbreak ye scavenge fer clan. If ye good scavenger, ye receive clan mark."

"Clan mark?" The big mouse showed me a bite mark on his shoulder and grinned.

"Aye, clan mark."

I swear if I get out of here, Arthur... "Out of curiosity... if someone wanted to leave..." The chief mouse looked back at me with a ferocious, menacing gaze. "Forget I asked." We reached a damp patch of leaves and sticks.

"This yer place." The big mouse said.

"I'm supposed to sleep here?"

Detective King

"Nice, eh?" I attempted a smile. "Ye know ye lucky, neh? Any other clan'd kill ye fer tresspassin'. 'Ere, all ye worry 'bout are the giants. Sometimes they make a lotta noise, like they fightin'." Setting aside the terrifying things he said, that last bit was interesting.

"Really? Did they make those holes in the wall?"

"Yeh, we think giants come 'ere to fight sometimes, with them metal sticks. Lotta giants die 'ere." The mice left me to my spot, where I looked up and saw the light from the holes turning to warm colours. There wasn't much daylight left. If I turned human in there...

Arthur here. What happened to Owen will become clear momentarily. Meanwhile, I had devised a plan with the girls to re-infiltrate the house. If we were lucky, I could get the jump on Willy and finally arrest him. Lily rang the doorbell as Elaine and I took our position at the side window. When Winston opened the door, Lily got into character.

"Mister! Please help—my cat is stuck in a tree and I can't reach him!" Her acting was horrible, like she was reading a bad script at gunpoint. Winston waved her away with annoyance.

"Go ask someone else—I'm much too busy." He began to close the door.

"Wait! I can... um... give some kind of reward! I know I have some money with me..." As she rifled through her purse, Elaine and I were sneaking through the window directly behind Winston. Anxious gestures to Lily to keep the act going seemed to panic her (she started hopping up and down), but I was only halfway through.

"Oh! My POOR CAT!" Lily Watson's destiny did not lie in a West End theatre. I fell into the house with an agonisingly loud thump. Winston started to turn around, so Lily—in a panic—grabbed his arm.

"Please sir, it will only be a minute!" Winston broke free,

scowling.

"Enough! Be gone with you!" He stormed back into the house and slammed the door behind him. I looked on from behind the stairs as he passed toward his study, where Willy doubtless waited. Mrs. Thomas was coming down the stairs and spotted me. Without words, I gave her a pleading look and gestured my head in the direction he went.

"Ah, Winston! Come here a moment!" She called. Winston stopped before he reached the study and let out an exasperated groan as he turned back to his aunt.

"Yes?"

"I... was just wondering what you and your guest may like for dinner." His face twisted in irritation, fully unaware that Elaine was reaching into his pocket and stealing his keys.

"That can w—" He paused at the sound of keys jangling. Elaine froze too. "Did you hear something?" I hurriedly gestured to Elaine that she should get out of there. She tucked the keys close to her body and ran down the hall. "Now that just sounded like footsteps. Is there someone else here?"

"I don't know what you mean dear, there couldn't be anyone else here." Mrs. Thomas said. Winston shook his head in confusion, then returned down the hall toward the study. I exhaled with relief and exhaustion.

"Thank you." I whispered to Mrs. Thomas. She nodded in response.

"What do you mean the door's locked?!" Winston's voice rang loudly from down the hall. I tried to keep from laughing. Elaine tossed me the keys.

"You look for Owen, I'll finish off Mr. Banks." I said. She hurried to the wall and began knocking, her ear pressed to its surface. Meanwhile, I made an intentional racket running up the stairs—Winston yelled something to the effect of "I knew it!" and followed me up.

My hiding place under a bed left little room to move—I held my breath as Winston appeared—standing still, like a predator preparing to pounce. A loud BOOM shook the entire house. I had no idea what had caused it yet, but the confusion gave me my chance. As he turned to the window to look at the source of the noise, I sprang out from my hiding place and slapped handcuffs on Winston's wrist—confining him to the bedpost.

"Never turn your back on someone who wants to arrest you."

"You damn brat! What did I even do?!"

"Your brother's dirty work. All those bullet holes, all those enemies your brother made, the fact you have a gun workshop in your cellar."

"How could you know that!?"

"All the gunpowder, the stuff's everywhere! The door's in your study, right? That explosion just now might have something to do with a certain thief and a certain weapons cellar."

"Damn you! You're working together, aren't you?"

"God, no. I want him behind bars. You'll be lively company for him, I trust." Out the window, I saw Willy walking into the garden, fire all around him, with much of the yard scorched and blackened. Elaine and Lily backed away from him, toward the fence at the edge of the garden.

I ran down, leaving Mrs. Thomas to look after her nephew, and saw the gaping hole in the wall, the residual fires glowing in the twilight. He turned his head in my direction, but I was already behind a wall. His eyes glowed an unnatural yellow. Whatever that creature was, it wasn't Willy, not anymore. I dodge out into the side yard, between the house and the hedge facing the street. The first light of the moon shone through clouds, and as I ran to get a look at the backyard—I tripped on something.

"Owww..." Owen raised his now-human head out of the grass and rubbed the sore I'd just made with my shoe. I turned toward him into a sitting position.

"Owen! You're alive! See, I didn't... leave... you..." *Oh drat, he's miffed.*

LionBolt

"Do you know what they did to me? I could've died!"

"But you didn't!" I caught a whiff of a putrid smell that made me gag a little. "What is that smell?"

"Mice are gross animals, Arthur. But more importantly, we need to help the girls out." I nodded and stood. Inching along the side of the house, I peeked into the backyard. Willy was yawning obnoxiously—his eyes returned to normal.

"Lily, where's your brother? I'm getting bored!"

"Shut up." Lily spat. I looked back at Owen.

"Fill me in, what happened?"

"Elaine found me, and was trying to figure out how to get me out of the wall, when Willy came in and made that huge hole. It was crazy bright and hot. When she heard the noise, Lily came in and Willy backed them both into the yard. He said something about playing a game."

"Everything's a game to him." I walked into the yard— Willy turned to me and his face brightened.

"There you are! I thought you'd given up! Y'see I was wagering whether I'd catch your ghost friend and your sister before you got tough guy. Looks like I won."

"Congrats, now leave them out of this. Surely someone who just inherited such a sum can afford to be generous."

"I knew you'd snoop around there. Alas, the money isn't mine to use, so I'm afraid I'm still a proletariat."

"Willy, what's the real game?" I moved in closer and beckoned for Owen to follow.

"Umm, I'd rather not in front of the girls." He said from behind the corner of the house.

"Oh, right, sorry." Willy walked up to me and pointed a finger gun at my chest.

"I'll let them go, if you come with me. I won the game fair and square, even if you didn't know you were playing."

"Actually, I cuffed him around the same time you blasted that hole, so it's really a tie."

"Whatever, come away with me. I'll ditch Scarlett, you'll ditch all the moronic blokes who torture you at The Yard. It'll just be you and me, like old times. We could travel anywhere we wanted, do the Around the World in 80 Days route, or wherever else you like."

"You think you can do these horrible things, burn down Arthur's house, and then expect him to team up with you?!" Elaine spoke with such force and anger, I was taken aback. Willy chuckled, and I smiled at her, flashing her a signal with my head to get out of harm's way before turning back to Willy.

"I can't run away, you know that. I have responsibilities, even if you can't understand that, and that includes stopping Scarlett. She's stealing spirits like the one inside you, right? Why?"

"Why do you care?!" He started pacing around. As he was focused on me, the girls ran to Owen and hid with him, after he put on his robe. "I'll cast this thing out if you'll just..." His head tilted down and he became silent. When he looked up again, his eyes glowed yellow, and I felt heat coming from him. He started levitating and fire sparked in the air. "No one's casting anyone out." It was Willy speaking, but it wasn't his voice—it was deeper, more twisted, more inhuman. "He gave you a chance—now you'll die with the rest of this sullied world." A wave of that dark, suffocating feeling. The ghost sense—stronger than I'd ever felt, It was all I could do not to pass out. My throat was being constricted, like I was being strangled from the inside. My head and heart hurt worse than I thought possible, but I couldn't scream, or see, or hear, or anything. I was drifting into nothing.

This is it, I'm dead. My throat opened, and I gasped for breath. The pain ceased and my sight returned. Owen was standing between me and the demon, holding up his cross and chanting a prayer in Latin. The demon laughed.

"You recruited the mouse-boy?! Why would she have any interest in you? I suppose she's a mystery even to me." Owen looked over his shoulder at me.

"Get the girls out of here! I can't hold him long and the

mice said a lot of people fight here, so I wouldn't be surprised if a gang shows up!" I struggled to my feet, wobbling as I did.

"Told us that a little late, didn't you?" At that moment, Owen was pushed back, barrelling into me just as a flurry of bullets rained into the yard from the street at the far side of the house. The girls ducked onto the ground with us as the demon ignored the bullets. They bounced off him, or were deflected back at their senders. It jerked and one of Willy's eyes returned to its original violet colour.

"Go on. I'm not giving up yet, Arty. I'm gonna make a new world for us, and you're gonna love it. Can't have you dying before you see it." I led my knights through the hedges and we rushed to the nearest police box.

By the time the force got there, any sign of the gang, or Willy, had gone, save for the aftermath of their fight. Winston was arrested, as I informed the chief inspector about the true nature of Richard Banks's death and dealings. Mrs. Thomas was left without a house, but I learned she had a surprise gift of a large sum of money from a Mr. Ernest Garland, which allowed her to live comfortably close to her nephew's new prison. The chief was sceptical of my methods, and of my companions—my 12-year-old sister and a 14-year-old boy in monk's robes, barefoot, and smelling of mouse piddle—but you can't argue with results, and he elected not to do so.

The image of Willy being possessed by that thing, turning into some inhuman creature with such power, haunted me. I couldn't help but wonder whether Willy was working against his will, if what he said was just a trap, or if he was lost beyond help. I hoped our next case would give me insight into the supernatural and guide me toward one of those conclusions.

Detective King

CHAPTER 12 — THE ADVENTURE OF THE NECROMANCER

Most people spend their Saturday getting together with friends or relaxing at home. My Saturday afternoon began by being shepherded into a dark cellar-like room that smelled of exotic incense. Charms and crystals hung from the ceiling and jingled as they swayed from the cold draught from the open door as we were let in. Intricate patterns lined the rugs, atop which sat a round table and chairs filled with a cast of two charlatans and two suckers. Everything in the room was fake, as were the smiles of the so-called 'spirit medium' and his assistant. I looked at Gwen, who came in beside me. We smiled at each other—this was going to be fun. There's a certain pleasure out of exposing frauds, though it wasn't necessarily mean-spirited—it's a public service after all. We approached the table, Elaine following behind us. The 'medium' outstretched his arms in welcome.

"Aha! Welcome! I see you two wish to receive messages from beyond as well! Charles E. Webber, at your service! Please, sit down." He wore a white suit and a striking blue pendant hung around his neck. His assistant, a woman with thick glasses and plain clothes, rushed over and took my coat and hat, as well as Gwen's.

"Thank you, miss." I said. She said nothing, hanging up our things on a coat rack, then rushing back to her spot beside her boss.

"My, you two are young to be seeking the guidance of the spirits!" Webber said. "May I ask—"

"We're 18." Said Gwen. "I-I simply must speak with my dear grandmother once again." The table gave sympathetic looks and words of comfort as Gwen began to tear up the brilliant actress she was. I was still a little too short to pass for 18, but her performance was enough to make them overlook that.

"Th-that's perfectly fine! I'm sure we'll be able to make contact with her before the day is out!" Gwen wiped away her 'tears' and smirked at me in satisfaction. Webber clapped his hands. "Well now, shall we begin?"

A hush fell upon the group. I should note the other participants in this seance—An old woman, who I heard being called Doris, sat next to me. Doris was very skittish, constantly looking about the room as if something were about to jump out at her, which was probably by design, to distract and 'amaze' the poor saps who believed in this sort of rubbish. She was alone and was wearing a black, veil and all, but I didn't think it was a husband she meant to communicate with, as her jittery nature suggested to me she was used to having a companion, and the look in her eyes told me this was an unexpected tragedy she was grieving, so it was more likely a child or grandchild. The other participant was a middle-aged businessman with a moustache that reminded me of my father's. His shirt pocket was embroidered with an 'R', and judging by the expensive material of his clothes and, let's say, generous girth, I deduced he held a high-paying office job. Good with numbers, most probably, since common sense was out the window by coming to this sort of place. Sure, Spiritualism was the day's fashion—politicians, authors, you name it bought into these lies, despite the good work of sceptics in exposing the fraudsters—but this place was a dump compared to the well-known mediums, so he was probably from around this area, which led me to the conclusion that the R stood for Riley Family Trust, and that this was Frank Riley, the owner of the small local bank. As a detective, I go into these games of deducing people unconsciously. Let's see how I did.

Doris trembled with fearful anticipation. Sweat beat down Frank's brow. The assistant took up a pen and small notebook, whilst Webber closed his eyes. He slammed his palms onto the table, causing everyone but Gwen and the assistant to jump. Webber slowly slid his hands toward the edge of the table.

"I am receiving a message..." He said, sounding like he was in a trance. The table slowly lifted off the ground, causing Doris to yelp in fear and cling onto my arm. "M-motherrrrr! Do not be afraid Motherrrrr!" If she were any more tense, the old woman would've squeezed my arm off.

"Benjamin! Is it really you, dear?!"

"It is, Mother! I know how you've grieved for me, but take comfort in knowing that I still live in the next world, watching over you!" Doris wept loudly while I attempted to push her away, as the old woman was twisting my arm in ways it shouldn't be twisted. "I know it can be painful at times, but try to remember our memories together. Can you do that for me?"

"Of course! Oh, my dear Benjamin." Oh, spare me, I may vomit from the sheer stupidity. And yet she and the banker looked so impressed. The table floated back down to the ground and Doris finally released me. Was Elaine laughing at me?! That hurt, you know!

"That was fascinating..." I said in as sincere a tone as I could muster. "Tell me, what sorts of things did you learn about the spirit when you were one with it?" Webber looked from me to his assistant, then back—she handed him a notebook.

"I suppose I should explain—I am unaware of what messages the spirits convey through me during a trance. That's why an assistant—like Cora here," He gestured to the woman. "Is necessary, to record the messages of the spirits" I leaned back, unimpressed, as Webber turned his attention to the dimwitted banker, showing him a cone he called a spirit trumpet from which muffled sounds supposedly from the spirits could be heard. Webber interpreted the spirit's words as being about the man's bank, so at least I was two for two on deductions.

"Elaine, is any of it real?" I whispered. She looked about to die a second time from boredom.

"I doubt you need me to tell you that." The shyster Webber basked in applause and accolades from the others. "What a fraud. You ready to show this trickster he's out of his league?" Gwen and I nodded.

"Oh, Mister Webber, you're amazing!" Gwen said. "I do hope you can contact my grandmother... she had something important to tell me before she passed. I must know what it was! Please!" The tear returned. Webber looked uncomfortable—probably due to the personal nature of the request, it would be harder to fake after all.

"Well, let's see dear... for a case like yours... Ah! Cora, fetch us the spirit slates." Cora strode to the cabinet, bound by ropes.

"Allow me to explain- this here is my spirit cabinet—it contains all sorts of specialised equipment for receiving messages. Spirit trumpets, talking boards, and of course..." She produced two slates, placing them on the table and binding the cabinet once more.

"Chalkboards?" I aimed to sound as annoying as possible. "Are the spirits running a school now?" Muffled chuckles were quickly hushed as Webber stood the slates upright with a thud.

"Very funny! And not far off from the truth, mister..."

Detective King

"James Rider," My favourite fake name. "and this is—"

"Anne Weston. James is my fiancée."

Wha... my mind went blank. I felt light and giddy.

"F-f-fff... you a-and m-me?!" Elaine kicked my leg, and I snapped back to my senses.

"Uh, Ahem. Right. Carry on, Mr. Webber." Gwen was laughing at me—I could see it in her eyes. I wanted to disappear like a ghost. Webber held up a piece of chalk.

"When placed in between these two boards, the spirits can produce written messages for us." He laid the chalk onto one of the slates, then placed the other directly on top.

"How would I even be able to write on that?" Elaine whispered, even though we were the only ones who could hear her. "It's completely covered!"

Scratching emanated from the slates, causing a hush around the table. The sound ceased, Webber carefully lifted the topmost slate, revealing a message written in chalk.

"My dear Anne, how I miss the time we had together. I needed to tell you how much you mean to me. My only regret is that I could not see you wed, so please, cherish your life with James, and think of me whenever you need strength."

Doris sobbed loudly, once again grabbing hold of me. If it were Willy in my shoes, he'd probably have kicked her to the ground, but I restrained myself. Webber leaned forward with his hands tented.

"Well, Miss Weston, what did you think of your grandmother's message?" Gwen and I looked at each other with a nod. It was time to end this.

"It was a nice sentiment, but unfortunately, it showed us just how 'authentic' this whole thing really is." Gwen glared into Webber's black eyes. There was something off-putting about them, as if they were devoid of life. Perhaps he knew his game was up as I placed my badge on the table.

"The real name is Detective Arthur Watson. Scotland Yard's sent us to investigate your practice." That was actually a lie—we'd been busting joints like this all week hoping one of them would give us some insight into actual spirits, but alas, it was becoming clear they were all frauds without exception. "I appreciate the elaborate measures you've taken, but in the end, you were sloppy." Webber slammed his fist on the table.

"How dare you! You've no right to come in here and make such baseless accusations against me!"

"Baseless?" I stood, taking on the role of professor. "Allow me to explain: Your first trick was quite simple." The table slowly rose above the ground, causing Doris and Frank to gasp.

"All you did was wait for someone to tilt the table a bit, as you just did for me, then all you had to do was put your foot under the table leg and lift up. That's why the table is so light." As I spoke, I demonstrated how easy it was to lift the table, and the others even tried it themselves. Gwen stood now.

"The second trick of the spirit trumpet was just a record playing in the background. There weren't real words, but Mr. Riley had no reason to distrust your 'interpretations'. Your last trick was a little more complex. The message was written beforehand, right? Probably by your assistant. Cora, was it?" Cora glared at us. "All you did was cover the message with a piece of black cardboard when you first showed us."

"Still," I said, "you are a decent actor. The scratching sound you made to imitate the chalk was a nice touch." I scratched the table, replicating the sound we were told came from the spirit writing.

"You're wrong. I'm no fraud!" Webber stood, trembling. "What I do is real! That one time, I know it was..." He looked around the table at the others. "Are you really going to believe these children over me, a professional?"

"I... want to believe you..." Doris said, teary-eyed.

"He is a detective..." Frank looked at my badge, glinting in the overhead lamp's light.

Charles turned away and banged his fist on the side of the spirit cabinet. He'd get no sympathy from me.

Detective King

"I expect you to reimburse your patrons... Oh, you wouldn't happen to know about any strange activity around the cemetery, would you?" My current official case involved a grave digging case. Though Spiritualists were suspected by the police, I found that unlikely, but it gave me cover to investigate these places for my own purposes.

"Get out." As Webber pointed to the door, Cora grabbed us and dragged us away. "You scum only seek to tear down our faith, disparage those that believe they can connect with those who have passed on. Get out." That response is why we didn't take Owen—he'd have been too sympathetic to their 'faith'. Elaine pushed Cora off us and took my hand as we stood in the doorway.

"You're more of a medium than he'll ever be." She said. I gave a salute, and the door slammed behind us.

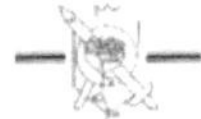

Sam waited with a car outside. He was often relegated to the chauffeur job, but he was a good sport about it. We weren't in the best neighbourhood, as noted by the sorry state of the road and worse look of the buildings, so a guard was appreciated.

"Any luck?" He asked.

"We exposed a shyster, but no lead on the grave digging case, or anything else." Elaine tugged at my sleeve as I spoke.

"At the end, as we left, his assistant pushed back against me. I think she could see me, maybe both of them could now that I think about it. There's definitely something weird there."

"Serious? That's new for a place of this sort." I paused in thought, then snapped my fingers. "Let's head to the cemetery—I think we've had enough fun in the seance parlours." Sam groaned and made a sour face.

"Alright, but I really can't stand this ghost stuff. Whether it's in a cemetery or around a table, it's all creepy." Elaine got a wicked look on her face—she grabbed Sam's hand and placed a slip of paper in it. Sam stood rigid, like he'd seen a—well, you know.

"Whaaat was thaaat?!" He glanced at his quivering hand at the note that read—*Hi, I'm Elaine!* We all couldn't help but to laugh, and I patted him on the back. "I guess I can't deny she exists anymore... N-not that I doubted you, of course."

The cemetery in question was guarded by two statued lions on either side of the wrought-iron gate. As was common in London during autumn, a thick fog hung around us, producing an otherworldly effect. As we crunched through piles of leaves, I noticed Elaine dragging behind.

"What's wrong? Don't tell me a ghost is afraid of cemeteries." I said, falling into step with her. She looked distant.

"Why did it have to be this cemetery?" So that was it. I couldn't imagine how difficult it must have felt.

"Do you... want to visit it?" She shook her head.

"No, I should focus on the present, not the past."

"Elaine... I think Owen mentioned this before, but... if there's an afterlife—" She ran head before I could finish.

"C'mon! We won't solve the case sitting around all day! Let's go!" She disappeared with the others into the fog. Eventually, she'd have to face that question. I wasn't exactly a man of faith, but for her sake, I could at least hope.

Several hours later, after the sun had set, we were still in the cemetery, camped out under a tree. I paced back and forth while the others sat on the ground.

"Arthuuuuuur, what are you even doing?! We've been sitting around all day!"

"Shhh! I'm thinking." The longer this grave robbing case dragged on, the more of a distraction it'd be on our larger investigation.

Detective King

"I should've packed lunch." Sam said, his stomach growling. "Or dinner."

"Can someone go over the details of the case one more time?" They all groaned.

"Ugghh!" Sam laid down in the grass. "A grave was found dug up last week with a body in it, but the body wasn't the one the grave belonged to. The only evidence found were strange markings believed to be spiritualist in origin."

"Which was inaccurate... Alright, I think I've figured this one out." The others perked up, staring at me in astonishment.

"How?" Elaine asked. "All you did was stare at the ground for hours and bore us out of our minds." I smirked and snapped my fingers.

"Elementary, my dear Elaine!"

"Never say that again."

"Oh, fine. But it really is simple when you know what to look for. Truth is, we've already met the culprits." Shock danced across each of their faces most deliciously. "I think I'll hold off on letting you all in just yet. After all, if you know the secrets of my process, I don't look as impressive."

"That's so dumb!" All three of them yelled.

"Shh!" I crouched behind a headstone and gestured for them to lower their voices. Autumn truly is the best time of year—it's so easy to hear when someone's coming thanks to the crunch of leaves. Charles Webber and Cora appeared out of the fog and stopped in front of a grave—Webber holding a shovel, Cora, an umbrella. Sweat beat down Webber's trembling face. Elaine crouched beside me, eyes wide.

"So it was him after a—"

"Not him." I said.

The shovel broke earth, a big cache of soil lifted into the air and discarded of. As Webber dug, his face looked grave and lifeless. Cora looked on behind him, drawing a circle arould the grave, in the counter-clockwise direction.

"She can't be—" Gwen watched in shock as the circle came

toward completion. "We have to stop her."

Webber put down his shovel, shuddering. Cora stood over the newly uncovered corpse and recited something in a foreign tongue—a spell, perhaps? Gwen leapt forward and the rest of us followed. Cora glanced at us dismissively.

"I should thank you—I would've had to dig myself if you hadn't given my little puppet here the push he needed." She sounded bored.

"Why are you digging up graves?" I said, "You—" Gwen pushed past me as I spoke and ripped a silver pendant off her neck. It glowed as she flung it at Cora, who effortlessly dodged it. A fountain of dirt welled up from the impact of the weapon. Cora brushed a piece of dirt from her shoulder and stared at Gwen with the look a teacher might give her most unimpressive pupil. I turned to Gwen in exasperation.

"W-what happened to negotiation?! We can't just—"

"That woman's trying to resurrect the dead. The time for talking passed a long time ago." Cora pretended to look hurt.

"Oh, you don't want to play nice with me? Then I guess I'll follow your lead." She shed her coat to reveal a tight black dress, discarded her glasses, and let her dark hair down, which part to one side.

"Damn." Sam was red in the face. Elaine smacked him with a twig. Cora looked over to Webber—he looked frightened and disoriented—and placed her hand on his forehead.

"Are you ready to submit to me now?" She said. Webber nodded, his eyes clouded. Cora pointed, and Webber charged toward us, the pendant around his neck glowing. Sam stepped between us.

"What's got into him?! I'll take care of this, go after her!" Cora clicked a button on her umbrella, taking its top off to reveal a spear. Gwen produced three daggers, they started glowing. Elaine and I stood back. This wasn't a mystery to be solved or a criminal to take down anymore, it was a battle. I may be bright beyond my years, but I was no fantasy-book

Detective King

warrior—I felt useless. Beyond the fighting, the circle around the grave glowed, a crackling sound pierced the air, and a dreadful scent, like burnt flesh, made me gasp for breath. Elaine poked me with the twig she still held and pointed at the circle.

"Shall we destroy it?"

"Sounds risky..." I took a step back as heat pulsated from the circle and the crackling grew louder.

"Then stand there like an idiot." Elaine said as she ran toward the circle. When she reached it, the light grew blinding, and she was pushed back off her feet. Cora looked over her shoulder at her.

"Good luck breaking the circle from out there! You may be a ghost, but you're no witch!" She dodged to the side as daggers zoomed past her. The spear sparked with lightning-like magic. Elaine was wavering as she got to her feet, and I rushed to help her.

"I think I've got an idea. If we can't break the circle from the outside..." A glance at the tree above us filled Elaine in.

"Arthur, take this!" Gwen tossed one of her daggers[3] at me (don't try at home, it landed at my feet and almost cost me my manhood).

As we climbed up the tree, Sam continued his fight with Webber. After taking a severe blow to the jaw, Webber swayed back and forth—like he was drunk—and pulled out a knife.

"Whoa! Hold on, no need for that now!" Webber grunted and came at Sam, who grabbed his arm. They struggled until Sam turned the blade onto Webber, cutting his arm. Sam leapt back and stared in shock.

"Th—there's no blood!" Webber looked unfazed and charged again.

"So you're already dead, eh?" Sam made a nervous chuckle. "That means I don't hafta hold back, right?!"

---

[3] I would later learn her daggers are called *athames*.

Meanwhile, in the tree—Elaine was walking effortlessly along the branch, while I clung to it, moving inches at a time.

"Elaine, you can't fly, right?"

"Nope. But I have no reason to be afraid of falling, so something like this is easy." I caught up with Elaine and looked down. We were directly above the circle, while the battles raged around it—Cora's spear shooting red lighting at Gwen, as she dodged and deflected with grace. The creaks and sparks made my ears hurt, and the smell of rot made me want to pass out even more than the height.

"Shall we drop in?" Elaine said.

"Ummm... ladies first?"

Elaine flashed an evil-looking smile and jumped, shaking the branch and tossing me to the ground with a yelp and thud.

I sat up after a moment lost to memory, and froze in horror at the black, swirling torrent around me. A raging storm, invisible from outside the circle, tore at me. I couldn't breathe—it was at once hotter than a star and colder than the depths of death. At the tombstone rose a figure, incomplete, not dead, not alive, with a single, flickering eye trailed directly on me. Elaine dropped to the ground at some point—because, after some moments of sitting in a daze, I found myself being shaken by her. I wasn't fully woken up until she smacked me with her stick, which left a little unintentional scratch.

"Arthur! We need to break the circle!" I looked around for the dagger, cursing myself for dropping it, when the storm subsided abruptly. Cora was waving her spear in an arch, then stepped into the circle. When Gwen tried to follow her she was pushed back, as Cora pointed her spear to edge of the circle again.

"Welcome to my circle!" She said, turning to me and Elaine. "Now I won't have to use my previous experiment as the sacrifice!"

"So it's true, you resurrected Webber?" She gave an exaggerated sigh.

Detective King

"But he was a failure—he ended up with a will of his own, save for when I place him under my spell."

Sam heaved Webber over to lie at the edge of the circle and dusted off his hands (they were covered in thick grey dust).

"You're right, he was a failure—he couldn't fight to save his life!" As he spoke, I sprinted behind the tombstone. Cora swung her blade in my direction, destroying the stone and making me stumble to the ground.

"Did you think I'd be that easy to fool?" She said. I smirked and nodded.

"You were." The glow of the circle turned dark and the rising figure of the corpse collapsed in a heap, devoid of any life. Bewildered, Cora turned to Elaine, standing with the dagger—the ground shifted beneath her—breaking the circle. Cora looked around at us Detective Knights in wild fear.

"But, you're just children... She... she won't allow this..."

"She? Who? Why is she making you do this?!" Cora stamped her spear into the ground, causing a great puff of smoke. Once it cleared, she was gone. Don't panic—the title of Detective Knights wouldn't hold much weight if we let her get away.

— ❖ —

Owen told it to me this way—

"Lily and I got tired of waiting for you, and we figured you were either in trouble or you were on one of your bouts of intense thought. Since it was probably the latter, we decided to search for you once I'd returned to human form. Lily knew where the cemetery surrounding the case was, so it was a natural first stop. At the gate, I saw the figures of two people in the fog. I couldn't make them out, but I went ahead of Lily to ask them if they'd seen you. One had a hood on, and the other looked real scared. The hooded one disappeared into the fog, and the scared one—that woman—started running until she bumped into me.

LionBolt

"'Sorry miss, you alright? Have you seen my...' And that's when you slapped the handcuffs on her. I didn't even see you come out of the fog!"

"You caught her! Good job, Owen!" I said to a very baffled Owen. Lily reached his side.

"What did... we miss?" She asked, puzzled.

"Just an average case of a psycho witch raising the dead."

"Oh, that's all?"

"So, will you tell us how you knew it was her?" Elaine asked. "Being able to see me couldn't have been all."

"Well, based on the indentation of the footprints at the crime scene, I deduced that a woman of about her build was at the scene. She came with a different man than she left with."

"All from the footprints?!"

"I could also tell the markings were pagan, not spiritualist. But what convinced me was when she took our coats at the seance. Good thing I kept my badge in my trouser pocket, because she searched through our things, keeping an eye on Elaine the whole time she did. It was obvious she was suspicious of us. With the assumption that something supernatural was at work, the only way she could've swapped out the body and left the scene with a different partner was if she killed her first companion and raised the original occupant of the grave." Sam shivered.

"That guy basically turned to dust after we beat her—I nearly had a heart attack!" Elaine ran her hand up Sam's shirt and he yelped like a puppy. "Don't do that!" Everyone but Cora and Sam laughed.

Something caught Lily's eye—she approached a gravestone, and I followed after she gasped. The last name was obscured by a wreath of flowers, but the rest was clear—Elaine. Born 29 January 1909, died 30 October 1918. Elaine grasped my hand.

Detective King

"My foster siblings place a wreath every year. I wish I could thank them." She usually acted so lively and strong. It was only when she let her pain show when she felt distant. Her hand was so cold, and while she looked sad, it was more of a numb sadness, like she couldn't cry no matter how much she wanted to. Was this how she felt for all that time before we met? I squeezed her hand, and we smiled at each other. Our group moved away onto the street in silence to turn Cora Fox into the nearest police station and put a close on the case of the necromancer spiritualist.

CHAPTER 13 — THE ADVENTURE OF THE NEWSPAPER COLUMNIST PART I

The morning paper is something of contrast. You sit in the peace and comfort of your home, maybe with a hot beverage and breakfast, as you read of the most gruesome and despicable crimes humanity has to offer on the given day. I set the paper down—as we'd hear about plenty of crime the rest of the day. Lily came down the stairs, and to my delighted surprise, was dressed in a school uniform. It was a welcome sight I'd not seen in some time, especially not with her smiling as she was.

"You're finally going back to school?"

"I only missed a few days."

"Or two weeks."

"You know we've been busy around here... and I needed a break." She's struggled with school for years—not because of her grades, she was probably smarter than some teachers—but due to more social issues. Elaine appeared at the top of the

Detective King

stairs, Owen on her shoulder. She hurried down to meet us.

"It must be nice going to school," she said. "I almost forgot what it's like. Maybe I'll tag along with you someday!"

"That sounds fun! We could pull off all sorts of jokes on people!" The girls giggled mischievously.

"You'll be back in the afternoon, right?" Owen asked.

"That's right! Don't worry, I haven't forgotten about yesterday."

"What happened yesterday?" I asked.

"It's a secret." She put her finger to her lips, then skipped out the door.

"Hey!" I tossed her lunch bag to her. She waved and disappeared down the street. "So absent-minded." I put my hand on Owen's head. "You can tell us about your date during the car-ride to our next case." It's fun to watch him get flustered.

"It was not a d—"

"Oh—looks like Sam's here." Owen grumbled as we got in Sam's car and headed to the scene of a crime. Along the way, Owen told us about Lily's antics the day before:

—⬩—

"Being a mouse can be really humiliating. When this curse got put on me, the scariest thing was probably how big everything looked, and how far I'd have to travel just to cross a room. And so, since I can't walk about alone, Lily stuffed me in her bag and skipped along as I bounced about and almost got sick.

"'Where are we going? Y'know, I'm not a pet you can just parade around!' I said.

"'It's a secret.' It wasn't fair. Wasn't as if I could get out of it. I think she noticed I was cross though, and I sorta feel bad for acting so sour. 'So... did you have friends at your church?' She said, breaking the silence.

"'When I was little, I had the other orphans, but when I started exorcist training...'

LionBolt

"'When was that?'

"'I was seven, I think... they discovered I had strong spiritual potential, so I was sent on the path God set out for me.'

"'But weren't you lonely?' That's not a happy subject, so I didn't answer. 'Well, you won't be alone while you're with us! Ta-da!' An old antique shop stood before us. I looked up at Lily with underwhelmed confusion. She giggled. 'My favourite store! You can pick out anything you want, my treat!'

"The store was filled with a ton of old stuff, really cool stuff. Toys, books, various trinkets all round the shelves and tables. It was dusty and stuffy, and the smell tickled my nose, but it was also kinda comfy. Lily made faces into a gazing ball—then we played hide and seek, where I hid in a model ship. There was a little statue of a knight that was really neat. It was shiny, despite the dust, and for whatever reason, I was drawn to it.

"'You like that knight?' Lily asked.

"'There's so much stuff I never knew about...' Lily smiled warmly. She gasped with excitement and hurried over to a bookshelf, then brought over a stack of books and plopped them on the table next to me with a big, dusty thump.

"'If you want to learn about the world, maybe we can get you some books?' One with a really pretty, colourful cover caught my eye, but I knew they'd be no use to me.

"'I memorised most of the bible by ear, but reading's always... hard.' I sounded stupid. Well, maybe I am a little.

"'Nonsense, you just need practice! We could read together.' She looked so excited. I couldn't say no, even though I knew I was just gonna make a fool of myself. I smiled and nodded, then I glanced back at the knight. Lily picked it up. 'I'll get this too. As a gift.'"

We stepped out onto a street in front of a flat block—Owen sat on Elaine's shoulder, smiling, Sam and Gwen followed.

Detective King

"So, that's where Lily took you yesterday?" Elaine said to Owen.

"She goes there every chance she gets—it's nothing special." I said.

"It was special to me—I've never really got a present from someone before, not like that anyway... she promised to read with me later, that's what she was talking about earlier." Sam, being unable to hear Owen beyond inarticulate squeaks, took a breath in, sizing up the area.

"So this is where the fella lives?" We were tasked with investigating the disappearance of a newspaper journalist. He'd been missing from work for over a week, but his disappearance had only been filed the previous day. Into the building we marched. It was old and in desperate need of a remodel, as it smelled of mould and looked water damaged.

"I'll look around his flat with Elaine and Owen after I have a chat with the landlord," I said. "You two go talk with his neighbours, see what you can find out." Sam gave an eager salute. Gwen nodded and smiled, more reserved than usual.

"Everything alright?" Sam asked her as they left.

"Oh—of course, everything's fine. Let's get a hurry on." She went ahead of him, in what I interpreted as a means to avoid discussion. Something was off, but... the thought of prying into her personal affairs was too much for me. I trusted her to come to one of us if something was seriously wrong. At least I told myself that.

The flat offered nothing but further questions, as it was empty, save for a simple chair and bed. He had no appliances in his kitchen, no clothes in his closet, not even bed sheets. I paced back and forth after Owen had scurried into every crevice and Elaine had phased through every wall with nothing to report. Nothing spilled, no sign of struggle—the only thing keeping me from saying it was clean was the immense amount of dust and cobwebs and a very pungent, foul smell whose origins I couldn't place.

"It's safe to assume he only used this place to sleep and

receive his paychecks, if he used it at all." I was more talking to myself than either of them. Sam and Gwen came in, looking exhausted. "Anything?" Sam grimaced.

"All we learned was he's a piece of sh—"

"He's not a popular fellow." Gwen interrupted. They proceeded to tell us of the doors slammed in their faces at the very mention of the missing man's name, with one woman even telling them— 'May God forgive you for speaking that man's name aloud!' before slamming the door on Sam's foot.

"Nothing on our end, either." I said. "It reminds me of..." Elaine had a distant look on her face, like she was trying to make sense of something. "Elaine?"

"This feels different—not like when I spirited away those kids. I sense... hatred... it's kinda scaring me."

"Then let's head to his place of work. Which is... Wha?!" I'd only skimmed over the file the first time around, but upon closer inspection... "It had to be that newspaper?" This case was going to be rotten.

⚜

The click-clack of a chorus of typewriters and a sense of imminent doom. I crept into the office building of The London Compass, stepping carefully, looking around. To be seen meant death.

"What're you hiding from?" Elaine asked. She and my companions walked in normally.

"I know someone who works here. Let's make this quick so we can—" Too late—I was tackled from, I don't even know where, and squirmed whilst encased in the embrace of my older sister Violet.

"Arty-bear!" she cried.

"Oh God, no." In front of Gwen too! *Just kill me now, please.* Violet rubbed her face on mine and squeezes me tighter, causing me to squirm more.

"You didn't tell me you were coming to visit your big sister at work!" Toward the end, she devolved into an insipid baby-talk tone like I was a child. I finally broke free of her clutches.

"I'm not here to see you! This is a strictly business tri—" She had taken my hat off and was putting her hands through my hair.

"You need a haircut! Why don't I get my scissors?"

"You'd end up killing me!" My so-called loyal knights were laughing hysterically at me, like my misery was the funniest thing in the world to them. "Everyone, this is my older half-sister, Violet." I said in a deflated tone.

"Oh, you don't need to say the 'half' part!" Violet said, ruffling my hair. An older, balding man strode toward the group, looking exhausted.

"Watson, what on Earth is the commotion? Who are these people?" Violet turned to the man, startled. She appeared almost to shrink at the sight of him.

"Oh, um, yes, um… this is… um…" Her voice was so meek and soft I could barely hear it. I extended my hand to the man, both as a courtesy, and internally as a thanks for ending my sister's reign of terror.

"You must be Chief Editor Hunt. My name is Detective Arthur Watson. I understand one of your writers has gone missing."

"I see, forgive me, this is quite terrible business, but to see your sister so excited…" I cleared my throat.

"Do you mind if we stay on topic, sir?" The less we talked about (or to) Violet, the better.

"Ah, yes, I apologise. Mr. Killian isn't exactly the most… well-respected in the office." Violet shuddered and shook her head.

"Every woman in the office has some story about him."

"That definitely lines up with his neighbours' testimonies." Sam said.

"Even so," I said, "we must remember that this man is a journalist. What sort of stories did he write?" Hunt and Violet looked at each other uneasily, sighing in unison. We were all lost for words when they handed us samples of the man's work. "You're sure we're talking about the same person, right?" Hunt scratched his head and nodded.

"I know, if we had anyone else to do it, he'd have been fired ages ago."

"But a women's advice column?!"

"I'm sure if the paper were willing to hire more women..." Violet said under her breath. Hunt looked at Violet with a raised eyebrow. "Ahh, I—I, um, I mean no... d-disrespect... s-sir."

"I don't think you said anything wrong though..." Gwen muttered. Owen poked out of my pocket and examined the paper.

"'F-five easy steps to please your man in—' what is this!? Would someone really kill him over this?" Violet grabbed Owen and lifted him up, petting his head and scratching his underside. Owen squirmed in futility.

"You didn't tell me you got a pet! He's so cute!"

"Ahhh! Stop! Don't touch that, that tickles! Arthur, help me!" I laughed at him.

"It's your fault for coming out like that!" *And that's what you get for laughing at me earlier.* Hunt cleared his throat, bringing everyone back to attention.

"If you're through turning my office into a circus..."

"My apologies. I had one more question—when did you hear from mister Killian last?"

"He contacted me on Monday, saying his next article would be late. He never said why, but he sounded agitated." I rubbed my chin, trying to think. Sam snapped his fingers and grinned.

"Whelp, we're not gonna find him standing around here. I have a few places in mind where we can search for clues."

"It better not be anywhere creepy!" Elaine said. "I have a weird feeling about this entire case, to be honest."

Detective King

Sam strode into the bar, with the rest of us following cautiously, looking around with anxious scrutiny. The bartender, a bald man with a moustache, raised a glass toward Sam with a smile.

"Sammy! What'll it be today?!"

"Hey Bart! I'm uh, not here for a drink today…" Some of the other bar patrons laughed. Bart nodded.

"I got ya, info or…?"

"A friendly visit."

"What are they talking about?" Elaine asked. I had to admit, I wasn't sure. Bart pressed a button, and a door opened next to the bar.

"Good luck findin' whoever yer lookin' fer." Bart said as he cleaned a glass. "Wait, are you bringin' in these kids too?" I flashed my badge with a cocky smirk.

"Whatever's back there, I can handle it."

Once through the door, I resisted the urge to arrest the lot of them. Jazz music blared as a woman in a sparkling, revealing dress sung on stage. Youthful vamps and flappers danced in the centre of the club, and at the tables—several couples necked with passion. Smoke hung heavy in the air, and I was pretty certain it wasn't tobacco smoke. I was incredibly suspicious of the pipes and paraphernalia on the tables.

"Sam, you knew about this place and you didn't report them?!" I said in a low voice between the two of us.

"Calm down—this place serves a purpose. You'd be amazed at how easily people talk when they're… we'll say giddy. I've come across plenty of tips here, so long as I (and by that I mean we) promise not to rat this place out."

"I don't like it, but I'll pretend I didn't see it this one time." We approached a… startlingly under-dressed waitress. I looked down and away as we spoke.

"Hey there, you're a tad young to be here, aren't ya?" She leaned in close to me. Gwen shoved me away and looked the woman in the face.

LionBolt

"We need to find a journalist named Sean Killian. Can you tell us if he's been here? Or if someone mentioned him?"

"Well, aren't you pushy? But if he's who I'm thinkin' of, he's a regular. He always gripes about his work, a real creep too. But last time he was in here, he said something 'bout findin' a major story. I paid no mind to 'im, since he was half seas over[4]."

"Do you know where he went from here?" I asked.

"He got in a cab and headed west, I think." I tipped my hat to her and turned to leave, but behind me the woman leaned in toward Sam and whispered something in his ear. The only word I caught was 'danger'. He nodded and tipped his hat—then we left.

"What did she say to you?" I asked on our way out.

"She's just concerned for us, that's all."

"Why? Is there something she's not telling the rest of us?"

"What are you suggesting?"

"Nothing—I'm suspicious of everyone, you know. Nothing new." I think I got under Sam's skin a little, but she was definitely hiding something from us, and everyone is a suspect, as you know.

———

We made a stop back home, and moments later Lily returned from school. She looked... about as I expected. She slouched and moved slowly, her bag dragging along the floor, a frown plastered on her face.

"Welcome home," we said at the same time, though in drastically different tones. Owen popped out of my pocket and grinned at her.

"Hi Lily! Did you have fun at school?" She looked about ready to cry, but managed a smile, though she couldn't raise her head.

---

[4] She means he was very drunk

Detective King

"Yeah, lots of fun." I sighed—this is how it always was.

"It'll get better, Lily." I was never good at comforting her. My attempts always fell flat, like that one did. I switched the subject back to the case. "'A major story', what could that mean? He was a columnist. Was he just spouting nonsense, or…?"

"He disappeared some time Monday night, after contacting Mister Hunt, and leaving the bar." Gwen said.

"Judging by the state of his flat, he never made it home… unless…" I headed back out the door. "I think I may have missed something. Let's go." Lily's face brightened up.

"I want to come too, I can help!"

"No need—I think I've almost found my answer. Owen, why don't you stay here too? I don't want you transforming out on the street." Owen looked grumpy, but perked up when Lily picked him up.

"Fine, leave us out of it." Lily said. "We have plenty to do on our own!" she stormed off with Owen. I sighed and shook my head.

"I just don't want you getting hurt." She was gone before I could mutter to myself. Elaine crossed her arms and stared at me with her head tilted.

"You let me come along." Elaine said.

"But you're already… y'know…" Elaine turned away, skipping toward the car.

"C'mon, you're never gonna figure this out by yourself! I have my own theory about the case, anyway." I had to chuckle at that.

"This should be good…"

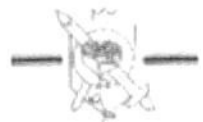

Using a pair of binoculars, I peered out the window of the flat and was astounded to find that I could see directly into a nearby building. What's more, the building was hopping with activity—people milled around looking busy, coming in and out continuously in every room, so that it looked more like a business than a residential complex. Men, women, even a child, who—if I didn't know better—looked like he was ordering people around.

"This wasn't Killian's home—it was a stakeout." I said, turning to my team. "He may have been a columnist, but he saw something in that building he thought was a big story. This is a conspiracy case."

"How can you be so sure?" Sam asked. I produced a crumpled sheet of paper and some paper sterling bills.

"At the bar, I had Elaine go through that woman's pockets. She had information on us and a tad more money than one would expect from her position. Someone payed her off to mislead us."

"You stole money from her?!"

"Anyway, here's what I think happened—Killian was looking into something he shouldn't have, found out something big, then got done in at that bar, no cab to speak of. I'm sure contacting the cab companies would just confirm that. What's troubling to me..." I looked out at the building across the way. "Is what he uncovered and where our journalist might be now."

"Well, thanks for cluing us into all of this. You always do this." I was surprised at Sam's resentful tone.

"Did I say something wrong?"

"Forget it." I shrugged—my genius was overwhelming sometimes, I know. Elaine, however, didn't seem convinced.

"I still feel something about this place. I feel... pain. Something happened here, and I think it's connected with the disappearance. My targets were random for the most part, but... something's telling me there's more to it than that. I think he was spirited away." Not impossible... but no evidence.

"Well, at least we can question the people at the bar—that should at least confirm whether or not my theory was accurate." I said. Elaine made a sour face and crossed her arms.

Detective King

"But... I know something happened here! You checked everywhere, right?"

"Yes! We looked everywhere, you looked on the walls, we talked to the neighbours, who I suppose are also suspects. The only place around here we couldn't have checked would be..." We all looked up together and at once, it made sense. The foul smell, like rotting meat... "Sam, make a call to The Yard. I've made an alteration to my theory."

LionBolt

CHAPTER 14 — THE ADVENTURE OF THE NEWSPAPER COLUMNIST PART II

"The corpse was hidden in the ceiling?! How on Earth is that even possible?" The chief inspector stared at the corpse in astonishment. Police and morticians crowded around the scene, and my team was forced to retreat outside.

"I haven't figured that out yet, sir, though I think it has something to do with those." I pointed to the file being sealed in a bag for inspection. It was filled with papers, presumed to have been typed by Killian, and was found with his body in a compartment between the ceiling and the building's roof. The chief looked exhausted.

"The trouble is, this case is becoming a bit too similar to another case in Mayfair. Both victims disappeared suddenly, then their corpses were found with similar injuries." He had signs of strangulation from what looked like a rope, but there was no way this could've been a suicide considering where he

Detective King

was found—as was the case in Mayfair—where the victim had been on his back porch.

"So you suspect a serial killer is on the loose?" I asked.

"Keep your voice down! We don't want the media sending the public into a frenzy! In any case, I'm assigning two inspectors to assist in the case, try not to slow them down."

"Very well, sir." I barely contained my frustration. Once I'd been dismissed onto the street, I kicked the ground in anger. I was more than capable of solving this case on my own, and there were aspects of it I thought might connect to my larger investigation involving Willy. "That woman had info on us, that's still true… perhaps we should look within at Scotland Yard for our suspect."

"Arthur!" Sam had just come into earshot when I said that and looked cross. "The last thing we need is to rush into an accusation we'll regret later."

"Are you saying I'd make a false accusation?"

"I didn't say that!" Gwen and Elaine came between us.

"Behave yourself, no one needs a bullheaded detective." Elaine said.

"Fine. I'd rather work alone, but I guess I have no choice."

"And since when are you alone?" Elaine scowled and tapped her foot.

"I didn't mean it like that. I just wanted this case to be done with. At this rate, I'll never take Willy down." I lead the way to the car, while behind me I overheard Sam mutter.

"He's such a kid sometimes." That hurt, and he knew it.

After that drama, I resigned myself to working with whomever The Yard threw at me, a hope that was quickly and mercilessly squashed as I stood waiting outside a conference room in Scotland Yard as my new team discussed amongst themselves, occasionally stealing glances at me through the window in the door to the point where I had no choice but to barge in and assert myself.

LionBolt

"Excuse me, I'm getting rather tired of waiting out here, and I'd really like to get started on the investigation." The men glanced at me, then returned to their conversation. Okay, we'll try that again. I pulled up a chair and sat, staring at each of them in defiance. "I know I'm not exactly popular around here, but we don't have a choice but to work together on this, right?" The two inspectors, sitting on my left opposite each other, looked from each other to me.

"I apologise, Detective Watson," Inspector Hopkins said. "we were just engaged in a bit of an argument. Perhaps you could help us settle it?"

"Who would you suppose is best qualified to lead this investigation?" Inspector Gregson said "An old failure, with no real accomplishments to his name, or—"

"A bumbling fool who owes his position entirely to his uncle's reputation!"

I was rather disappointed with them, though they were infamous for their bickering. Hopkins was a greying middle-aged man with a moustache and glasses. He'd just started as an inspector during the time of Holmes and was an avid student of his methods. Gregson was the nephew of another well-respected inspector of Holmes's time. He was considerably younger, dark-haired, thin, and tall. He rejected many of Hopkins's tactics and possessed a large ego thanks to solving a high-profile larceny case that I'd solved by reading reports in the papers when I was nine-years-old. The others at the table were TDCs—a young man with russet hair and glasses, and the familiar face of Timothy Dartmouth, who hated me more than anyone else in Scotland Yard. Tim leaned in close to me, but he didn't whisper, not with the loud arguing of the inspectors causing such a ruckus.

"Say, why dont'cha tell us why you're here? You're sixteen, right? I get that you've got lucky a few times, and maybe that's impressed some higher ups, but I'm not convinced. Sooner or later you're gonna see you're in over your head, and then you'll wish you had that extra six years of school like everyone

Detective King

else.”

“Tim! Stop being an arse!” Hopkins said, interrupting his tirade against Gregson.

“I haven’t a clue what you mean, sir.” Tim never took his eyes off me.

“Nice to see you again, Tim.” I said, “How’s about we rush through the introductions and get to work, alright? After all, I’m sure all of you want to be here as little as I do.”

“Right,” Hopkins cleared his throat. “You’re already familiar with most of us. Russel, introduce yourself to Detective Watson.” The red-haired trainee looked flustered and fiddled with his glasses.

“Good day, I’m Russel Bridges, TDC, but everyone calls me Rusty. Let’s all, um, get along.”

“I agree, Rusty Bridges.” The name made me laugh a little. Gregson stood and looked down over all of us.

“With that out of the way, let’s share our information.”

Pens scribbled on pads of paper. Hopkins and Gregson stared intently at me, only looking down occasionally to write. Tim stood by the door with his back turned toward the rest of us, staring at his watch and tapping his foot. Rusty paced back and forth near the window, looking uncomfortable.

“—That’s my full report.” I said. “I’d like to look into the victims’ personal affairs and habits in more detail, and of course, I need to see the other victim.”

“That won’t be necessary,” Gregson said. “You’ve fulfilled your primary duty on this case already.”

“I don’t understand. I’m still assigned to this case—I should be equipped with all the information available.” Hopkins placed his hand on my shoulder, like I was a kid reaching for something on a high shelf, and he were a parent telling me to stand aside and let him handle it.

“Son, have you ever worked on a homicide investigation before?” I brushed off his hand.

LionBolt

"The first time was when I was 8 years old, a woman who lived in the neighbourhood was murdered by her son. The motive was inheritance money. I figured it out before the police even showed up." Everyone in the room, even Tim, looked astonished by that—their mouths open and their eyes wide.

"I admit, I'm not sure how to respond to that." Hopkins said.

"You really dealt with dead bodies when you were only a child?" Rusty asked.

"I guess I was born to do this."

"Oh, shut up." Tim said under his breath. I admit, that was a tad smarmy. Gregson threw his hands in the air.

"Fine, we'll let a kid work on a homicide case. What the hell. Both victims were killed via strangulation, most likely a rope. Their necks were both broken. The case in Mayfair was originally suspected to be suicide, but the location was suspect and when this case popped up, it became clear something else was afoot. There are no known connections between the victims, but both were found with papers." Gregson produced copies of the documents. Some words were scratched out, but the ones found in Mayfair read: *Many mythical creatures and spirits emerge throughout the mythologies of the Irish. A belief in magic, and of the so-called Otherworld—an ethereal plane similar to other forms of afterlife found in religion and mythology the world over—are commonplace in the pagan annuls of belief. What is of importance in this case is the figure of*—then the rest is scratched out. While it was interesting to me, given the strange creatures and worlds I'd seen thus far, it seemed of only scholarly importance to the murdered. The document Killian held, however, was more grounded.

An attack is imminent—they seem to believe in the magic of old, as do I, having witnessed miracles through my observations of their actions. When they strike, they will have no mercy. God help us. Spirits haunt me, and I fear past sins are coming for retribution. They have unleashed something

Detective King

upon me that shall be my end. One last observation is necessary, but I cannot stand the voices any longer. The roof—that's all he wrote.

"Was he talking about the house visible from the window?" Gregson pondered aloud.

"We've still no evidence he was observing them..." Hopkins said. "What about the roof bit? What does that mean?"

"He went on the roof? To observe whatever he was investigating." Tim said.

"That house was so busy, and so easily viewed," I said. "I find it unlikely he was observing anything else, but I agree he might've gone on the roof after writing this."

"And was murdered there." Gregson sounded satisfied. "The roof certainly makes it easier to deposit someone in the ceiling."

"Was it whoever he was observing?" Rusty asked.

"Probably, though no one seemed to like him much, based on Watson's testimony." Said Hopkins.

"The first passage, about the Celtic mythology." I said. "The murders are so similar, there must be a connection, what was known about the Mayfair victim?"

"Emmanuel Hawk," Hopkins said, "53 years old, a lawyer—mostly dealing in financial disputes, very technical sort. He lived with his wife in Mayfair for twenty years, well-liked by his neighbours, active in social clubs. No living relatives, no known connection to Ireland or any sort of mythological study."

"Perhaps it was a personal interest?" Rusty said.

"Then why seal it in a file, in the same manner as Killian's?" I said.

"We can't rule out coincidence," Gregson said, "but it is worth investigation." Hopkins rose and rubbed his hands together.

"Alright, now we have a homicide investigation! Follow me, you'll each learn a lot from this case, I'm sure of it!"

LionBolt

Gregson stood on his toes in an attempt to loom over Hopkins.

"I agree, Inspector Hopkins. When I've solved the case in full, you'll be well served to study my methods."

"Or mine, gentlemen." I said, striding past the both of them as we headed out. It was essential to assert myself as not only an equal, but as an authority.

"Let me sock him, just once." Tim said to Hopkins. "He could use it." Hopkins chuckled.

"Only if he fouls up." Tim grinned, staring into the back of my head like a hungry wolf.

As we filed into the newspaper office, I hid behind my colleagues as Violet passed, gleefully dragging Gwen along. Earlier, I'd asked her to take Violet out somewhere—the last thing I needed was for her to make a scene in front of the other detectives. The editor, Edwin Hunt, met us with a tired expression.

"Welcome gentlemen. I hope you find what you're looking for. After all, it must be important for you to interrupt my work again." I raised my hand.

"May I ask a question, Mr. Hunt?"

"Watson, how... pleasant to see you again."

"I want you to confirm the victim's residence, as well as his business expenditures from the past few months." The detectives looked at me with disdain for speaking out of turn.

"Boy, learn your place!" Hopkins said.

"My place is as an investigator on this case, sir." I said it with a dose of faux innocence that I knew infuriated those who thought themselves better than me. All the while, Elaine was busy digging through the files on Hunt's desk. She held up a handful of files and I smiled in triumph. "Now if you would, Mr. Hunt?"

"I can say with certainty that his address was the correct one—that was where we sent his checks anyway, although he'd only recently moved there. Unfortunately, our financial documents are…" Elaine handed me the files, and I held them up.

"These, right?" They all looked so shocked. Sure, it was cheating, but it got the job done and their stunned faces were so hilarious.

"How did you…?!" Hunt wrung his hands and fumbled with his glasses. "It doesn't matter—you'd find out, eventually. You see, Killian… was married."

"And why on Earth didn't you share that with us from the beginning?"

"Because she died last year. Sarah Hawk was our advice columnist before Killian. He ended up taking over after—" The other detectives jumped at the name.

"Did you say 'Hawk'?"

———

We gathered at the Mayfair crime scene. A light rain began to trickle onto the back garden, where we observed the site of the murder.

"What a sorry bunch you all are!" I said. "You mean to tell me not one of you brilliant Scotland Yard detectives looked into the connections of the man's relatives?!"

"That's enough, Watson!" Hopkins's brow was furrowed in a scowl. "You didn't research your victim's relations either!"

"My investigation started yesterday! You've had a week!"

"May I remind you that you still answer to me, boy!" Gregson snorted in amusement.

"We'd be better off with a smart-mouth brat than a senile old—"

"I've had enough from you too, George! Honestly!" Hopkins lit a cigarette and let out an agitated groan. Elaine had come with me and pulled on my shirt sleeve to get my attention.

"I feel traces of a presence here. A spirit is connected to

this case, I'm certain of it."

"I'm not convinced." I said, "After all, I think I've pieced together much of this case already." Hopkins laughed.

"Well then, let's hear it!" It's frustrating when other people overhear your conversations, especially when your speaking partner is invisible to them.

"I believe Sarah Hawk was murdered last year. In his writing, Killian mentioned something about 'past sins', so either he's responsible for her death, or thinks himself responsible for whatever reason. In any case—the group Killian was observing was involved, and are organised enough to silence him and attempt to throw the investigation off through false witness testimony, like in the... establishment I mentioned."

"And Emmanuel Hawk's connection?"

"Hawk wrote his bit about mythology as if he were answering a query from someone. Either they were corresponding with each other in a sort of vigilante murder investigation that got them both killed by this organisation, or they were communicating with a third party. I think that's likely, as it was this third party that required the redactions."

"This supposed third party is whom?"

"That I don't know yet, but—" Tim laughed, in a very obnoxious fashion.

"You're nothing but hot air! There's no conspiracy here, no third man. We have no evidence that the people he was observing have done any wrong, no evidence Sarah Hawk was killed, the very document you cited paints a picture of a Sean Killian slowly losing his mind, he was delirious." His face was red with passion, and he barely breathed as he berated me. "And worst off, you've failed to mention how the victims actually died!"

"Both were strangled via rope, with Hawk tossed onto his back porch here, while Killian was placed in a ceiling that was already open. You saw the sorry state of that place—I asked the landlord about the condition of the building, including whether the roof leaked—which of course it did, but one flat's ceiling had recently been patched up. Whether Killian went on the roof or stayed inside, he was taken into the ceiling compartment while repairs were done on the neighbouring flat."

"Why hide it?"

"To delay the body's discovery."

"Why would that matter?"

"Because whatever Killian has uncovered, whatever scared him so viciously that he feared to stay in his vantage point—is very much time sensitive. He says so in his written statement."

"Hooey!" Tim said. "Your theory is based on a fantasy! Nothing but assumptions about the victim, with little evidence." Hopkins stepped forward.

"I'll take it from here, Tim. Let's assume you're right in that Killian was investigating some criminal organisation, or at the least something unusual that caused him to poke around where he shouldn't have, like at the establishment you cited earlier. What of Hawk? His body was not concealed, and while there's no evidence of a struggle at the flat." Hopkins led us to the side yard of the house. A row of flower bushes were trampled and muddy footprints showed a trail leading into the bushes and one would assume through the window. "A break in is clear from the evidence. Setting aside the documents, which were not stolen from either man, mind you—why would this killer be so much sloppier? And how was Hawk connected to Killian's investigation by this attacker?"

"The documents are the key to everything. Both documents mention spirits—"

"All that proves is that Killian was delusional. To leap into a groundless conspiracy is irresponsible and, frankly, is disappointing, Watson. Have you considered that waitress' information came from the fact that you're a well-know figure in the media? A teenage detective and son of John Watson, there are few who don't know of you, so why is it such a surprise that someone would recognise you?" The inspectors started leaving, satisfied with their arguments against me.

"At least let me stake out the house," I said, causing them to turn back around. "let me see what spooked Killian so bad. The connection is there, you must see it!" Tim chuckled and put his arm around my shoulder (more so my neck).

"I agree! Let's put Watson's ideas to the test! I'll stakeout with him and see if there's some shadowy organisation at work here. Of course, if there isn't, we'll have to look for other suspects, with other motivations for killing poor Mr. Killian. If I recall, someone's sister works for the very same newspaper as Killian. Wouldn't she want that columnist position real bad?" I pushed him off me.

"Shut up. Violet has nothing to do with any of it."

"She did say as much..." Rusty stood in the doorway. I hadn't noticed he wasn't with us—shame on me. "I trailed Ms. Watson—she mentioned wanting a columnist position, and didn't have many kind words for the victim. What's worse, there's been another murder." We all looked at him in shock. The waitress from the bar was found dead. I sent Sam and Owen back there to follow up with her and the bartender, but when they got there, it was a police circus—she'd been slashed through the chest, as if with a sword, but there wasn't any blood, like the blade was so hot it cauterised the wound instantly. Sam and Owen had met up with Gwen and Violet while they were at a cafe, and from there Rusty—who had been trailing them—heard of the crime. "How did her friend know about the murder? Sam, the TDC, didn't mention it." Owen must've told Gwen about it.

"Well, there you go!" Tim said, puffing out his chest. "A different means of murder, but nevertheless, it directs back to your familiars, Watson. Is it not conceivable that your sister killed Killian for the columnist position, stuffing his body in the ceiling as you described, but the victim's former brother-in-law happens to witness the crime, or she reads something of him in the scratched out portions of the document? She kills the man to cover her tracks, or has him killed. I see no

Detective King

issue yet."

"Why would she kill this waitress?"

"She knew where the bar was," Rusty said. "mentioned it was on Westbridge in Battersea. Perhaps that's where she lured Killian from, and how the waitress got info on you, but then she got nervous and had her taken care of as well."

"That's absurd!" I said. "Once we've finished a proper investigation, my sister's name will be cleared. I can assure you of that!"

"And if she's guilty?"

"Then I'll place her in handcuffs myself." I stormed out, as Tim, and even the inspectors, laughed at me. Elaine came along close behind.

"Arthur, listen to me. I feel a dark presence at both these places. I know a spirit is involved, I'm sure of it."

"They already think I'm a fool, Elaine. They'd be more than happy to throw Violet in prison just to take me down. I won't let them. There's an explanation to all of this—we've almost reached it."

"You're not listening to me!"

"Because I know I'm right!" She glared at me, then turned her back.

"Fine, go on your stakeout without me, then."

"Fine by me. Find me evidence for your theory, then I'll believe you."

"I will." What a stubborn assistant I was saddled with. Why did I have to prove myself to everyone, even Elaine? Why couldn't they accept me as the Detective King I knew I was? I'd show them. Before long, they'd all have to apologise to me, I was sure of it.

—※—

Needless to say—the stakeout was tense. At nightfall, we settled into the same flat Killian (purportedly) spent his final days. We had a telescope set up, three spots on the floor, and a very negative atmosphere. Tim and I pushed each other as we both tried to peer through the telescope. Since he was quite bigger than me, he won out, so I stood beside Rusty instead.

"Not one light on in the joint. Looks like you're gonna lose our little bet." Tim said with an ill-concealed blood lust.

"It'd really please you to see my sister dragged off?"

"If she's the crook, yeah, that means justice has been done. Not only that—you'd probably lose your job."

"What did I ever do to you? I know I can be boastful, but you've hated me since we first met." During our first encounter, Tim had tripped me heading into the classroom. He led various other attacks against me after that—ranging from stealing my clothes from the locker room to dumping a cauldron's worth of something sticky the ants they sicked on me seemed to like very much.

"You represent everything I despise in this world, that's all." Tim said casually. "I've been working to get here for all my life, even then I'm the disappointment of a family filled with business leaders and judges. Then here you are, years younger and already a full detective. I want you to feel the struggle I had to endure until that smug look on your face disappears forever. Understand?" He looked at me with a grin, head cocked to the side.

"If you think I've come all this way without working for it, you're a bigger fool than I thought. Now give me a look." I shoved him out of the way, but there was no change in the dark house. Tim groaned loudly and paced back and forth. After another eternal hour of no change and supercharged silence—a light. One light flickered on in the house. We all crowded around the telescope to get a look and when I did, it felt like I'd been punched in the gut. The room was empty, save for an old man sweeping. After a while he left and turned the light off, then he moved to the next room, and again the room was empty. All that waiting, my entire theory—lost.

"No, no, we need to go over there, this is wrong." I was frantic, embarrassing myself. Tim and Rusty shook their

Detective King

heads.

"There's nothing there." Rusty said, with an expression you might give a pitiful child who's lost a toy.

"I won't lose to you!" I charged out of the flat and scrambled down the stairs. Whether they were following, I couldn't tell—I was vaguely aware of tripping and falling on my face, but I got back up kept running because it was my only choice. I couldn't be wrong. Something must have happened—there was some twist. I reached the dark, empty house and banged on the doors. When no answer came, I forced a window open and stumbled in. The room was dark and vast, but more than anything, it was bare, save for a decade's worth of dust. I stood there, alone in the darkness, and screamed. Tim and Rusty jimmied the door open and gazed at me in the doorway for a long while. I wasn't myself, I was something much worse, something worthless, but what scared me was that this worthless creature was closer to the real me than any boastful Sherlock-wannabe. The janitor came down the big wooden staircase and looked at the scene in surprise. Tim stepped forward and attempted to explain our situation.

"This building'll be turned into new housing," the janitor said, "no one's lived here since before the war. If you saw people here earlier, they were probably the renovators."

"Right, so sorry for the intrusion, sir. Good night." Tim tipped his hat and brisked out. Rusty took me by the arm.

"Wipe your face and apologise to the man." When did I start crying? Was I really so weak?

"S-so sorry, sir. I'll pay to fix the window. Good night." I barely wheezed it out. I handed him my contact information and rushed out. We stood under the light of a street lamp, Tim and Rusty staring down at me, reminding me how much shorter I was than them.

"Well, I knew you were just a kid, but that was sad." Tim said. "Your eyes are still puffy—get a grip! Things don't always go your way, that's the adult world! You think this is all a game for you to win?" Rusty grabbed Tim by the arm.

LionBolt

"Enough."

"No, he needs some sense knocked in him. You want to be some big-shot who's respected by everyone, don't throw tantrums every time someone levies a harsh word or two! Are you going to cry again? Do you want your mother to come and make everything better?"

"That's enough, Tim!" Rusty lifted my hat off my head and leaned down to look me in the face. "Hey, calm down. We all make mistakes, we can't be right all the time." I couldn't respond—I was hysterical, the boiling point of months, more like years of stress and anxiety, of reaching for a goal I never really understood. I was consumed by the idea of being the best, of being respected as an authority. Now the mask was off, ripped away by reality. "How's about we take you home?" Rusty said. "We can figure out the rest later."

"My sister..." I choked out. "Is innocent. Of that, I'm sure."

"That's something the investigation will determine." Tim said. They ushered me into the car and taken home, disgraced.

Chapter 15 — Healing

I couldn't look the others in the face when they asked what was wrong, especially not Elaine, not after what I'd said. I shut my bedroom door and laid in the darkness, cursing myself. Then the door opened and someone sat by my side.

"How bad was it?" Elaine asked. I didn't answer or look at her. She groaned and shoved me off the bed. "Now is that any way the Detective King is supposed to act?" I shifted myself away from her.

"That's just a dumb dream, leave me alone."

"It is not dumb!" I was surprised how angry she sounded. "It's that ambition of yours that saved me. Does it make you do dumb things? Absolutely. Are you a stubborn, arrogant, selfish jerk sometimes? Sure. But the detective I know doesn't give up so easily, that's why I'm still here."

"You'd be better off going wherever's next."

"I chose to follow you. It's up to you to live up to that trust. You're not acting just for yourself anymore, there's more at stake now. Violet's innocence, and everyone who's going to get caught up in Willy's plot. We're counting on you."

"I don't want to be counted on!" I glared at her with fury— an anger directed not at her, but at myself and the miserable world around me. "Most people my age care about their grades, getting dates, their local football club. Why do I have to shoulder this responsibility? I wish I'd given up a long time ago." Elaine shrunk away, looking hurt.

"And leave me?"

"You know that's not what I meant."

"Why did you become a detective in the first place? The real reason?"

"My mum told me to change in the world, to be like King Arthur. Detective work is all I'm good at, so I got saddled with this. I hate being a detective, dealing with such atrocities and horrors. I'm sick of it." Elaine shook her head and scooted back by my side.

"I don't think that's true. I know you, Arthur—better than you think. You love solving problems, and bringing bad guys to justice. You love being praised for your intellect, and you get frustrated when you come up short because you care about your work. Maybe you were saddled with this, but I don't think you'd be anywhere else if you could choose. You want to be the next Sherlock Holmes, the Detective King, right?"

"If my own sister gets hanged because I can't compose myself—"

"Then don't let that happen. You're not alone Arthur. You never have been." Lily and Owen peeked in from the door.

"You saved my life and gave me a home, Arthur. Don't give up when there's still work to be finished." Owen said.

"If someone's responsible for mom's death, you need to bring her to justice. If you have to face some challenges along the way, so be it. We'll help." Lily said. My cheeks felt hot and I couldn't help but smile.

"I'm embarrassed. I made such a scene in front of my colleagues, and you. But thanks, all of you." They all laughed.

"We know you need your hand held sometimes. No detective is perfect!" Elaine said.

"Alright, enough. Lily, call Sam and Gwen. Let's check in

with Violet and clear up this mess."

My knights were gathered around me on the sidewalk outside Violet's flat. The lights were off, but this was too important to wait.

"Where's Gwen?" I asked.

"She never picked up the phone." Lily said.

"Maybe she's still with Violet? They were together when I saw them." Sam said. Onto her doorstep, I reached for the knob when Elaine gasped and pulled me back.

"You can't go in there! I knew I sensed something wrong! It's dangerous!"

"Then I have to go in there! If Violet's in danger..."

"There's nothing you can do against something like this!" She trembled as she held onto me. "I'm afraid... of losing you. Let me go, I'm a spirit too, I can—"

"Then you'd be in danger. This is my fault for not listening to you earlier and letting the real culprit run loose. I need to take care of this."

"Arthur, you still don't get it! You don't need to shoulder that responsibility by yourself!" I grabbed the doorknob as she spoke and immediately I felt intense pain, and a rising anxious feeling that made me want to scream. Owen leaned on his cross and winced.

"I feel it too, this isn't right." Something was pulling me, drawing me toward the door. I tried letting go of the knob, but I was frozen in place. My knights were reaching out to me and yelling, but I couldn't hear them, and soon they got darker and darker, further and further away as the darkness swallowed me whole.

CHAPTER 16 — WILLY — THE OTHER LONDON

Scarlett knelt at the grave in silence for a long while before placing a rose before the headstone.

"For all that you suffered, I will end suffering and create the world we were promised in scripture and take what was stolen from you. Mary." I stood some distance away, occasionally glancing at my watch. She'd come to this small plot atop a hill several times before, almost every week since I joined her revolution, yet not once did she explain why. I couldn't fathom a reason she would grieve for Mary Morstan—John Watson's first wife who died shortly after Arthur's older sister was born—I was sure the Watson siblings had some connection to Scarlett, some key to her revolution, but what I couldn't figure. Might as well ask once more, right?

"I ask this every time—but who the hell are you, really?" Usually she didn't respond or gave some strange, vague answer like 'the one who will unlock the gateway' or some ethereal crap like that. This time was different. She stood and smiled at me.

"Would you like to see? It's about time you know the full

truth."

"I hate when you get all philosophical, but if you're willing to finally fill me in..." She took out a key from—who knows where and waved it in the air. Then she took my hand, and we jumped forward together. At first I thought it had suddenly become night, but as I looked around me, the sky swirled with colour like a painting and strange creatures floated and flew through the air. We overlooked a city marked by enormous trees surrounded by buildings with strange, organic shapes. Lights fluttered and danced in the city—a soft, sweet-smelling breeze flew by—the wind had an almost musical sound. It was an enchanting sight. "This is an Otherworld?" I asked. Two short figures wearing tall hats hustled toward us. I was taken aback when I saw their faces—one had the face of a dog, the other a cat. He halted and bowed to Scarlett. She looked at me with that mysterious, confident expression she used around everyone else.

"This is OtherLondon. My domain—the refuge of those who slip through the cracks of reality." She led me—flanked by the cat and dog—through the city, which was alive with creatures of every shape and size. Most wore wizard robes like the cat and dog—they came in a variety of colours, but were designed the same way, flowing down to the ankle, while an additional garment was worn over the shoulders and many topped it off with a hat. It felt like Halloween, only no one wore a mask. They really were wolfmen, lizardmen, harpies, you name it. One fella with a giant set of wings nearly hit me in the face while I tripped on another's tail. Smells of spices and unfamiliar earthy concoctions spread around me as the crowd chattered on all sides. When any of them saw Scarlett approach, they'd stop anything they were doing and immediately bow to her. As her presence became known down the street—the chatter fell silent and rows of magical beings lined up to bow to their queen. One fella found himself stuck in the middle of the road. Not knowing where to go, he jumped right through me and bowed from behind us, appearing translucent for a moment. At the end of the street—in the centre of the city—was a grand tree, with a massive estate snaking along its trunk. The place looked very much like Buckingham Palace—the gates were even the same, but it was at least 10 times larger, featuring hanging gardens and waterfalls on its various levels. A vast set of doors ushered us into a grand hall, adorned with colourful banners, lavish chandeliers and artwork, and more servants than I could count. I had countless questions, yet I found myself speechless. I followed Scarlett up a steep, massive staircase. We passed floors of halls, gardens, outlooks over the city—hell, the palace itself was a small city. We walked up a long way, but I never felt tired, and we reached the top in what felt like a minute. Leaves of every colour, even outlandish ones like pink and blue, formed a natural mosaic around us. Beyond the leaves was the city—sprawling out in every direction, its lights looked like fireflies dancing about. On the roof itself were ornate fountains, with the water flowing upward and floating around in the air, forming intricate patterns. At the end of the roof was a lone girl. Scarlett led me to her, her face concealed by a hood.

"It's about time you met." Scarlett said, "My fifth horseman, I suppose you could call her, as you can never have enough help in a revolution." The girl looked away, out at the city below, and sighed heavily.

"You're Red?" she said.

"I'm William. You are?"

"A lap dog, a slave, call me what you will." She turned toward Scarlett. "All is proceeding as expected, he only knows what he's allowed to know."

"And he trusts you?"

"Without question. You'll uphold your end?"

"Of course, dear. I only want the best for Arthur, same as you."

"Wait, wait, wait!" I interrupted. "What are you talking about? What about Arthur?!" Scarlett patted me on the head, but I swatted her hand away.

"Arthur is an important piece in the plan. You know we collect spirits, yes?"

"Of course, I was step one of that."

"Actually, you were step five-thousand or so. We're building an army here in OtherLondon. Can you feel the power this place lends you?" It was true—I felt lighter, stronger, like I could run forever, or tackle the sun.

"So you'll invade our world from this one?"

"No no, then we'd lose our advantage. We're going to merge this world with yours. The only way to do that is with a bridge between worlds. One stone in that bridge is that thing around your neck." She pointed to my locket. "Another is the one I took from Arthur." She held up the sun locket. "And the final is a soul with a foot in both worlds."

"You're saying that's Arthur?"

"Possibly. I sense something from him. His connection to John can't be coincidence."

"And what's your connection to the Watsons?" Scarlett looked away with a wistful expression.

"I care deeply for that family—to which I've sinned greatly against." That's no answer, but what did I expect.

"I want your word Arthur doesn't get hurt." I said with a growl. If Arthur were harmed in any way, everything would be for nothing.

"That's exactly what I want." The hooded girl said. "We're to build a new world—combining this one and the other. A babel from beyond."

"It sounds like our goals intersect..." I said. The girl came up close, so I could see her face—red hair and blue eyes.

"If you hurt Arthur, or anyone else unnecessarily, I will kill you."

"My, you're a feisty one! Believe me, I want a world of peace and equity for everyone—especially Arthur." The hooded girl turned away. "Hey, what's your name, anyway?"

"Anne Weston." Obviously a fake name. She knew

Arthur, so it wouldn't be hard to figure out who she really was. A small, furry servant rushed from the stairs and blew a trumpet that was too big for it.

"Ah, that would be Ash." Scarlet clapped her hands and a large door appeared out of thin air. It opened and Connor walked through, along with at least 50 men and women, all carrying various weapons.

"Hey Red!" Connor waved at me with a big grin. "Yer detective friend almost caught us! You shoulda seen the fit he had when we gave him the slip!"

"I can imagine. Nothing frustrates him more than appearing to be wrong when he isn't. Everything's in place for the operation?"

"With Lugh[5] as witness, we're ready to bring hell!" The hooded girl took out a key and sliced in the air, much like Scarlett did when we entered OtherLondon. She stepped through and disappeared. Scarlett tossed me a key of my own.

"Don't lose it. Should someone else find it, it'd mean your head." Scarlett said.

"Got it." I slashed like they did, but nothing seemed to happen.

"Just walk forward, it'll work." I did as she said, and sure enough, I was back in London. Soon whistles and sirens started blaring, and I became aware of men in red uniforms running toward me. I glanced behind me at Buckingham Palace.

Ah, now it makes sense. I slashed with the key again and disappeared.

Scarlett's preparations were impressive. The resources and power she'd built up over the years were growing by the day, and to be her general in such a magnificent undertaking was

---

[5] Celtic God of Light

an honour. That is—if I trusted her. Her presence was a mystery—every day leading to more questions and always with an underlying uneasiness. Was I scared of her? Course not! She was a riot—and if I'm gonna follow anyone, it might as well be someone entertaining. I wanted to see what new form the world would take once her plan was achieved, but that didn't mean I wanted the same things as her—I wanted my vision for the world and I would follow Scarlett so long as those visions aligned. And so, my own scheming was necessary (in any case, it's more exciting when you cause trouble).

I tracked down Arty and saw him get swallowed into an Otherworld, his friends rushing in after like idiots. Coin flip's chance they'd make out alright, I'd step in if things took a foul turn. But first, my attention turned to the fellas outside the flat—a couple of half-witted wannabe rozzers who'd make most excellent pawns. They crouched behind a post-box—their jaws agape and their eyes wide in an unsightly display of ignorance.

"Could you tell what happened?" The tall, dark-haired one said.

"I haven't a clue. What should we do? This doesn't feel right." The scrawny redhead in glasses said.

"So let's run away because we got a bad feeling." The first one said sarcastically. "Come on, if that brat went in, so are we."

Their names? I asked the demon.

Are we going to kill them? It asked.

Of course not, we're going to use them.

You know, the more we kill, the stronger I become. You should kill more, it's good for your health.

Their names, psycho-demon?

Timothy Dartmouth and Russel Bridges. Want me to divulge all their greatest fears and secrets?

Nah, that's the fun part—I'll expose those myself. I sprang from my hiding place on a roof and grabbed Timothy Dartmouth by the arm as he rose from the safety of the post-box.

LionBolt

"My God, Rus—" He looked down and noticed I wasn't Russel.

"I wouldn't go in there if I were you." I said with a polite grin. "Not without me, that is."

"Who the hell are you?!" I unhanded him and raised my hands.

"Whoa, whoa. Easy there, I just wanna help you out a bit. You do want to get the upper hand on Arthur Watson, am I right?" Dartmouth laughed under his breath.

"That's tempting, but after the show he put on earlier..." Russel sprung up behind me and grabbed my arms. Timothy took me by the jacket collar. We smiled at each other.

"I tend not to trust anyone who approaches me out of nowhere in the middle of the night. Talk."

"I'm an old friend of Arthur's. I happen to know a bit about the shit he's been getting mixed up in, so I figured you'd wanna hear what I have to say."

"Your name is William Manders, isn't it?" I laughed.

"You must really hate Arthur if you've done that much research on him. Or perhaps you're really in love with him." He stepped on my foot and dug in hard.

"What about you? What do you gain by talking to us? I should arrest you right now."

"But you won't, or should I say you can't." Shadowy figures with glowing eyes appeared out of nowhere, slowly growing in height and build. They were spirits from OtherLondon that I'd taken through with me. They were grunts with little intelligence, but they'd be far too strong for any normal person to overtake. "You're gonna act as an inside man for me, Timmy. We both wanna mess with Arty, so you shouldn't have a problem with it. But even if you did..." A shadow grabbed Russel and flung him into a wall. He screamed in pain and fell to the ground. Timothy's eyes remained defiant. Impressive. "Calm down, he'll be fine—maybe a few broken bones. Meanwhile, why don't I tell you a story filled with ghosts, witches, and a talking mouse?"

Detective King

CHAPTER 17 — CLUES AND CONSPIRACIES

I felt numb, like I was disconnected from my body. The world was dark, but there were steaks of light all around, stringing together in patterns that reminded me of a spiderweb. I managed to glance down at the cocoon of light string constricting me. My knights streamed in with tendrils of light creeping behind them. I wanted to warn them, but nothing came out when I tried to speak, and soon everyone but Elaine was unconscious and entwined in the web, much as I was.

"Arthur! Owen! Lily! Sam, anyone?!" Elaine called out for us frantically. I couldn't answer her—a powerless bystander once again. "Who are you?! Why are you doing this? Please, just give them back to me!" She must've been talking to the ghost. "I was like you. I was filled with anger and sadness. The world was like a black, endless pit. I had no one, and it was scary—because I felt consumed by hatred and jealousy. So I did bad things too." A voice echoed from the strings.

"You know nothing of what I've suffered. They deserved to die. After all, my own life was robbed of me." It reverberated unnaturally, like there were a hundred voices speaking together. As the ghost spoke, the blackness of the void splashed with crimson, and chilling screams rose from all directions.

"That doesn't mean you can kill people. Whatever injustice or evil hurt you—if you decide to hurt people too, you're no better than those you hate. I know you understand... Sarah." The red splatters shot out like blades, stopping just short of Elaine. She closed her eyes and tensed up before opening her eyes as a woman appeared from a cloud of mist before her. She was slight and her skin was pale, almost see-through. Her hair was knotted and messy, and her white dressed was a tattered mess—like a doll that'd been abandoned for many years. The ghost's face came close to Elaine's.

"It's you who needs to understand. Understand the worthlessness of life, and the depth of my pain. A pain you should well understand." The red spikes exploded into a red fog which Sarah disappeared into. "I was used by everyone. They worked me, and worked me, yet if I tried to speak my own mind, I was silenced." The fog dissipated and the ground below Elaine collapsed into water. She splashed into it, sinking deep into its depths until Sarah pulled her up and hovered over her—her face only barely above the surface. "I was drowning in a world ruled by thieves. My accomplishments were stolen. Those who claimed to love me only used me. And in the end, they even stole my life from me." Sarah pushed Elaine down into the water, which shifted into roaring flames circling around her, from which Sarah reappeared. "Tell me what worth there was to my life? What justice is there in letting those pigs live, whilst I anguish in endless solitude?!" Elaine stepped toward Sarah and grasped her hand. The flames fell away, turning into a cascade of flower petals.

"No life is worthless. I used to think the same way you did." The scene around them faded into black. "After I died—I felt so lost, like there was no meaning to any of it—that there was no way to fill this void inside." The black of the void turned to white, starting from Elaine's feet, and expanding to encompass everything. She smiled. "Now I know I only felt that way because I was alone. I needed to blame someone, so I blamed the world—but instead of wallowing in my despair and hatred, I should have been doing something about it. I should've been looking for the meaning of my life, instead of assuming there was none."

"You're just a child, spouting idealistic nonsense. I lived through what this world really is. We are all puppets to a pointless fate." My body was pulled forward and hung down like a marionette in front of Elaine—along with the others, including Violet. Again, I tried to call out to her, or move my body, but it was hopeless—It was up to Elaine to save us.

"Arthur! Everyone! Please, you know you don't have to do these awful things, you can find peace now! Just let them go." Sarah looked away and cast out her hands. The ground became chequered and a large, red queen chess piece appeared before her.

"I don't want to let go. I was nothing in life, but now in death, I have power. Even if it's wrong, I won't give it up! When that woman appeared to me and asked me if I wanted revenge against God, I gladly said yes, and I would again." The chess piece moved toward Elaine, fire swirling around it.

"Woman? I think I know who you mean—so I can tell you she's just manipulating you. Did you really feel such despair before you met her? Didn't she put these ideas in your head?" Sarah didn't answer, instead she waved her hand again and the chess piece charged at Elaine, causing her to jump out of the way. Elaine looked up at me and the others.

"I know I can get through to you, with a little help. Besides—taking two turns in a row is cheating." Behind Elaine, two bishops, a rook, a knight, two pawns, and a king manifest in white, each with a name on it. "Each of us has dedicated ourselves to living for each other. Owen lights our way with his undying faith. And Gwen puts all of her emotions into her magic." The bishops move across the board. "Sam charges head on into battle to keep us safe." The rook slides close to the queen. "Violet and Lily work hard every day, so that one day they'll make something amazing of themselves." The pawns bounce forward one space at a time, then transform into queens. "Arthur leads us, like the king he says he'll be, and I'm his knight, who will fight for him until the end! Checkmate!" The knight moved into place and as all the pieces surrounded the red queen, it glowed and shattered. Sarah looked enraged, but tears flowed down her cheeks. She touched her face with surprise.

"I don't understand. You were abandoned—all of you. God has not shown you any mercy, and yet you trust each other, care for each other. Why? Why bother with this wretched world and take the risk of relying on someone who can break your heart?!" Elaine grasped Sarah's hand and smiled.

"If we just open our eyes, we can see a wondrous world around us, with incredible people, and a bright future. We shape how we view the world, its people, and ourselves. By moving past the sorrow and suffering we may see, we can find peace, and see the world as beautiful again."

"I'm afraid. I don't want to disappear, but I've sinned so greatly."

"Then make up for it now by doing the right thing. Then you can finally find the peace you've been searching for this whole time." Everyone was released from the strings, and the void fell away into Violet's flat. I could finally move (after hitting the floor hard and painful), and as I struggled to look forward I saw Elaine and Sarah embrace, as Sarah turned transparent and twinkling sparks of light radiated from her.

"I'll accept whatever punishment I deserve. Looking back, I never hated anyone, and I didn't want to kill anyone, but those dark emotions took hold of me and I became something evil. That's exactly what that woman wanted. Stay away from

Scarlett, don't let her use you."

"Do you know why she's doing this, or where she is?" Sarah floated upward and disappeared, leaving only twinkling lights. Her voice growing fainter and fainter.

"She's preparing for war and needs spirits to do it. Thank you, Elaine. I hope you too find peace." The last of the lights twinkled out as the others awakened. I reached out and took Elaine's trembling hand.

"You're the best knight anyone could ask for." She sat down and leaned against me.

"Does that mean you heard everything?" I nodded, while Owen sobbed loudly (he's such a softie).

"You're so strong. You didn't run away from your past... Like me."

"What do you mean?" Elaine asked. Owen wiped his face.

"Nothing, I just think I'm ready to face some things of my own." Sam struggled to his feet and squinted in Elaine's direction.

"Is that... was that Elaine?"

"Can you finally see her?!" I asked.

"N-not really, it was only for a moment. But I feel like I should thank you, Elaine." He smiled and tilted his head in the wrong direction. Lily helped Violet stand, swaying as they rose.

"Arthur, you have a lot to explain for."

"I'll gladly tell you everything, but it's a bit of a long story, so I'd sit down first."

We marched out of Violet's place in a cheerful mood, relieved the case had been resolved.

"Next time you come visit, I expect more ghostly stories, Arty-bear!" Violet called from her doorstep.

"Hmm, I wonder who you're talking to, because I don't answer to that." The others laughed at me.

"Y'know, not a lot of time passed—we could grab dinner!"

LionBolt

Sam said, pointing to his watch.

"We should check on Gwen first. She never showed up after all..." Elaine and Lily giggled amongst themselves. "Laugh all you want, nothing wrong with being concerned for a friend."

"What friends you have, Arty-bear!" The voice was tinted with malice as Tim emerged from the shadows. "You're talking about Gwen Adler? And you all are Samuel Tristan, Owen Lot, Lily Watson... and Arthur Watson in the middle of them, conducting illicit obstruction to an ongoing investigation." His stance was aggressive—his feet planted firm as he leaned forward as if ready to pounce—but I noticed he was shaking.

"You met Willy, didn't you? That's how you learned everyone's names." Tim stuffed his hands in his pockets.

"I don't know who you're talking about." He jerked his head upward as a signal, and I nodded.

"Well, be careful if you ever do meet him," I said, loud enough for Willy to hear. "he likes to play games with people. It's often his goal to give himself as many trump cards as possible, but I'd say my hand's still stronger than his."

"Not if you're crying every time things don't go your way, nor if you're going behind The Yard's back. I'd be within my right to take you in right now." I walked past him, stopping just behind him.

"Says the guy in Willy's pocket. What'd he do?"

"Enough to tell me you're no threat to him."

"We'll see. I think I have my own trump cards." I looked back at my knights following close behind me. "Whose deck will you choose to be part of?"

"Whichever is the safer bet, but I'd rather fold than lose out to the likes of either of you."

"That may be for the best." We departed from each other and I left with my team in tow.

Detective King

Hopkins scrunched up his face, his fingers pressed onto the bridge of his nose. He took a deep breath.

"I'm still having trouble with this—what exactly happened again?" Tim and I sat across from the inspectors in the conference room, smiling, with Rusty beside us with his arm in a sling.

"In our investigation we came across the true culprit, William Manders." Tim said.

"He and his thugs attacked us, causing Rusty's injury." I said.

"Although I have no memory of the incident. It's all very troubling." Rusty looked down at his arm and winced.

"And you were investigating... together?" Gregson asked.

"We came to an... understanding." Tim said. I smirked and placed my arm around Tim's shoulder.

"Yup, we're the best of friends now! Isn't that right, Timmy?" Tim glared at me before clearing his throat.

"Th-that's right, mate!" His tone was as if he'd called me a curse, then he punched me in the gut harder than one would if they were playing with a chum—but we kept up our fake smiles nonetheless. Gregson and Hopkins looked at each other in confusion and shrugged.

"Whatever, now we have our suspect, assuming your evidence pans out." Hopkins said. "What was his motive, if I might ask?"

"As you know, he's been engaging in a series of attacks on business leaders." I said, going through the lie Tim and I crafted. "We think Manders is amassing a group to carry out a larger scale heist, and Killian had found out."

"We think he's enlisted Irish separatists," Tim said, "which is why Killian had his brother-in-law research Irish mythology and superstition, which led to Hawk getting caught by Manders as well."

"And the waitress?"

"Must've found something out from Killian." Her death was in truth still mysterious. It wasn't Sarah's doing, but her dying so soon after my visit was no coincidence. Hopkins and Gregson looked thoughtful for a moment.

"I don't like it... it seems off." Gregson said.

"There are the negotiations going on..." said Hopkins. The government was in the process of negotiating a treaty with the Irish republicans to establish a free state in Ireland and end the fighting that'd been ongoing for nearly two years.

"True, there are some radicals that would resort to terrorism to keep the fight on..." Gregson said. "But to be linked to this case feels... off. I can't put it any other way."

"If I may..." I raised my hand, "I think there's a bigger plot at work here, and if you'd allow Tim and I to investigate and confirm our suspicions, I'm confident we could avoid a major incident." The inspectors looked pensive again.

"It's the Chief's decision, but I don't see any issue..." Hopkins said.

"I agree, so long as you both take full responsibility if you're mistaken, or fail to stop anything... unforeseen." Gregson said. We both saluted.

"Of course." We said together. Rusty nodded to us and saluted with his free hand. The inspectors rose to leave.

"Then we'll leave it you." Hopkins said. "Watson's in charge, as the highest in rank. That alright, Tim?"

"Wouldn't want it any other way!" He said through gritted teeth. The inspectors left us, and as soon as the door closed behind them, Tim and I pushed away from each other. "That was humiliating!"

"Same here, but all went according to plan."

"So how do you intend to catch your supposed Irish nationalists?"

"Odds are there's some group planning something, and if there is there's a decent chance Willy's got some hand in it. Worst case—we nab Willy by himself and say his terrorist cell fell apart without him. Easy."

"If only you were as a good at detective work as you are at lying."

Detective King

"I prefer manipulative narrative." Rusty glanced at us with a frown.

"I don't enjoy being left in the dark." Tim patted him on the back.

"Some weird stuff's been happening to our friend, Arthur, and we're going to help him bring the guy who did this to you to justice." He said, looking at Rusty's cast.

"Why do you sound so insincere? And why lie to our superiors?"

"Would you believe a ghost was the real culprit in Sean Killian's murder?" I asked. Rusty stared at me like I was a ghost. He glanced at Tim, who nodded in agreement with me.

"I don't understand any of it." said Rusty. "But if you need me to believe in ghosts, I guess I'll play along." I wouldn't call Tim an ally, and the new investigation we'd just launched wasn't what it seemed. There was no guarantee he'd really cooperate in stopping Willy, since he could easily choose to side with him and discredit me. Rusty was oblivious to all of this, as per Tim's wishes, but while the arrangement was a dangerous one, it was an extra two sets of eyes to search for Willy and Scarlett[6]. I was still convinced I saw something suspicious in that flat block, and I was certain something big was about to happen that we needed to stop at any cost.

I commandeered dad's study and set up a large cork-board which I'm fond of using to organise my thoughts on complex cases. The study was a small room next to the sitting room—book shelves mostly filled with medical writing and my father's own work about Holmes, along with a large desk of

---

[6] I suspected her name was Scarlett already, as it was the same name as the shadowy boss Willy alluded to in a previous run-in, Sarah simply confirmed it.

LionBolt

dark wood (I'm a detective, not a woodworker) took up of the space in the study. I wrote notes and tacked them on my board, with occasional help from Elaine or Lily.

Let's go over the facts we know, shall we? Scarlett is plotting a so-called revenge against God, whatever that means. To achieve this—she is gathering spirits, demons, and the dispossessed, like Willy, or Cora the necromancer, who wish to overthrow the current order of things in this country. She looks exactly like my mother, sounds like her too. Mum died from the Spanish flu in early 1918, just before I turned 13. While nothing strange or nefarious was suspected at the time, the way Scarlett looked at me, the way she spoke was so malicious, so murderous—I couldn't help but suspect some link between her current plans and my family tragedy of almost 4 years prior. Willy unleashed a demon that had been sealed away in Owen's church for centuries and is now semi-possessed by it, giving him supernatural powers, but not always total control. Willy is working for Scarlett and is amassing large sums of money and supplies by killing or terrorising prominent members of business and the criminal underworld, as witnessed by his actions against the Banks brothers, though his loyalty to her is shaky, given his offer to run away together. Finally, he attempted to coerce Tim to act as informant within the police (who knows if he's the only one Willy's pressured). All of this points to the build up of a large scale operation in which they use spirits to attack the foundations of British society.

As I laid out these facts, having assembled them for a nighttime meeting, my knights looked on pale-faced.

"When you put it so plainly, it's rather daunting." Sam said.

"I think she killed our mother." Lily said.

"We don't have any hard evidence of that yet…" I said.

"I don't care, I can feel it. She's done such horrible things and turned Willy into a monster. This is a murder investigation."

Detective King

"I sort of hope you're wrong, but my gut agrees with you."

"Either way, they killed Father Michael, and Mr. Banks, and who knows who else." Owen said. "How are we supposed to fight demons and killers?"

"I've been thinking about that..." I smirked and produced my work of genius—a diagram representing the truth of all these occult happenings. As I stepped away to allow my colleagues to witnesses, my greatness tacked onto the board, I was puzzled when they started laughing.

"What is that?!" Elaine gasped between laughs. "Did you consult with a toddler?" I felt my cheeks turning hot.

"Wha—This diagram represents how Otherworlds work—I believe they're the key to this fight." I admit, my drawing skills are to be desired—the lines were a tad squiggly and upon a second look, it was... busy. I was in a hurry, and I'm a detective, not an artist!

"What's that scribble in the middle?" Gwen asked (at least she attempted to keep in her amusement).

"Th-that's a ghost..." I said quietly. "The diagram's not important." I ripped it off the board to end the ridicule, "the point is—ghosts live between this world and another, a world they can manipulate and control. This works two ways though—Elaine was able to pull people from our world into hers, while Cora pulled a soul from the other world to reanimate corpses—proving both worlds can influence each other, and even merge, like Elaine's park, or Sarah's world and Violet's flat. Clear so far?" Gwen and Elaine nodded and smiled, while the others looked less sure. Owen raised his hand.

"The other worlds aren't heaven or hell, right? Where did Sarah and that Minotaur boy go after they disappeared?"

"I don't know. My understanding is that ghosts are restless spirits who have some reason to materialise in both worlds, so maybe we pass somewhere else when we're at peace..."

"You don't believe in that though, right?" Owen's assertive attitude was surprising. Glancing at Elaine, I could tell she was uncomfortable with the conversation.

"I don't believe, I look for evidence." I said, "Cora awakened souls that weren't previously ghosts, so either those spirits were in a resting state, or they existed in the other world and simply couldn't connect to this world—either way I need more evidence to make a determination." Elaine sighed. I knew this topic was difficult for her, being closer to 'passing on' than any of us.

"So how does this help us fight them?" Sam asked.

"It gives us a direction. We know they're using the Otherworld, and the power it gives spirits to stage their attack, but it also gives us a direction to attack—if the other world is cut off from ours, they lose their leverage. The question is how we bring down Otherworlds. Up to now, we've only stopped them by convincing the spirit to relent, except in Cora's case, which gives us an important clue. Otherworlds can be influenced by magic, after doing some more research (inspired by the documents we found with Emmanuel Hawks's body), I've learned that magic has been used to communicate and influence the Otherworld since ancient times, right Gwen?"

"To practice magic is to take fate and nature into your own hands, yes."

"Not really man's place..." Owen muttered.

"It's not always a choice we're able to make." Gwen sounded annoyed at Owen—best to move on.

"If we're to fight, we need to be able to cut off their world—and by extension, their power—by force. Once we can do that reliably, we'll have a strategy against them."

"What about Willy's demon?" Lily asked. "It acts through him, rather than a world."

"The only thing that's worked against that thing is Owen's exorcism." Owen looked down and scrunched up like a student who doesn't want to be called on by the teacher. "Can you do it?" I asked.

"I don't know... I'm not good enough yet, I'm too

sullied."

"Owen, that's not—" Lily reached out to him, but he shuffled away. I cleared my throat. I'd talk to Owen about it later...

"More than anything, we need to learn more about the demon's power, but for now, focusing our strength on the spirits is our best chance. Sound good?" My knights didn't sound enthusiastic, but it was better than stumbling blindly against an enemy we didn't understand. Elaine raised her hand.

"I'm curious about one more thing—who was the spirit that attacked us at the park after I released Lily and the kids?"

"We went there plenty of times since, so I've still no idea, other than it must've been involved with Scarlett. It seemed powerful, but we managed to escape that one without magic."

"Did it just let us go?"

"Or perhaps there's an exit in every Otherworld. Only way to know is to get experience. That's why..." I reached behind the desk and heaved a massive stack of papers onto it. I patted the top as I caught my breath. "This here is every potentially supernatural occurrence from the past year. Anything reported to Scotland Yard, mentioned in a non-tabloid newspaper, or happened to be overheard by myself or one of my contacts throughout the city is collected here. Our job is to investigate each one."

"How long did it take you to collect that?" Lily asked, looking more concerned than shocked.

"Oh, just 10 or 12 sleepless nights, no big deal. Sam helped a great deal." Sam sighed, looking tired.

"And who are these contacts?" Lily asked, sceptical.

"Police officers, store clerks, nurses, children off the street, really anyone who would tell me anything, or agree to keep a look out for a small fee."

"You're going to bankrupt yourself." Lily said, exasperated.

"I won't starve with you and Marianne as my cooks." She

stuck her tongue out at me. "OK, everyone take a profile, whichever's most promising, we go after!" We were on the right track—I could feel it. The mystery of my mother's death, the witch woman Scarlett, and my demon possessed former friend would all become clear, and I'd finally be rid of this supernatural nonsense.

CHAPTER 18 — LILY'S DIARY PART I

17 November 1921

My mouse in shining armour. He never fails to brighten my day. He's so sweet, and whenever I look at that knight figure on the desk of the study, I can't help but to smile and think of him. I certainly needed lifting up after the day I had.

My desk had scribbles all over—they wrote some horrible things—and some junk that wasn't mine filled the inside, so I had no space for my own things. The usual girls crowded around me, with their queen, Rachel, sitting on my desk like a throne.

"Lily! You've been gone so long, we thought you died! Oh well. So we're keeping some stuff at your desk—hope you don't mind." The girls all laughed as Rachel tossed a skirt at my face. "Stitch that up for me? Thanks. Oh, maybe wash it too, it could use it." As they laughed, Rachel leaned in close. "If you ever skip out on us again, some rumours might spread around that you'd rather not want." Then the bell rang, and they went to their own seats, looking like good little girls in front of the teacher.

Enough about them, and I don't want to even mention my stupid brother leaving me out of his mysteries. In the evening, none of that mattered. I got to sit with Owen and a book in the study.

"Just then she heard something splashing about in the pool a little way off," I read "and she swam nearer to see what it was; she soon made out that it was only a mouse that had slipped in like herself."

"'Would it be of any use now', thought Alice, 'to speak to this mouse?" Owen read. "I don't really get what's going on, but it's definitely interesting. We certainly didn't have books like this back home."

"When I first met you, I couldn't help but to think of Alice in Wonderland—I'm sure you see why now. Hey, tell me more about you. Like... your favourite colour?"

"Yellow, it reminds me of Easter."

"How old are you?"

"Thir—no, fourteen. I'm still not used to saying it, since my birthday was only a few weeks ago."

"But that was right before we met you! You should've said something!" I was a little cross with him about, though maybe I shouldn't have been.

"It's no big deal. I didn't even know when my birthday was until..." He trailed off and looked back at the book.

"It's okay, you can tell me."

"I'd rather not, just forget it." We fell silent for a moment, though it felt like a long while.

"When Elaine and I visited your church... the priest was so relieved to hear you were safe, and he mentioned someone named Margaret..." Owen's eyes got wide he sat quietly, like he was searching for words, then he stood and marched toward the door with his head down. "Wait! You don't need to leave!" He didn't look directly at me, but I glimpsed a tear.

"Just forget about it." Then he shut the door behind him.

Detective King

I put my head in my hands. What had I done? Why do I push people away? His face broke my heart, and I didn't know why. I looked at the knight on the table again. So brave, like Owen was when he protected us from Willy. I needed to be brave too and make things right. I wasn't going to let him close the door on me, because we still had plenty of chapters to get through and a promise is a promise—we'd read it together.

LionBolt

CHAPTER 19 — INTO THE OTHERWORLD

After 2 weeks of following every lead, we could and barely surviving a variety of spirits[7], we came upon the deciding case. The treaty negotiations with the Irish were quickening in pace, and an agreement was expected (or hoped for) any day upon the arrival of December. Tim and Rusty did their part, keeping track of Willy's movements, with Tim even meeting with him to maintain his trust. Whether he was letting Willy in on our plans was unknown to me, but I made sure not to tell Tim enough to jeopardise anything. On one particularly cold morning, I received a message from Tim telling me to meet him at an address in Brixton, saying he knew where Willy's hideout was and that we needed to act fast. I thought it odd. First of all, I didn't trust Tim, but more than anything, his letter was... cordial. Usually correspondence from his read something along the lines of—*You dumb bloke, your maniac mate stirred up a street riot AGAIN!*—then he'd usually lob some

---

[7] Perhaps I'll write these cases down someday?

Detective King

expletives in my direction, but in this letter he didn't curse once! Lily was already at school, and Sam was called in to The Yard, so I arrived in Brixton market with Gwen, Elaine, and Owen. Tim was indeed there, so far so good, but he looked tense. We huddled together next to a food stall.

"What's she doing here?" Tim pointed his thumb at Gwen.

"I'm a Detective Knight, thank you very much." She said.

"You're no detective. I suppose you've got the mouse in your pocket too?" Owen popped out and saluted him. "So weird. I've been staking this place out for a week, I'm certain he's staying here."

"So why not report it officially? I see no inspector." I said.

"Because that'd break my deal with that devil. That's why I need you to go in there, as if you found him on your own. That way if you mess it up, I'm in the clear."

"You can't walk that tightrope, Tim. Eventually you'll fall."

"I'd rather you take the fall for me—in that spirit..." He pointed into an alley. "Third door on the right. If I don't hear from you in 12 hours, I'll assume you're dead."

"I'm sure you'd be so sad." I said sarcastically.

"Of course, I'd be disappointed if I didn't get to do it myself." I tipped my hat and headed down the alley, but something nagged at me and I stopped, turning back to Tim.

"Oh yeah, where's your partner?"

"He's at The Yard, not that it matters."

"His arm feeling any better?"

"What, are you, an old woman starved for gossip? Don't worry about Russel, focus on your own job." I nodded and went down the alley.

"That's not Tim..." I muttered.

"I thought so..." Gwen said. "What happens in 12 hours?"

"We're going to find out." I halted before the third door. "Elaine, follow Tim." She still looked stunned at my deduction of false identity.

LionBolt

"But what if this is a trap?"

"This is definitely a trap, but I need to know where that fake goes, and who he really is." She nodded. I picked Owen out of my pocket and handed him to her. "You too—best not to be alone."

"How will we know if you need help?" He asked.

"Hopefully we'll meet you back home when we've finished, but if you don't hear from us by tonight, have Lily report us missing to Scotland Yard." They left us and hurried after the fake, albeit with reluctance. I turned to the door and after a deep breath and a silent prayer to no one, I turned the knob.

A river flowing in mid-air was my first clue this was an Otherworld. The door disappeared, replaced by a misty grey horizon and several rivers crisscrossing above and adjacent to us. Beneath us was grass, which squished as I tread as if it'd just rained. The rivers made a trickling noise that echoed in an unnatural tone—like little voices speaking to each other in an unknown tongue. We walked forward cautiously—then stopped—a sound in the distance gave me that terrified, anxious feeling and a pain in my gut. That was the first time the ghost sense was triggered by a sound, but it was a noise that'd strike fear in any man—a tortured, hungry howl of a creature I could only imagine the enormous size of. It was followed by another howl, this one slightly different—deeper, like the first was an exclamation, and the other a threat.

"Th-they sound far off," I said, trying my best to sound braver than I was, "besides, if it was Willy who sent us here, I don't think he wants to kill me—he's said as much." The howls sounded again—closer. "Even so, let's quicken our pace." We hurried past the curious rivers, each shimmering with countless fish of every colour. We followed the one directly above us, from which we could see the fish quite clearly, and I'm sure it would've been beautiful (and maybe romantic) had the dread of whatever made that howl not been dogging us, growing closer and more severe with each howl. My father faced down a supposed demon hound during one of Holmes's investigations—but this was something truly supernatural, enough to make Gwen tense up at each sounding of the hounds.

"Do you know what's making that sound?" I asked her.

"I have a few ideas, none of them good."

"Swell." We reached a turn in the river, and as we turned, I saw our reflections in a wall of water before us. I stopped and looked closer. There was us... and something big behind us. I turned in terror—nothing, just mist. Gwen snatched me by my coat and lugged me away from the river before us—our reflections obscured by that big something. A howl so loud my ears rang, followed by an intense pain in my chest—Gwen struggled to make me move as my eyes fixated on the hulking beast that jumped out from the water and stared us down with its row of fangs and fiery eyes. It was taller than me, slinking forward with massive claws. Its ragged pelt was white, except for its blue feet, red tail and purple hind legs.

"Don't look at it." Gwen said. "Don't make it think you're a threat." We backed away slowly, as the hound matched us step for step, inching closer. Something fell on my head, and we backed up to an enormous tree, which stood surrounded by the rivers that flowed in every direction. I glanced down at what fell on me—a hazelnut. "I know what this is..." Gwen said, leading me to the far side of the tree, "The rivers should lead to a well—if the stories are true."

"Does that help us?"

"According to the stories, it's a well of wisdom, though stories about the Otherworld aren't always reliable."

"Well, we're kinda facing down a hell-hound—" Another howl, so loud I thought my head was going to split. The howl turned into a low growl, and we turned slowly to see the beast behind us—then turned back at the beast circling the tree from the other side. "Make that two hell-hounds."

LionBolt

"When they charge, kick it in the face and run for one of the rivers." Gwen said, getting into a running stance.

"What if it bites my leg?"

"Then you'll be down a leg." She glanced at me and winked in that cute way of hers. This was not the way I envisioned our first adventure, just the two of us. The hound in front of us pounced, and we dived in opposite directions. The other hound raced toward me, so I kicked its face as I was told, moving away just before it could snap its massive jaws on my leg. Stronger than I expected—the river carried me along with the fish at the speed of a bullet. Even so, the hounds followed from outside the river, keeping pace just behind me. The river zigzagged so much I got dizzy—desperate for breath, but when I started to sputter, I found I wasn't drowning—I could breathe natural and easy. I spotted Gwen riding a nearby river, which soon converged with mine. She grabbed my hand as we fell into a whirlpool at the confluence of all the rivers—the well. It was a gigantic hole, with the rivers turning into waterfalls as they fell into it. The hounds halted the edge of the water, their eyes locked onto me. As they stared, they opened their mouths, and I swear I could hear two voices, speaking in unison, echo in my head.

"Save our master from the witch of Emain Ablach." What that meant I hadn't a clue, nor did I have time to think it over as we went over the falls into the well.

Everything was white, like I was floating in a sea of milk. Small orbs of multicoloured light sparkled around me, starting soft, then glowing brighter as a voice whispered in my mind.

One truth, one wisdom, one question, one answer. After a moment of utter confusion, I realized what it was trying to say—Gwen said it was a well of wisdom, so perhaps it was offering to answer a question? Might as well try.

"What must I do to keep my promise? To be the Detective

Detective King

King?" What was I thinking? I should've asked about Scarlett, who she was, her plans, how to stop her, how to save Willy from the thing inside him. Instead, I go back to that childish promise to Mum? The white of my surroundings filled with colour, like watercolour paint spilling onto a canvas—a scene formed.

I saw myself standing atop a building (or maybe a cliff—it was fuzzy). The only things in focus were myself and Willy, facing each other, Willy with a ragged, deranged expression, while I looked strangely calm—serene even. I said, "I'm sorry, and I forgive you, too." Then I fell from the ledge and...

I gasped for breath, my entire body shook violently and I felt sicker than I'd ever felt in my life.

In the vision... did I die? Why would it show me that? How would that make me the Detective King? What would that mean if I were dead? Did it mean anything, anyway? My mind raced, my heart pounded. Is it saying I should stop with this playing at detective, give up? I looked around—I was sitting on the side of a street I didn't recognise—the sky had patterns and unnatural colours (mostly purple and yellow). The buildings around me seemed intertwined with trees and rose into strange shapes, while the people walking about were all dressed in robes, like they were playing at being Merlin. I was still in the Otherworld (or I was asleep or dead). I leaned against a nearby wall as I stumbled to my feet. Where's Gwen? Cloth fell on my head, and I screamed (I think you can understand I was more than a little on edge). The cloth fell away and Gwen stood before me, giggling, though her expression soon turned to one of concern.

"I'm sorry, I didn't know I'd scare you so bad."

"N-no, I-I'm alright..." I wasn't alright. She picked up the cloth, which upon a second look was the same sort of robe the townspeople wore. Gwen was wearing one too.

"Put this on, you're soaking wet," I looked down—it was

true—I hadn't noticed I was drenched, "and around here people wear magical garments, you'd stick out dressed like that." She turned away, and I reluctantly began to undress. "Did something happen? You're taking awhile…" I couldn't keep a grip on anything—I was struggling to undo my shirt buttons.

"Wh-what did you see in th-the well?" Gwen took a long while to answer.

"I saw us sealing Scarlett away in an Otherworld—one where she can't hurt anyone anymore." She was lying. I could hear it in her voice, but I wasn't about to press it, at least not then. I managed to get my clothes off and slipped the robes on, despite the trembling. "What did you see?" Gwen asked.

"I died." She turned to me, eyes wide (good thing I'd finished dressing).

"Th-the well is simply knowledge, not a set future," her voice shook. "I'm sure we can avoid it, I…" She was shaking nearly as much as I was—then she hugged me tightly. I didn't see it coming, but as she embraced me in her warmth and her sweet scent, the trembling stopped and I calmed down. "Don't die, okay?"

"I'll try my best." She knocked me on the head playfully, then took my hand. We walked through what looked to be an entertainment district, with lights flying around and forming impressive patterns, and robed figures juggling balls of fire and water before combining them into a cloud of floral scented steam—to the applause of the crowd. Peeks inside the buildings lining the street revealed what appeared to be a wild game of chance involving a massive roulette board, played by a roaring crowd, an amphitheatre with the actors flying around and spreading sparks of glitter through the air, and what looked like a racetrack—only instead of horses they raced large winged creatures I didn't recognise, with a strange mixture of feathers and scales, and legs resembling a lion's. The people were all dressed in robes, though in varied colours (Gwen and I wore them in black). I yelped in surprise when I saw one of

Detective King

their faces—it was that of a lizard. Looking around, there were people with faces of various animals, alongside those who looked human, though even amongst the human-looking ones some of them had blue, green, or pink skin, while others had pointed ears or a third eye, or were transparent, or some other abnormality. Gwen chuckled and walked closer by my side.

"It can be overwhelming the first time you see this place."

"You know where we are? This is far more complex than any Otherworld we've seen so far—how could you not mention a place like this?!"

"OtherLondon is a space for the witches, wizards, and spirits to live and gather outside the confines of Earth. What happens here is separate from our world and is usually sealed off from Earth for all but those who know the secret of entry. This is the first time I've entered on my own, but I understand this place has laws and customs like anyplace else."

"So you're saying it can't be used to plan anything nefarious?"

"If the witches who rule here were to take her side, it could. I didn't know how to get here and the specifics of this place are still murky to me, and that's why I didn't say anything—not until I had more information. I'm sorry." *Don't look at me with those eyes...*

"It's fine, I guess. Do you have any idea on how to get out of here?" I fumbled with my robe, trying to tighten it. "This thing's looser than I'd like, and I don't know how Owen stands to walk around without shoes—I already have a blister."

"Well, the map of OtherLondon should correspond with that of our London, so maybe we should start by going somewhere we're familiar with." We reached a corner where a sizeable group was gathered, a flashing light floated above them. The light turned from yellow to red and a long vessel pulled by those same flying creatures that were being raced pulled up to the corner. People streamed out of it, then the crowd boarded the gilded car. Gwen led me onto it, and away into the sky we rose. "Think of it like taking a streetcar or a train." Gwen said. I looked out at the lights and sights of this strange city that was part fortress, part forest, and part modern city. Creatures flew, floated, and glowed in the sky around us, making whooshing and bubbling sounds. I glanced within the cart at the strange assortment of magical beings commuting with us and wondered whether the more stunning sight was inside or outside the carriage. After a couple stops, we had our relative bearings and rode up to where we approximated was Marylebone (not far from home in our world). The area looked like a giant park, no pavement, just grass, while (what I assumed were) residential buildings rose like small overgrown castles, the kind of scene one might've seen on the moors in ancient times. Lights glowed from the tops of these structures, and strings of lights connected each house so the entire field was alight with warm, flittering light like a kingdom of fireflies. Jaunty music, singing and cheering from a large group in the centre of the field caught our attention. Most notably—they weren't wearing robes, but normal clothing.

"What do you make of them? Is that violin?" I said to Gwen.

"Fiddle, if I'm not mistaken. Shall we visit with them?"

"If you think they can help us get out of here." We started walking up to their bonfire, as the group danced and sang and waved several flags, mostly a blue one with an orange sun in the corner and rays expanding out from it. We tried to get someone's attention, but it proved difficult to break through the merrymaking. Gwen grasped my hands, pressed herself against me.

"Wh-what're you doing?"

"Just one dance?" She wanted to dance? With me? Really? I'm a sorry dancer, but she led me through the steps patiently, and though my heart was surely about to burst from my chest any second, I found myself enjoying myself.

"W-we still n-need to f-find a way out..."

"Worry about that when the music stops." We waltzed

about until we were in the midst of the group, by the fire. Her eyes shone as her presence overtook my entire world. I could dance with her for days and never tire. What would she say if I asked for a kiss? Not that I'm interested in such distractions as romance... yet the question consumed my mind.

"You... you look nice..." *What was that?! You look nice?* I hate myself sometimes.

"Thank you, Arthur. You're quite the gentleman." The song wound down, and the group applauded and cheered. I was a tad disappointed it was over, but then Gwen leaned in and kissed my cheek. "Thank you for the dance, Detective King." The only response I could muster was a dumb smile. A group banged on some metal to grab the party's attention, and a boy climbed atop a tree stump, to roaring cheers. He couldn't have been older than 10 or 11, with ginger hair and freckles. He wore a white tunic, like I'd seen in old medieval paintings of the Celtic people, open on the bottom and coming down to his knees, with big sleeves and a sash coloured green, gold and orange. The boy raised a sword to even more boisterous applause.

"Mo chairde—my friends, tomorrow is our day! Tomorrow Eireann lives, as England turns to ash!" Cheers. "For centuries our people have suffered, been beaten and cursed, but 'morrow we show 'em what the Fianna can do!" Their screams of joy were deafening. "You all know where you need to go. Red?" My jaw opened wide as Willy stepped onto the stump with the boy.

"G'day! Hope you lot are ready to lay down your lives in Westminster." The left half of the group yelled in the affirmative. "Remember, the spell lasts just 10 minutes, so make the most of it and don't dawdle. That's all I need the say, I think." Boisterous applause for a half-arsed speech.

"And the rest with me!" The boy said. "When we've finished our Wild Hunt, we'll have a feast for the whole country in Dublin." He lowered the sword and was handed a mug, which he took a huge gulp from. He swayed to and from precariously and his tunic got dishevelled so that one of his shoulders was bare. "Now let's get drunk!" The loudest cheer of all, the music started up again, the dancing continued, everyone took a drink, including Willy and the boy, who stumbled off the stump and sat on the grass laughing and drinking more.

"Time to go." Gwen said. I nodded, keeping my eye on Willy as we ducked away from the militants. We hid behind one of the little castles and peeked back at the revelry.

"What was that about?" I asked.

"They must be Irish revolutionaries."

"Willy was with them, which means—"

"—A jolly good time." Willy stood behind us, frightening me out of my skin. He laughed and slapped his knee. "Sorry, couldn't help it. I knew you were there the whole time—I recognise that sloppy haircut of yours anywhere. What happened to your hat?"

"Got a little wet and ruined. What's this about, Will?"

"A little chaos, that's all. A relatively minor part of the campaign, but a fun one nonetheless. Though that brat promised me a taste of Irish beer—he was faking it, it's just apple juice." Gwen threw an athame dagger onto the ground and snapped her fingers. A circle glowed around Willy. He looked over his shoulder at the other athames in the ground. "When did you... very well played. How many of those do you have? Every bit of magic takes sacrifice—what are you sacrificing?"

"None of your business."

"Your blood? Or your soul?"

"Create an exit for us with your key."

"Why don't you do that yourself? I know you have one yourself. Oops, was I not supposed to say that in front of Arty?" I looked at Gwen, who was biting her lip.

"I don't know what you're talking about." Willy shrugged and took out a key, which he slashed through the air.

"Let me go now?"

Detective King

"What are they planning tomorrow?" I asked.

"What happened to the fun of the surprise?! You're a mystery lover, you should know better than anyone else. Be up at sunrise and you'll see without a doubt. Now…" His eyes glowed yellow and flames engulfed him, confined to the circle until it broke. The flames faded away and Willy stepped backward out of the circle, bowing and tipping his hat. "Tally-ho." Then he scurried off back toward the bonfire. Images of the vision and his face from within it filled my mind.

"Hey, Willy!" I called. He stopped and looked back at me. "Take care of yourself, alright?" He grinned.

"Same to you, mate!" Then he continued on his way. Gwen took my hand, and we took a big step forward from where Willy had been standing. At first I couldn't tell what had happened—I was being smothered in some kind of cloth. After beating back my silky attacker, I realised where I was—in a clothes rack in a boutique.

"We're back in our London." Gwen said. I laughed and looked down at my cloak.

"How dandy. Pick out something nice for yourself, I'll pay." After dressing to the nines and creating a tab with the tailor (with my badge as proof I was good to my word), we found ourselves back in London, late in the night. A few blocks down the street was one of those new telephone boxes—what a joy it is to live in modernity and luckily I had the good sense to keep my wallet of coins in hand when I abandoned my clothes in OtherLondon.

LionBolt

CHAPTER 20 — NIGHT BEFORE BATTLE

First call was to Scotland Yard, alerting them to the upcoming attack on Westminster.

"Who are they? They mentioned the name Fianna. I've not heard of them before, but they're connected to William Manders." I said. "How do I know of this? I heard it myself, as part of my investigation. Where are they now?" That's a tough one to answer—I couldn't say they were squatting out in a different world. "Somewhere in the borough of Westminster, I don't have specifics on that, other than they plan on an attack tomorrow, so they can't be far. There's also another regiment of them attacking someplace else, but I don't know where yet... Riots, what riots? Too busy for rumours? This is a concrete threat, at least boost security around Whitehall and Parliament... no, I don't have any other witnesses, other than a civilian, but..." We went on like that for far longer than was useful to either of us. I hung up the phone in frustration. Our adversaries were smart, if nothing else—keeping the police force preoccupied with civil unrest. I put in another four haypennies and called home, craning my neck slightly to reach

Detective King

the mouthpiece, which couldn't be moved and was designed for someone taller than me.

"Arthur?! Do you know what time it is!" Lily was difficult to interrupt when she got this cross. I let her berate me for embarrassing her with filing a missing person report and staying up half the night.

"Are you done? Good." I cleared my throat. "Detective Knight Lily Anne Watson, Your king has a proclamation—"

"It's almost 2 in the morning, save the theatrics, Art." I snapped open my pocket watch—I hadn't realised. That poor tailor serving the strangers who appeared out of nowhere in his store at midnight...

"Fine. You said you wanted to help me, right Lily? Today's gonna be rough, dangerous. Are you sure you don't want to sit this out?"

"How could I? With you sounding so excited, I can't just sit out on the fun!" I put the earpiece down for a moment and smiled. *That's my sister alright.* I explained the situation to her.

"Once the sun rises, we should be on the move. You got everything?"

"Right, I'll be there."

"Good, now can you put Elaine or Owen on the phone? I want to know what happened to them today." I waited a while before Elaine's voice came through the telephone.

"'Bout time we heard from you! Here's what happened after we separated—"

⚔

We followed Tim a long way—he took the tube back to Scotland Yard—with a real blank stare the whole way. Whenever someone approached him or anything, he spoke to them like normal, but then he'd go back to that blank stare. He picked up some papers and left The Yard, then he went to a neighbourhood I'd never visited before, went in an alley, and gave them to a woman wearing a hood and carrying a staff. It wasn't Scarlett. Neither of them said anything, either.

LionBolt

She tapped her staff on his forehead and left, then about a minute later he blinked a lot, like he'd just woken up and looked around like he didn't know where he was. Then he looked real irritated and went to a flat in Waterloo, where we figured he lived with Rusty as his roommate, since he was already there. Tim said something to Rusty that was pretty weird though—

"Is one's life more important than one's duty?" He asked Rusty.

"I don't think so. Why?"

"Just some stuff weighing on my mind…" He got quiet for a long while, then he said— "Would you think ill of me if I did something wrong for your sake?"

"I can't see what I would ever have you do wrong. What's this about, Tim?"

"Just confessions of a sinner." Then he turned the conversation to how Rusty's arm was healing. I think he was under some kind of spell, from that woman, then after he gave her whatever, he was back to being himself.

What a strange twist—another piece in the mosaic of Scarlett's organisation, and another supernatural impossibility to keep me up at night. I bade Elaine farewell and returned to Gwen, having used up my entire wallet on the phone.

"It's too far to walk home, it's too late for the tube, and we're not getting a cab this late either…"

Into the old bed-and-breakfast we went. After ringing the front desk bell a few times, an elderly gentleman came out to sleepily greet us. I promptly smacked my badge on the desk.

"Official police business." I said, in as authoritative a voice as I could muster. "I need two rooms. You'll be compensated by the department later." The old man's eyes grew big and bright.

"Ooh, tell me, what is it, burglars, a kidnapper, something more sinister? I love crime stories oh so much—you know my cousin met Sherlock Holmes on one of his investigations some years ago…"

"Really, which one?" Gwen coughed, loud and deliberate. I cleared my throat and reassumed my 'I'm a police officer' stance. "Classified police business, sir. Hope you understand." The old man handed us the keys with the most excited grin. At least I made his day. As we were about to go into our separate rooms, I remembered one last question I had about the events in Otherworld.

"Hey, Gwen—have you heard of something called Emain Ablach? I think that's what they said…"

"Who said?"

"The hounds, as we were going into the well, I swear I heard them say something about a witch, and that name."

"Emain Ablach is another name for Otherworld. Specifically it means the Island of Apples. It's basically Irish Avalon."

"And there's a witch there?"

"Not that I've heard of. You know the King Arthur stories better."

"Right… perhaps Morgan le Fay? Who knows, maybe I was hearing things after all." Gwen smiled and waved goodnight. We didn't have long to sleep, and I was more exhausted than I could remember, but I still ended up staring at the ceiling for a while—a natural response after seeing yourself die before your eyes, I suppose. I dreaded the sunrise, because I knew however hard this day was, the next was going to be much worse.

CHAPTER 21 — LILY'S DIARY PART II

23 November 1921

There's a big gate that leads onto school grounds. I hate that gate in the morning because it means I have a full day of dealing with the other girls ahead of me. In the evening I love the sight of that gate more than anything, because I can finally go home and get some peace. This morning, however, wasn't like most mornings. I felt a shiver and looked behind me as I passed the gate—Elaine was hiding behind the school walls, Owen on her shoulder. From what I can tell (and Arthur agrees) things Elaine touches are invisible to people who can't see her, so no one was alarmed by a floating mouse. I smiled and waved at them, but they disappeared behind the wall. How odd—what were they planning? I shrugged and turned back to the school. A group of girls, including Rachel, stood by the school doors with arms crossed. I walked by with my head down, as I always did, hoping with little conviction they'd leave me alone that day. But of course, one of the girls tripped me, and I fell flat on my face. The girls all laughed, because they're terrible, while Rachel squatted down and held my head up by my hair.

"Aww, Lily, you fell! God, you're clumsy! But I guess you belong on the ground—it definitely suits you. You should stay down there and never get back up." Then Rachel let go of me—she was pushed back by what looked to her to be an invisible force. It was Elaine coming to my rescue. "What the—what was that?" I started to tear up as Elaine held Rachel back and Owen sprang forward and crawled up her leg. "Ewww! A mouse! Get it away!" Owen bit her before she threw him off in my direction. I caught him and hugged him, maybe tighter than I should've—he is pretty small when he's like that. But that was the moment my mouse in shining armour came to save me at last.

"Thank you." Is all I could get out, though I wanted to tell him so many things, share everything with him. The other girls all screamed and ran away. Rachel glared at me.

"You're so disgusting! I knew you were a rat, but this? Teacher's going to hear about this—then you and your rat boyfriend will get what you deserve!" Then she ran like the coward she was. Elaine helped me to my feet.

"I'm sorry, are they going to get you in trouble?" She said.

"Let them. I won't let them hurt me anymore. Besides," I ran my hands through Owen's soft fur. "I have a better friend in you than any girl alive, and a little knight to protect me. My rat boyfriend!" I laughed, for the first time maybe in years I laughed at school. Owen covered his face and twitched his tail.

"I wanted to apologise for before. I wasn't ready to face my past, but for you... I'll find my strength, somehow." I embraced him and rubbed my face on his, which probably embarrassed him.

"No, I'm sorry—I shouldn't have pried."

"Will it be okay for you to stay here?" Elaine said.

"If I stay, I'll be in trouble, but if I leave, I'll probably never be able to come back... Will you stay with me?" They both nodded without hesitation. I strode into school, Elaine by my side, and my little knight in my arms, ready to face whatever may come. I'll never let anyone make me feel powerless again. My friends believe I'm strong, so that's what I'll be for them.

5 December 1921

What a day today was, I'm exhausted but if you think I can fall asleep after everything that just transpired you owe me a sixpence (I know you're just a diary, don't worry about it). The events of the day can wait—I'm sure Arthur's rendition of events will be more informative—I want to detail what happened in the early hours of the day, just after I received a call from Arthur filling me in on the plan that would start at sunrise. I got dressed and was about ready to get a breakfast started when I found myself in front of Owen's door. My hand was on the knob.

What are you thinking?! I thought. You can't barge into a boy's room while he's sleeping! I was thinking this as I was turning the knob and sneaking in. Okay, you went in, but no more—let him sleep until we have to go. I got to his bedside—he was a restless sleeper, sprawled out with the sheets mostly kicked off. His hair was so messy and his expression so peaceful—he's so cute. I did gasp and nearly ran out when I saw him, however, as he wasn't wearing pyjamas. Don't worry, there were enough blankets to cover the important bits. If I woke him, he'd be much too embarrassed—I really should go. I have a terrible habit of thinking things through as I take action, so that I hadn't decided to leave him be until I'd touched his shoulder and shaken him awake. His eyes opened and he yawned.

"Lily? Five more min... aah!" He sprang awake and scrambled to cover himself. "What are you doing in here?!"

"Sorry—but get dressed, I want to show you something."

Detective King

I met him in the hall—his face was still red, his hair sticking up, and his shirt was buttoned wrong.

"Let me fix this for you, you need to do it from the top down." I said. He batted me away as I started unbuttoning him.

"I'll do it! Sorry, you just keep surprising me." He fixed his shirt, and I led him onto my balcony. "Where are you leading me?" There's a ladder leading up to the roof on my balcony, which I started climbing.

"To another surprise," I said. On the roof, I had a blanket spread out, where I sat and beckoned Owen to join me. "This is my secret hideout, not even Arthur knows about it." Owen sat next to me and shivered as a breeze hit us. It was December, and he was barefoot, and without a coat or anything (perhaps I should've warned him we'd be going outside). I had an extra blanket and put it around us. We snuggled close together, facing the direction the sun would rise. "I love to watch the sunrise from here—it's so peaceful. Or sometimes I'll come up here to think."

"What do you think about?" The red in his cheeks looked to be more from the cold than embarrassment now.

"All sorts of things… like why you sleep in the nude." I had to tease him a little. He hid behind his knees, turning even redder.

"I'm a mouse in the morning—I don't want to get stuck in my clothes and suffocate!" He gave me an embarrassed smirk as I laughed and shoved him a bit.

"I also think about school… about those bullies… and how you and Elaine stood up to them."

"Sorry about that—you got suspended because of us."

"That's not the important part. You helped me stand up when I was pushed down. You saved me." He looked away, hiding a sad face.

"I've been thinking lately, too. About how much stronger you are than me. That night, you asked me about my past… I've spent all this time trying to cover my eyes to it, but… I think I could gain the strength to look at who I am through you."

"I'll listen… if you want to talk about it." Owen took a deep, troubled breath and began his story.

CHAPTER 22 — LILY'S DIARY PART III: OWEN

They would say I was hyperactive, too loud, too silly, but I was 7, and even though I didn't have parents or a family of my own—I had everyone at the church. The other orphans, the nuns, and especially Sister Margaret. She was the most important person in the world to me—I told her everything, and was always by her side.

"I saw—I saw a butterfly in the courtyard!" I'd bounce up and down, so excited over the littlest thing. She'd kneel in front of me and listen to everything I said with great interest, then she'd always pat me on the head.

"That's amazing, Owen!" she'd say. She'd help me clean up after meals—because I was a very messy kid—and she'd make me feel better and stay with me all night if I had a bad dream. Really, the only place I was quiet and behaved was in the chapel during prayers, but Sister Margaret was patient with me no matter what, and I loved her very much. When I was 7, everything changed. The priests took me into a small, dark room with a cabinet in it. The moment I stepped into that room, I was gripped by cold. I started shivering, my teeth chattered, there was a horrible churning in my stomach and my head hurt really bad—it's what Arthur calls the 'Ghost Sense'. But worse than any of that—I heard a voice, from nowhere and everywhere, ringing through my head, calling my name. As soon as they let me, I ran out of the room and threw up. That was the test to see if I had spiritual potential—the requirement to be an exorcist. I'd passed, showing a stronger sensitivity to spirits—in this case the demon—than anyone ever had at the church. They told me I'd have the chance to become an exorcist when I was older, and Sister Margaret was especially proud—so even though it was scary, I was happy. That week, a missionary from America was visiting. I wasn't allowed too close, but I saw him from afar. All the priests and nuns would gather around him, so I figured he was real popular or important. He was young looking, and I remember he wore a black hat (remember, I was only 7). His name was Benjamin Dawson, and while everyone was excited about his visit, Sister Margaret was the only one to keep her distance. She would sigh and look out into nothing for a long time, which she never did—so I was worried about her. On the last night of Mr. Dawson's visit, I saw Sister Margaret from down the hall, and being the mischievous little boy I was, I sneaked around—hiding behind corners and columns—following her. She went into Mr. Dawson's room, so I peeked in from the doorway.

Sister Margaret slapped Mr. Dawson across the face, tears streaming down her cheeks. I was so scared—she'd never had that sort of face or done anything like that before.

"You promised me! We were going to run away together. You said you loved me and then you left!"

"Margaret..." He smiled and laugh, despite his bruised cheek.

"I was alone... I couldn't bear to face myself. A sister with child is nothing but a sinner."

"A child?"

"I was scared. Desperately, I waited and prayed for you to

come get us, but once I realised you weren't coming, I..." Her voice shook... and I guess mine is too. "I had the knife... in my hand... but I couldn't do it. I fell to my knees and asked God what to do. His answer was my son." She said. We both cried. This couldn't be true. Sister Margaret was a nun—she couldn't have a son! There was a feeling in my stomach, in my heart, I knew, but I didn't want to accept it until...

"What is... his name?" Dawson asked. Sister Margaret smiled.

"My curious, energetic, and ever sweet boy is named Owen. Yet he can never know the name of his mother." The room spun—my whole world was falling apart—it couldn't be true. I stepped back, unsure what to do, or who I was anymore. When I ran, she saw me and called out my name, but I didn't look back.

I held Owen's hand as he told the story—it was cold and trembled terribly. His whole body was against mine and I felt every quiver, every painful word and memory.

"After that, I started my exorcist training. I told them I wanted to start right away. If my life was born out of sin, it's all I can do to devote my life in service to God."

"But that's not your fault. It doesn't matter what your parents did, or if your birth was right or wrong, which it wasn't, anyway. You're here, and you deserve to live your own life." I don't know when I'd started crying, or when I'd taken both his hands, but I couldn't let him hate himself, no matter what.

"You're right, that's not my sin... My sin is much worse. I'm so weak that I haven't spoken to my mother since that night. I couldn't face her, couldn't even look her in the eyes. Sometimes she tries to smile at me, or she'll leave an orange or something in my room, but... I give her silence. She loves me, and wants the best for me, yet I'm so horrible I won't even look at her."

LionBolt

"That's something you can set right. When you're ready, let's go see your mother together. Okay?" Owen let out a breath—the cloud of vapour from the cold hung in the air for a moment. He looks at me and smiles, despite the red eyes and sniffling nose. The sun rose higher, casting the sky into beautiful hues of violet, pink, and orange. The light hit Owen's toes and instantly caused him to glow with light. He emerges from the blanket as a mouse a moment later and I picked him up. "Thank you for sharing with me. Say, I know this curse is a nuisance... but I kinda like you this way too." I said.

"It isn't so bad anymore... so long as I'm not alone. And I can still appreciate views like this, even if it makes me a mouse." I kissed his head, turning him red again. Someday we'll kiss when he's human, I know it. Then Elaine burst into laughter, making both of us jump—I nearly dropped him. Elaine was standing on my ladder, leaning onto the roof.

"How long have you been there?!" I asked.

"Sorry, didn't mean to spoil your moment. I overheard everything back to your phone call with Arthur, so..."

"Elaine!" A loud boom sounded from the distance. It came from the direction of city centre, so it must have been an immense explosion to be heard from home.

"That came from where Arthur is, didn't it?" Elaine said.

"I guess he wasn't goofing us. Let's go." Elaine led the way off the roof, and we were off on a new and dangerous adventure.

Detective King

CHAPTER 23 — WILLY - BATTLE OF THE TREATY PART I

May I have your attention, ladies and gentlemen—The fun part's about to start, so if you would, please hold on to your hats and enjoy the ride.

The explosion got their attention first. Connor led his army into the heart of Whitehall—home to all the fat cats in government, setting fire to the lot of them. The police set up a barrier, and that chubby chief inspector tried his best to keep order, I'm sure—but when you're faced with a mythical sword that can slash an enemy through the heart at a distance of several dozen feet, not much you can do but bleed out. All in all, he did his part, and was off to his next target without issue. For my part, the invisibility spell proved quite nifty. Within the Palace of Westminster, there's a famous centre lobby in the shape of an octagon that we passed as the explosion sounded. The building shook, then all was still until one of those damned detective inspectors sent his boy in the direction of the House floor. I thought that blond hair looked familiar—it was Arthur's chap, Samuel Tristan. How fun! I decided to up the drama by fanning out my men, knocking out unsuspecting officials so it appeared people were dropping like flies unprovoked. We took out that inspector too—Hopkins is his name if I got things straight.

Sammy got to the House of Commons first, all frantic and panicky. He was stopped by the sergeant-at-arms at first, but was released and allowed to approach the prime minister, who stood at the edge of the floor in his usual spot on the government side of the house (personally—government or opposition, Liberal, Conservative, Labour, I think they're all deficient, inadequate and corrupt, but that's just me). We smashed through the door onto the floor as the invisibility spell wore off. I was dressed spiffy with my favourite top-hat, trench coat and walking stick (I'd stolen it from a royal tomb. Not sure whose it was, but I liked the idea of that which was a king's was now the property of a commoner like myself).

"Good morning gents!" I said with a bow. "Sorry for the racket. Just a little warring early in the morning is all." I skip-stepped to Sammy-boy and the prime minister. Sam snarled at me and tried his damnedest to punch me in the face. Alas, it was no trouble to dodge. "I remember you, you're Arty's mate. He should be meeting my comrade-in-arms soon, if he's where I think he is."

"I'm not lettin' you get away this time, you'll have to get past me if you want—" I pushed the bloke aside and sat the prime minister down by my side. He was usually so stately—the image of a leader, the man who got us through the Great War—well, when your life's being threatened, I suppose you wouldn't be newspaper picture ready either. Officers and MPs tried to rush us, but they were driven back by my militia.

"My Irish friends don't seem to like you very much, sir." I said to the PM. "Frankly, I don't care for you myself. Certainly, you'll get an earful from them in due time—but I've got special grievances to raise, if you would be so kind as to listen."

"I—I will not be cowered by rebels or terrorists and I've no interest in what justifications you've imagined for yourself."

Detective King

He said.

"Oho, big talk sir, I appreciate that. Yeah, I suppose the blight of the working population of this country is imagined. As is the routine assault on the rights of those you've colonised." Shouts and jeers erupted from the MPs behind us. They were silenced by my troops as they raised their weapons. Sam grabbed my arm, and I stared at him, utterly unimpressed.

"I'm not lettin' you ignore me." He said. "Push me down as many times as you want, I'll get back up."

"The army should be here straightaway," The PM said, "end this foolishness, boy! You don't want to be killed over this." I grinned and showed them some fire and my yellow eyes.

"I don't plan on dying, but I'd rather die than get locked up again." Sam stepped between me and the prime minister.

"So you're just gonna hide behind those powers of yours again?" He said. I turned my fire off.

"What could you mean by that?"

"It's rather easy to beat around us normal blokes when you've got that demon runnin' round in inside of you." With a smirk and a whistle, I turned away—my hands behind my head.

"I know what you're doing. I'm no fool."

"Then whether you take the bait is your own choice." I liked his style—no nonsense, just action. It deserved a reward. I turned back to him with a smile.

"Alright Sam, I'll duel ya—one on one, no powers. So long as I can keep the exits sealed." Sam slipped off his tie and clenched his fists.

"Fine by me, so long as you and your goons back off and don't come back once I've beaten you!" I took off my coat, showing off my locket and my scars, and tipped my hat slightly.

"I'm a man of honour, but you know you won't even knock my hat off, let alone win." Sam rolled up his sleeves.

LionBolt

"It's time someone taught you a lesson, kid." We charged at each other—I landed a blow square in his jaw. Sam reeled back, wiping blood from his cheek—his eyes like two exhilarated wildfires of grey. Sam launched a barrage of strikes at me, all dodged easily. I countered—lunging forward, but he blocked me with his arms. He had more skill than I expected, but my hat was still safe and sound. The parliamentarians shouted and cheered around us. The prime minister looked beside himself. Sam attempted a tackle, pressing his body into mine. I shifted my weight and threw Sam across the room. He landed on the opposition front bench, having lawmakers scramble away to avoid getting hit. I strolled over to him, not winded in the slightest.

"I've still got my hat on." Sam spat out some blood. He flashed me a murderous glare.

"You think everything's goin' your way. But there's no way in hell that your revolution, or whatever shit you're preaching, is gonna get anywhere." He took a swipe at me, but he was fading fast—it wasn't even a challenge to dodge. I elbowed him in the back, and he fell to the floor, but staggered back onto his feet. Determined, I'll give him that. "Is all of this for politics? Is turning Britain red worth all this bloodshed?" I uppercut him, flinging him high in the air. He landed, and I dragged him onto the speaker's chair. Then he smiled, despite the bloody lip and swollen eye. "I think... you're still all messed up... from your dad. We all know he was a crook." I pounded his face. "You took... the easy way out. You turned to crime... and Arthur left you to your self-destruction." I kneed him in the stomach—knocking his wind out. No way was he getting up in the state he was in. I leaned in close.

"The ravings of a thug who knows nothing about me. What about you? You climbed out of a ditch. Maybe you belong back there." Sam laboriously reached up and grabbed my hat.

"Got it." Then he dropped it and passed out. I had to laugh and give him a round of applause as I put it back on. I turned to the members of the Commons.

"Anyone else care for a round? No? Alrighty then." I pranced over to the prime minister and took him by the arm. "You're all I want sir, we're just gonna do some negotiating."

"You're insane."

"There's a difference between insanity, and being willing to do what must be done." The barrier I'd placed on the exits to the chamber dissipated. I dragged the PM out, followed by my armed men. Sam laid unconscious and bloody on the chair, a smile on his face to the last—when all was set and done, I hope they give the lad a medal or something (not that such a thing means anything).

I leaned back in the rear seat of a luxury car, the prime minister beside him.

"You'll never get past the army."

"We don't have to." The car drove into a tunnel, where it turned and descended deep under the city into a labyrinth of underground passageways.

"Where are we? And where are you taking me?"

"These are the postal tunnels. I had an inside man give me a map. As for our destination, I think you can probably guess."

"You aim to turn me over to the Irish extremists, then? Good God, son, has evil overtaken your heart so that you could do such things to your own country? Do you care nothing for the people you've hurt or killed today? I'll ask you one last time, stop this foolishness before you've taken it too far." I leaned forward, hands tented, my eyes fixed on what was in front of me (currently the back of a car seat).

"There's no going back now, I've made my decision. For better or worse, I will stick to what I believe to be right. I don't think myself evil, and I don't want to hurt or kill anyone. Believe it or not, it pained me to fight that fella earlier—I know he's a good man. I'm even pained to hear my prime minister call my actions wicked, even if I may think similar things of your own policies."

"What do you aim to achieve? What is the meaning to all of this?" I leaned back again and stared at the car ceiling.

"What's the meaning to anything? Is there any point to what we do, say, or think? Are we nothing more than ants running around in every direction until eventually we're crushed by something bigger? You heard what Mister Tristan said about my father, right?"

"That he was a crook? Who was he really?"

"I assume you know of the gentlemen thieves, A. J. Raffles and Bunny Manders? Everyone seems to." The old man placed his hand on his forehead.

"You mean to say your father was one of the most successful thieves of the nineteenth century?"

"Yup. William Manders is the name. My dad wasn't perfect, but he was a loving father. To see him get dragged off and locked away... my eyes opened to what he'd been fighting for that whole time. It wasn't about stealing from others, it was about exposing the sins our society is built on. The men they stole from living in luxury, abusing the power they'd bought and making those who worked under them—the working class—suffer. In a real sense, it was they who were the thieves, not my dad or Mister Raffles." Mr. Lloyd George leaned back and turned to the window, his hand to his chin, a serious expression reflected in the window.

"I think I understand you a tad better, but I still cannot accept your actions as anything but unjustifiable."

"That's alright, sir. All I want is to create a better, more equal world, but it's human nature to reject that which runs contrary to their understanding of justice."

"Justice is abstract, there is no one right answer."

"All we can do is look at our world, and within ourselves, and figure out what answer we believe most right." The conversation trailed off after that—until we reached our destination in Knightsbridge.

Detective King

CHAPTER 24 — BATTLE OF THE TREATY PART II

After what amounted to a nap—we were back on the street as the sky lightened, turning varied shapes of pastel colours, despite the clouds hanging over the old city.

"First step—figure out where..." I yawned, making Gwen laugh.

"Stop, you'll make me..." She yawned too, bigger than me. We shook our heads to wake ourselves.

"F-figure out where that boy plans on going. If they're splitting up and aim to disrupt the treaty negotiations, and with Willy in Westminster, I think it natural they'd target the other side of the negotiators as well."

"According to the newspapers, they're based in Knightsbridge."

"Right. I've already told Lily to take Elaine and Owen there, so if we head there now—" I was interrupted by a boom sound that shook the ground, and came from the direction of Westminster. A plume of smoke rose on the horizon. "Looks like it's begun."

"Why don't I try to find Lily and make sure they're safe,

while you go on ahead to Knightsbridge." Gwen said.

"I'd rather not split up, but I agree things are about to get chaotic." Gwen left for the direction of home, while I faced the predicament of travelling on my own. With such a major attack taking place, I doubted the tubes were running, there weren't any street car lines nearby, and walking to and through Hyde Park would take too long... I glanced at the telephone box again and groaned. After scrounging around for 2 pennies' worth of coins (technology is expensive), I stepped back in and reluctantly called Tim for a ride.

After what Elaine told me about his behaviour, I couldn't exactly trust Tim. He treated me with the same unbearable defiance, same sharp words and dirty looks, but underlying all that was something else—his words didn't hold the same bite, his eyes held a weakness that diverted his gaze from me. He had a tell, as all people do—he'd wring his hands like he was nervous—he felt guilty about something. Rusty rode with us, and Tim kept glancing at his cast. I observed all this from the back seat of the car, and as we approached the headquarters of the Irish delegation—in an upscale 18th century housing complex—I couldn't stand it any longer and spoke up.

"Do you remember meeting with me yesterday, Tim?"

"O-of course," lie, "What of it?"

"Where did we go then?"

"Investigating..." That was so pathetic, I almost laughed. Tim glanced at me, flicking his eyes in Rusty's direction. I nodded. *Not in front of him*, he was telling me. I'd just have to ask later.

The leaders of the Irish negotiating delegation were not exactly welcoming, but we were ushered in nonetheless after we explained the situation. Their chief diplomat, Arthur Griffith, looked gravely concerned whilst he made a call, then hung up and turned to see us standing in single file.

"It appears what you say is true. An attack has been

launched on London. What I don't understand is why you believe we are a target." Tim and I both stepped forward, which turned into a brief jostle between us, which I won.

"Mister Griffith, I understand we are technically still at war, but understand these attacks are being conducted by dangerous radicals with connections to the criminal underworld. They have no interest in peace. That is why they will aim to capture the negotiating parties from both sides."

"How old are you, son?" Was that so important right now?

"About sixteen years and eight months, sir. I understand that my age is difficult to accept, given my status."

"Oh, do you?" Tim snorted under his breath.

"Forgive me for asking, but why have you been sent instead of someone more..."

"I was the first to undercover this plot and deduce they would target you. It's thanks to me you haven't been arrested yourself, as any attack from Irish revolutionaries is likely to reflect rather poorly on your delegation, sir. I have, for the time being, convinced Scotland Yard otherwise." That was a bluff, but not entirely untrue. Griffith looked exasperated. He turned away from us and polishes his glasses, mumbling to himself. I noticed some of the Irish guardsmen staring out the window at the fog. I recalled it hadn't been so foggy just a few moments earlier when I was outside, but it looked like night out the window. Squinting, I could make out a vague, shadowy figure in the fog, which drew closer and larger, as it darkened the window—which soon cracked, indeed all the windows in the room cracked at once. The guards in the room formed a line and drew their guns, us and the delegates behind them. All was still for a long while, then the windows burst, and mist billowed in. As it cleared, the guards were face to face with revolutionaries, weapons drawn. Griffith was held by the arms by two men, and in front of him stood the boy I saw in OtherLondon, now dressed in a formal shirt and Irish-style kilt.

"Dia Dhuit—good day, gentlemen! Are you enjoyin' the

show we're puttin' on 'ere?"

"You're just a child!" Griffith said, "Are you alright? Who is making you do this?" The boy cocked his head, looking puzzled.

"No one's making me do anything. Y'see, we found out you were about to settle for dominion status, rather than fight for our republic. You were about to agree to an oath of allegiance to the king, and even allow the north to break away in favour of the crown. We had to do something, right?" The delegates and my colleagues looked dumbfounded, but it was clear to me what sort this boy truly was—I could work with this. I knelt before him to look him in the eye.

"You're a child prodigy, aren't you? People used to look at me like that..." I gestured to my colleagues, "or I guess they still do. But you can't use your intelligence to hurt people like this. You kidnapped those men, right?" I nodded toward the terrified looking government ministers, likely plucked from Whitehall during the explosion earlier. "I've come to learn the most outrageous explanation is often the right one, so I'll come right out and ask you—what sort of magic have you been using?" The boy smirked.

"Well done, mister! You were the one dancing with us last night, weren't you? Where's your girlie?" It was my turn to look gobsmacked.

"Th-that's true, I crashed your celebration. My friend should be along momentarily—"

"She looked like more than a friend, the way she pecked yer cheek..." That little brat... I had to cool myself. It was simply a distraction tactic, nothing to get twisted up about.

"Th-that's not important. What's your name?" I didn't care what the kid's name was, but behind me, the others were attempting to sneak out without his notice. The boy laughed.

"That's not going to work!" He drew his sword and pointed it at them. "Not on Ash! That's my code name, nifty, eh? Red should get here with the prime minister soon, then we can hammer out a new treaty... or just kill you both. Either

Detective King

way, we win." Tim stepped forward and pushed me aside, standing before 'Ash' so he could look directly down upon him.

"That's far enough, brat! Is this nothing but a game to you? If so, you need to get a grasp of reality!" He points to the militants that followed the boy in. "And you pikers! You're gonna take orders from a kid, just like that? Where the hell is your pride?" The soldiers laughed in unison. "Did I say something funny?" Serious expressions replaced the laughter— the soldiers alert once more.

"We stand ready to die for Lord Connor. He is the prophesied saviour of Eireann." One of them said. The boy flashed the soldier a glance and put his finger to his lips.

"Code name!"

"Sorry, Lord Connor." Connor shook his head.

"Oh well. Whaddya think boys, should I teach 'im a lesson?" He pointed to Tim with his thumb. The men cheered and howled. Connor chuckled and lightly flicked his sword. Something thumped onto the floor. Rusty and I looked on in horror as the delegates yelled in shock. Tim looked bewildered before slowly looking down to see his left hand on the floor, blood spilling out of his arm. He looked like he wanted to scream, but couldn't—instead, his mouth hung open as the colour drained from his face. Rusty screamed for him.

"You—You're a monster!" I held him as he tried to lunge for Connor. "If Tim dies from this, I don't care if you're a kid, I'll—" Rusty stopped when he noticed how I was trembling. Of course, it was frightening. When it's Willy, there's a part of me that knows he won't consciously try to kill me. This kid had immense power, and no barriers.

"D-does your power come from your sword?" I asked him. He flicked blood off it casually.

"Bzzt. Not quite right, mister detective... Are ye familiar with the ways of old—the ways of war in legend?"

"I don't follow."

LionBolt

"The great heroes of Ireland, Cu Chulainn, for example, they would fight wars through one-on-one combat—duels. I always thought that was the best way to do it, it's so neat." He pointed his sword at me and flashed a mischievous grin. "I've taken an interest in you, what's-yer-name."

"Arthur. Arthur Watson. I am..." I spread my arms wide in a grand gesture, despite how I was shaking, and my instincts screaming at me to run. "... the greatest detective in this country." The boy laughed.

"I'm honoured to meet'cha then! What say we have a duel, you an' me? If'n ya beat me, I let everyone go. If ya lose... well, I win!"

CHAPTER 25 — BATTLE OF THE TREATY PART III

According to my knights, their quest to reach me as I faced down an unexpected and dangerous foe was fraught with its own danger. First of all—traffic. Lily made the mistake of trying to take a cab to Knightsbridge, but in the explosion's wake there was mass panic, and so the roads became a wall of automobiles and a chorus of horns with no escape.

"It'll take nearly an hour just to reach Hyde Park at this rate." The cab driver told Lily, "Sorry miss, whaddya wanna do?" At that moment, Lily caught a glimpse of a familiar face. She opened the door and tipped the driver (perhaps more than she should've). Gwen spotted her too, and they met in the middle of the street, surrounded by the swarm of noisy cars.

"Arthur sent me to find you!" Gwen said.

"So he's made it... but what are we to do?"

"I think I can get you there... though I should ask if you're sure you want to go. Dangerous things are going on, the army's even involved..."

LionBolt

"I'm helping my brother, and that's that! He doesn't have any kind of special powers or magic like you. He can die... And if I lose him, I'll be stuck with the thought that if I were there, I could've done something." Elaine took Lily's hand.

"I don't think you need any powers to make a difference. You don't even have to be grown up. I'm invisible to most people, Owen's a little mouse right now, and you're young and small enough to slip past most adults. We can be spies or release hostages, like Arthur wants. Take us to Arthur, Gwen—please." Gwen sighed and held out her hand.

"Alright, hold on to me, both of you, and don't let go no matter what." Lily and Elaine took Gwen's hands, Owen in Lily's coat pocket. Gwen whispered some magic words and drew a card from her pocket—which began to glow.

"Wait, what are you going to d—" Owen couldn't finish his question as they shot up into the air, Gwen having tossed the card onto the ground, which created a magic circle at their feet. She took out more cards and tossed them down in the same way, creating steps in the air that they could bounce on. The others screamed with fear.

"I guess I should've warned you." Gwen said with a chuckle. Lily and Elaine—after the initial shock, started enjoying it and laughed as they bounced through the air, while Owen hung onto Lily for his life, his eyes closed.

"Tell me when it's over!" As they approached the Irish HQ, they witnessed a massive flying creature, with a body like a tiger, huge talons, jaws, and wings—gliding through the air.

"What is that thing?!" Lily asked.

"I have no clue." Gwen said, trying her best to avoid its gaze. "It's not attacking anything, it's just flying around..." Owen bristled up and peeked out of Lily's pocket.

"Something about it... feels familiar."

"How is that monster familiar?!" Elaine asked.

"I don't know... it's looking for something, or someone." As if to confirm Owen's suspicion, a flash of light came from nearby Hyde Park. The creature flew down to it, shrinking as it did, so that it was too small to be seen upon landing.

"It reminds me of a falcon returning to its master." Gwen bounced down to get a closer look. A man in a white suit and white hat met the creature, which turned so small it could fit in the small jar he held out toward it. He then slashed through the air with a key and disappeared. "He's gone into OtherLondon."

"What's that?" The others asked.

"I'll fill you in later—let's get to Arthur. He'll be interested to hear about this."

"Y-you want to duel me? What would you gain from fighting me?" I asked the boy before me, who struck me with more fear than most adults ever could.

"It's not about gaining anything. Like I said, duels are cool. If we're gonna fight each other, let's have some fun with it!" I glanced at Tim, who'd fallen unconscious and was having his wound wrapped up in Rusty's coat.

"This isn't 'fun'. He's delusional, he's sick!" Rusty's face was red with fury.

"C-calm down, Rusty." I said, "Okay Connor, I'll fight you, but no swords, and you promise to let us go if I win, right?" Connor sheathed his sword and handed it to one of his soldiers. He gave me a little bow.

"Wouldn't be a real competition if there were no stakes." Elaine dropped from the ceiling, landing behind Connor's soldiers. She looked around, gasping, when she saw Tim. She sneaked past Connor's men, emerging behind him, who bounced about as he unbuttoned his shirt in preparation for our duel. I gestured with my hands to keep a low profile, but she didn't seem to get it. Connor removed his shirt, revealing a bony, scarred body.

"A-are you sure you want to do this?" I asked, disturbed at the thought of beating up a weak child, but Connor looked confident, even smug.

LionBolt

"I've been battered by war, with no one to rely on or to protect me. The only way I could survive was to get power."

"What is that power?" Connor smirked as his hair turned white and his bony frame bulked up, becoming that of a strong, healthy boy.

"I'll tell ya if'n ya give me a good entertainin' fight." I meekly raised my fists, still unsure of this whole duel business. Connor charged at me in a flash, faster than my eyes could follow. He knocked me back, but Connor's men pushed me back toward him as they'd encircled us. Connor landed a punch on my cheek, flinging me to the ground. I groaned and staggered to my hands and knees, winded and sore.

"Come on, mate." Connor bounced around like an excited little kid. "I want a fight, not a massacre. Here, I'll give ya a free shot, go ahead." I tottered to my feet and raised my fists, shooting a glance at Elaine—that signal she got. I charged at Connor, reeling a punch, but he stepped aside and I crashed into Elaine, who was coming up from behind him. "That was dirty. I'm disappointed in you, Art."

Gwen and Lily discretely slipped through a window in the back of the room—Lily gasped and rushed over to Tim.

"Who are you?" Rusty asked, bewildered at the young girl who'd suddenly appeared.

"I'm someone whose read every medical book in my father's study." An unappreciated prodigy, just like her big brother. As she got to work tending to Tim's wounds, Connor took notice and smiled.

"How many girls were you plannin' on sendin' after me?"

"So you can see me?" Elaine asked.

"Yeah. It's part of my role as a Horseman to have a special connection to the departed." He said, as if reciting something from a textbook.

"Horseman? Could that be a title in some organisation?" I asked. He covered his mouth with fake apprehension.

"Oops. Guess you don't know about that stuff."

"You mentioned someone called 'Red'. That's a code

name for another Horseman, right?" Connor turned to the side and look away as if disinterested, his hands behind his head.

"Maybe so..."

"And your code name was Ash, yes? If they're colours, perhaps it refers to an ashen grey, or..." I muttered to myself as I deduced what this revelation entailed. Owen popped out of Lily's pocket and scurried over to me, making Connor cringe as he passed.

"Gross! A mouse! Don't touch it!" Owen peered back at him, aggravated.

"I'm not a mouse, I just look like one at the moment." He then turned to me, "In the Book of Revelations, there are the four horsemen of the apocalypse. There's a red one, a black one, a white one, and a pale, ashen coloured one. Could that be it?"

"Excellent, Owen!" I scratched behind his ear in the spot he liked, his leg thumping involuntarily. "An apocalypse is a pretty hefty goal. Not the sort of thing led by someone who should be in school. You're part of something much larger than terrorism in the name of Ireland, aren't you, Connor?" Connor glared at me with a scowl.

"I thought we were in the middle of a fight. If you're not gonna play by the rules, I'm calling it off." I raised my hands and nodded.

"I understand. Just one last thing- Is Red's real name William Manders?" Connor charged at me, hitting me in the torso, and knocking my breath away.

"You should know, you saw him at our party!" I coughed and staggered to my feet.

"But now I've confirmed his code name." He swung at me again, but this time I managed to dodge and landed a counter-punch in Connor's stomach. I got him as hard as I could and he wheezed.

"If you're not holding back, I won't either. Even if you are just a kid." Connor laughed heartily.

LionBolt

"But I am holding back..." Connor began to glow, growing to the size of a man, his hair growing longer, mist gathering at his feet. Connor's men cheered with glee. Griffith looks speechless.

"You- you can't be... the hero of the Fianna from legend..." Gwen had been ushering hostages out the back window, but halted as Connor completed his transformation.

"He... he might be stronger than her!" Connor now stood quite tall, so that I had to crane my neck to see his face. He spoke in a voice that was not Connor's, but that of a grown man, that rung in an unnatural, almost metallic way.

"My quest is to protect Eireann, as it has been since time long past."

CHAPTER 26 — BATTLE OF THE TREATY PART IV: THE BOY'S LEGEND

Visions flashed in my mind, coalescing into a story. I saw Connor, a year younger, being pushed down into a pile of trash in an alley. A group of three men wearing the black and tan uniforms of the Auxiliary Police Force stood over him, laughing.

"Dirty brat! We saw you starin' at us! Think yer better 'an us, eh?" One of them said. Connor trembled with fear, but stared the men in the face with defiance.

"I-I'm not afraid of you! My papa said yer all nothin' but fluthered[8] and thick in the head!"

"And where's he at now, eh?"

"Ya threw 'im in jail for nothin'! Now mum's gotta..." One of the men smacked Connor across the face.

---

[8] Fluthered = Drunk

"Yer dad's a no-good rebel. He deserves to rot, like the rest of this city. It's about time we show 'em what happens when ya mess with us." Connor wiped a drop of blood from his nose. In the distance, screams and shouts arose. He looked out from a corner of a building to see a massive fire take shape. The Black and Tans added to the spreading flames, cut the firefighters' hoses, and even fire on those fighting the flames. Connor ran in fear.

He shuffled through the door of a small shack of a home. The door was barely on its hinges—the walls were cracked, and the wooden, nail-ridden floor creaked loudly. A large, burly man pushed past him, flashing a snarl at him. His mother sat upon a bed, combing her hair, looking exhausted. She coughed violently.

"Connor, me hero, you alright?"

"They're burnin' the city, mum."

"God save us. May Fionn Mac Cumhaill[9] return to save Eireann." Connor sat next to his mother, and she caressed his head, ruffling his hair.

"He's really gonna come an' save us someday?"

"Aye, when we need him most, he'll emerge from his cave of slumber in the mountains and defeat the enemies of Ireland." It was similar to resurrection legends surrounding King Arthur, which in turn amounts to Christian allegory, but I won't tire you with my love of the legends.

"What if someone went to find him?" Connor asked. She shook her head and kissed his forehead.

"He'll come in good time, now off to bed with ya."

The dark blue sky of twilight hung over Connor as he climbed into a horse-drawn wagon and hid in a barrel. As the wagon took off, he looked back at his home.

---

[9] Pronounced *Fin Ma Cool*

Detective King

"Sorry mum. I'll come back soon with Fionn Mac Cumhaill. We can get papa back then too."

The scene shifted—the wagon reached the mountains during mid-day. Connor shivered as he got off the wagon and snow fell in big flakes onto an already white landscape.

"The cave should be around here, I guess." He walked into the wilderness.

After quite some time, an exhausted Connor aimed a slingshot, armed with a rock, at a rabbit. He fired and narrowly missed—the rabbit ran off. Connor looked defeated and fell to his knees, the snow piling up ever higher.

"Where are you? I don't want to die yet. I'll save everyone, I will." He wandered down a hill, then tripped into the snow. He looked up at a small opening in the next hill, where he crawled and collapsed at the cave mouth. A light shined before him, bright and warm, and he attempted to stand but stumbled back down. He reached out and grabbed an old, rusted sword that was lying on the cave floor. "Please, Fionn Mac Cumhaill, I need you." His eyes closed, and his breath ceased.

Then he opened his eyes and sat up, disoriented, his hair turned white.

"Didn't I... die?" In Connor's hand rested a silver sword, shining blue. "This is..."

"You wish to save your homeland, little one?" A voice echoed from nowhere.

"Are you the hero from the legends?" Connor asked, wide-eyed.

"You shall have my power, and I shall act through you when the time comes. Lead Eireann to victory, be the hero you seek." Connor started to tear up, but held it in and smiled.

"Yes sir! I'll become a hero! No matter what it takes!"

The visions ceased, and I returned to the room as it was

LionBolt

before, as if no time had passed at all. I stood between the spirit and Elaine, my arm extended outward to shield her.

"Arthur, he's possessed by a spirit." She said, "It's... not like anything I've ever felt before. Don't fight him." I looked back at her and smiled as I shivered with fear.

"If it's a spirit, he can hurt you, too. I'm not letting anything happen to you, or anyone else here." The spirit before me pulsated with power—a feeling of suffocation and pain arrested me, growing stronger each second.

"Boy, do you intend to continue our battle?" Fionn Mac Cumhaill said, "I advise you yield, lest you face a death without meaning." Gwen whispered into Lily's ear, then strode in between me and Fionn, just as I was about to respond to him.

"I wish to duel with you in his stead." She said.

"G-Gwen!? Y-you can't, er—you shouldn't. He's too dangerous." Gwen looked over her shoulder and winked, making me turn red. She stared at Fionn with ferocity.

"I'm rather dangerous myself." Fionn seemed impressed, but shook his head.

"I like your spirit, but a lady has no place cutting into a fight amongst men."

"If you feel that way, this will be a rather one-sided fight indeed." Gwen flashed out three cards in either hand. She tossed them from her right hand in the air and whispered some words. They glowed, and each shot out beams of light that curled around Fionn's body. Gwen ran close to his massive body and transferred another of her cards into her right hand. It morphed into a dagger of light—which she stabbed into his stomach with a yell. The room fell silent. Fionn inhaled deeply before bellowing out a hearty laugh.

"Watson! You've got quite a woman here!" What am I supposed to say to that!? Gwen leapt back, looking cautious. The light dagger dissipated, leaving only a small gash.

"As expected of a mythic figure."

"Mythic *hero*." Fionn corrected (though I wonder if that

was Connor shining through). I rushed to Gwen's side.

"B-be careful."

"Take this and toss it down when I say so." She placed a stone in my hand, then charged toward Fionn, who dodged her flurry of attacks.

"Miss, I hope you give up soon." He said, "I'd rather not kill anyone more than I need to."

"Feel free to strike me down, I'm beginning to doubt your ability to do so." Gwen said. Fionn laughed and swatted her away with his fist as she jumped to attack. She was knocked back into my arms.

"Gwen! Are you alright?!" Gwen broke free of my grip and stood on her own—her gaze fixated on her enemy. Fionn grabbed his sword from a soldier—it grew to accommodate his larger size. He pointed it at the wall, and it glowed bright blue.

"I can see all, lass. No scheme of yours can work against me. Allow me to show you the might of Eireann." He slowly raised it toward the ceiling.

"Do it now." said Gwen. Fionn slashed the sword as I and my knights tossed our rune stones onto the ground. A bolt of light shot from the sword, bathing the entire room in white and blinding me for a moment. When the light dimmed, a circular, singed hole was left in the ceiling, revealing the grey sky above, as Fionn was halted in place—a magic circle at his feet—anchored by the glowing rune stones dropped in a circle around him. Lily, Owen, Elaine, and I each stood triumphant by our respective stones. Gwen crossed her arms and looked smug.

"You thought you'd show off and intimidate me, but it was then that your loss was assured." She said.

"This won't hold me forever." Fionn said, rather unconcerned.

"No, but the fact remains that I've won our duel. By the time you realised what I was doing, you were already putting all your strength in that admittedly impressive blast." Gwen backed away from him and pushed me forward. "I feel you're best suited to get Connor back out here." I wasn't sure of that, but I took a deep breath and looked Fionn in the eye.

"Okay. May I speak to Connor, please?"

"I am both he and not he. Speak."

"Connor, why did you accept this spirit? You've let him consume you."

"We made a contract, power in exchange for blood." *That's not Connor.*

"I'm not talking to you! I'm talking to the boy you're using to commit atrocity!"

"Connor's decisions are his own!" I took a step back, unsure how to get through. Elaine took my hand.

"I did some bad things, too. I didn't know what else to do—I was so confused and scared. And you were too, weren't you, Arthur?" I nodded.

"I was... It felt like my life was empty, with no direction to go in, and no one to lean against. How did you feel when you met your spirit, Connor?" Fionn contorted and squirmed as he struggled to break free.

"I... He... Grrr..." His expression shifted and the boyish expression of Connor returned to his face. "I... was scared too. The stories said a hero would save us. We were being burned and beaten. I was afraid that if I didn't do something... mum and papa would..."

"Does a hero attack and kill people like this?" I gestured toward Tim, who laid unconscious as Lily tended to his wounds. "That's not a hero's work." Connor/Fionn looked down, unmoving for a long moment, then he slowly looked back up, resembling Fionn once more.

"What of you? I see within you the desire to be a king. What does that mean to you?" I was taken aback—I tried to speak, but my voice failed. How could he know that? And what did it really mean to me, after everything that's happened. I still wasn't sure myself.

"That's for him to figure out." Elaine said, still grasping my hand. "As for you, you don't need to rely on spirits and power. Become strong and good on your own.”

"You don't need to hurt anyone anymore." Lily said from Tim's side.

"Have faith! Evil only has strength when there's fear in your heart!" Owen squeaked.

"Let them make peace. Then you can see your parents again." Gwen said. Connor shrank to his original size. Fionn's voice rang out, disembodied from Connor.

"Should you cast me out, our contract through Geis shall be broken, and you shall return to your state as I found you: starved and frozen to death."

"Then make a new contract." Elaine said. Connor nodded, returned to his normal size, muscles depleted.

"Give me some time to grow up first... until then, can you lay dormant? Fionn?" A long pause.

"... Very well... May you truly become the hero you seek..." the voice echoed distantly until it was no more. Connor staggered forward before collapsing. Elaine and I rushed to help him up—then Willy appeared—at my side as if he'd simply materialised there (though he probably just walked up without me noticing).

"Meet me at the museum when you get my sign." He said. I was about to answer him when Connor grabbed Willy's sleeve.

"Red... have you raised enough hell yet?" Willy chuckled and pulled away from us.

"Of course not!" He pointed to the ceiling. "BANG!" A blast of fire tore through the ceiling and into the sky. The revolutionaries cheered and charged outside as the British soldiers swarmed in. Gunfire rang out as I rushed to my knights.

"Come on, let's get everyone out." Rusty propped Tim up and dragged him out, Griffith close behind, out the back door. Willy reappeared beside who else but the prime minister himself amongst the smoke and debris!

"Go on and get your peace, David, sign a treaty." Willy

said to Lloyd George, "I've gotten my chat, and in the end, true justice will prevail." Who the hell did he think he was addressing him by his first name!? Willy tossed the prime minister in my direction, then disappeared into the smoke. I ushered him after the others, looking back at the carnage unfolding outside. No sign of Willy, save for a single flame burning what was once a carpet.

"Will... You better not burn my house down again."

Detective King

CHAPTER 27 — WILLY — TIRED OF HATE

The evening paper mentioned a gas explosion, a traffic jam, and the unfortunate passing of a Scotland Yard Chief Inspector. Though it was far from unexpected, I'd hoped they'd be able to report on my big fight. I sat down with a book in the British Museum Reading Room, or more precisely the OtherLondon version, which stretched up into an endless tower of bookshelves, with columns of tree trunks and soft yellow light filtering through rows of windows that snaked through the tower. Flowers grew around the chairs and little furry creatures maintained the library, wheeling around in carts, endlessly sorting books of every shape and size. One of them came up to me, with big brown eyes, enormous ears, and a cute tuft of fur on its head.

"How d'you know I lost interest in it?" I asked, holding up the book, which had billed itself as a mystery novel but muddied itself in some rather silly fantastical nonsense. The creature snatched the book in its jaws, displaying sharp rows of teeth. It snapped it so quickly I feared it was going to take my hand off—then it scurried off into some far off cranny of the library. As I watched it, someone slid into the seat behind mine, the chilling feeling she elicited in my heart when near gave away her identity. "We lost pretty badly, huh? Arthur and company taking down Connor like that. Isn't even in the papers."

"On the contrary, Red." Scarlett said, "We performed marvellously. They're afraid, and so they've silenced the media. It will only be a matter of time before we are out of the public conscious, but its subconscious... That is where we have struck a fatal blow. The living will become just as restless as the dead and the time for change will be upon us."

"You sound like a lunatic when you talk like that. So, you observed everything that's happened—is Arthur the one you're looking for—the bridge or whatever?"

"That's what I'd like to confirm tonight, if you'd allow me to join you."

"I was just going to mess with him, nothing spectacular."

"The boy entered OtherLondon unaided—we can't let any opportunity pass. He is her son after all."

"Don't talk in riddles, witch! What does she have to do with it?!" She leaned close to me and whispered in my ear.

"Pick something to steal tonight, and perhaps I'll tell you if you choose wisely."

"I hate you."

"Good, a devil should hate." She left me and I was alone with the library creatures and the monster inside me once again.

"I'm tired of hating..."

Too late for that. You've chosen your path. The demon said in my mind.

"You need me as your vessel. I hold the power here, not you. If I'm to be a devil, I'll be my own kind."

Then you will ruin yourself. Negative emotion drives the restless—it brings the world of the dead, the world humans fear most—closer to their realm. If you cannot stand it, you will go mad and I will claim control. It all depends on your strength.

"I'm plenty strong, even without you."

You could be stronger...

"How?"

By allowing yourself to hate. Give into your fear, your aggression, your lust, everything. Abandon this idea that everything will go back to the way things were when you were a child. For your own sake.

"If I do that, he's lost to me forever... I've not given up yet, I'm gonna get through the darkness and create a future of light for him, for everyone."

This is why I hate humans, and teenagers most of all—so idealistic, you romanticise everything. Makes me gag.

LionBolt

CHAPTER 28 — THE PAST

Back to the museum—my second home when I was young. My assumption was that Willy had one of two things in mind: trap me or mess with me. Either way, I couldn't let him go, not after everything he'd done. Naturally, I alerted my superiors, and the museum was surrounded by nightfall. I, however, entered alone with my knights (wouldn't want to scare him off). We entered the pristine marble lobby, the entrance to the circular reading room before us, with wings branching off in either direction.

"Okay, I was thinking we should split up in—" Owen and Lily ran off together, treating this like a school trip. "—pairs." I glanced at Gwen and shuffled my feet. "S-so Gwen, I-I was thinking the tttwo of us c-could..."

"AHEM." Elaine tugged at my arm. "It's no good to leave me on my own!" She dragged me closer to her. "Even if you're sweet on her, I'm still your assistant, right?" Thankfully, she didn't say it loud enough for Gwen to hear (if she had, I'd have found the nearest Otherworld and let myself get lost in it forever), but you can imagine the fierce look I gave my assistant.

"Actually, I think I'll patrol on my own, if that's alright." Gwen said, wandering off into a wing of the museum. I sighed, defeated in my chance at salvaging a decent evening with my sweet—I mean, my valued colleague... who am I kidding? You know I love her by now.

Elaine and I strolled through the rare coins and medals room, taking in the glittering artefacts behind glass cases. It wasn't a part of the museum I was particularly interested in, but Elaine seemed very intrigued.

"They're so beautiful! Hey what's in the next room?"

"I believe the Central American artefacts... but that's not important. If I were Willy, what would I be fixing to steal?"

"You're all work, Arthur. I've never been here before, let me explore. Why did Willy tell you to come here, anyway? Couldn't he just steal whatever he wanted without anyone knowing his plans?"

"He doesn't really care about anything in here—he just wants to mess with me. It's like a game to him— 'Can Arthur catch me before I make off with the loot?' It's not the first time he's challenged me like this." Elaine got close to the glass of a display and looked upon an artefact (a Roman medallion, if I'm not mistaken).

"Tell me about you two. What happened to make him... him?" I stood by the doorway, thinking over whether I should dodge the question again. I sighed.

"You deserve to hear the whole story, I guess. Just don't think less of me, okay?"

I was 8 years old. I'd gotten shoved into the snow by a group of other boys—nothing unusual for me. One of them kicked me in the back.

"Think yer smarter'n th'rest of us?" A common complaint.

"Bloody plonker!" The other said I wasn't sure what a plonker was, but I assumed it wasn't pleasant. Their words were mostly drowned out by the pain, as they kept kicking me until I started crying, when the kicking stopped. I was too afraid to look up, but the shadows on the snow showed the bullies getting attacked by another kid. That was new—was it a bigger bully looking to terrorise me, or had someone actually come to my rescue? A hand reached out, and I looked up tentatively. That was the first glimpse I got of Willy, standing there with a bloody nose and lip, and a goofy smile.

"C'mon, let's get outta here!" He said. I took his hand, and our friendship began. Willy had just transferred to my school, and neither of us had ever really had a friend. I loved reading and had an admittedly morbid obsession with crime stories (my father was John Watson, it was unavoidable). Other kids thought Willy had a scary face, and while it never came up between us, I suspected he'd been picked on for his skin colour, too. I say picked on, but Willy wasn't the sort to let anyone bully him, so most kids, including the bullies, feared him, leaving him an outcast. We were a perfect fit—we finally had someone to keep up with our intellects, and so we were inseparable.

When we were 10, a certain incident changed how I saw Willy, but it would be some time before anything became of it. We were walking home, in a fine mood as the term had ended and we were to be on break.

"'He sent his arrow flying, striking the king's sack of gold!'" I read from a little copy of Robin Hood, in a most dramatic, over-the-top delivery.

"Yes! You're quite the showman, Arty, you should be an actor."

"Right, we skipped two grades so we could recite Shakespeare for a living. Besides, I'm too shy."

"Ah, you can get over that. For me, I'd rather be like the characters in the story, fightin' for good an' takin' names!" I laughed and bumped him on the head with the book.

"Even if it makes you a criminal? Robin Hood is a thief after all." Willy shrugged, stopping by the gate of his house.

"I'd say doin' what's right is more important than

followin' the law." Willy's father then appeared at the door. He was definitely younger than my father (though Dad had his children later than most). Willy's father walked with a cane, as he'd been injured in the Boer War. He was balding, quiet, and I'd heard next to nothing of his wife, but I figured it better not to pry.

"Willy! Don't just stand out there—invite your friend in!" Willy opened the gate and beckoned me to follow.

"Good day, Arthur." Mr. Manders said with a cheerful smile.

"G-good day, Mr. Garland." All will be answered in time.

The house was a fine one—the parlour being decorated in relics of the Boer War, from rifles, to an army helmet, and even a lion's skin (though I had my doubts as to its authenticity). Willy's dad limped to the coffee table and lifted the lid on a platter, revealing an assortment of biscuits and sweets.

"Help yourselves!" He said. I nibbled on a biscuit, trying to get past my anxiety.

"What's wrong, Art? You always seem... off at my house. Although I guess you're always a bit off."

"Am not. I just can't quite figure it out. Your dad's a journalist, right?"

"Yeah, what of it?" We got up and ascended a steep carpeted staircase, roofed by a colourful stained glass window.

"Well, based on general salaries for his field, he shouldn't be able to afford a house like this unless he's rather famous."

"There you go thinking about everything like you're Sherlock Holmes."

"How else am I supposed to succeed him?" We reached the top of the staircase and, as I followed Willy to his room, I noticed the door to his dad's room was open. My curiosity overtook me, and I took a peek inside. There I halted—like I'd seen a ghost. I stood speechless for a moment as I gazed upon a cigarette box sitting atop a small table. I picked it up and inspected it.

LionBolt

"What're you doing?" Willy said, poking his head into the room.

"I remember hearing about an old unsolved case, where a pair of thieves stole a trove of jewellery by hiding them in a cigarette box." Willy grabbed my arm and led me down the hall to his room.

"Alright, enough crime fiction for today! I wanna destroy you in chess!" I looked back, still troubled by the old cigarette box, but left it be and followed Willy into his room. I didn't bring it up again, but it bothered me in the back of my mind for years after. There was something he wasn't telling me, some secret he kept hidden. I knew that box, and the Boer War veterans it was associated with, it all added up. I was too smart for my own good, and it would soon kill our friendship in the worst way possible.

Every summer I went down to my family's vacation house in Surrey, and while the war was on and London faced bomb raids from German zeppelins, Willy would join us on summer holiday—an arrangement we were more than happy with. It's an area with more trees than people, and while there was a town a few minute's walk down the road, we were left in the tranquillity of nature, with a wide field spreading around the stone house, which was then surrounded by forest. We could still hear the faint sounds of war, whether in London or across the channel, and those far away sounds were frightening to me, but some of my fondest memories came from those summer days in the country. I was never an athletic person, but Willy would sometimes convince me to put down my books and play with him outside, chasing each other in the field, exploring the woods, or swimming in the deep pond at the forest's edge. The earthy scent of the grass was invigorating, especially after rain. It happened during one of those summers, when we were 12. We arrived out of breath at the pond, having raced each other across the field. The sun shined brilliantly through the leaves above us, and cicadas sang in a symphony all around. Willy lost the race, arriving just after me. I lied down on the grass and raised a fist in triumph, while Willy put his hand on his knees and panted.

"You almost got me…" I said, "you're getting faster, Will." Even though he was easily more fit than I, he never once beat me in a race (perhaps it was all the running from bullies and criminals I'd already done at that young age).

"You're getting slower 'cause you're always inside reading." I sat up and took off my shoes and socks.

"And what do you do all day? I've noticed you getting into fights recently." He looked unconcerned as he undid his shirt.

"Sometimes it feels good to let loose on someone. Nothin' really wrong with it so long as you don't go too far." Willy flashed me a mischievous look and shoved me into the water. I emerged, sputtering, my clothes soaking wet. Willy stood at the shore laughing. I growled and grabbed Willy's ankle, pulling him into the water with a splash. We laughed and splashed each other until a shadow appeared over us.

"Boys…" My mother looked distraught. I'd never seen her with such a sad expression, "come back to the house… something's happened." She was looking at Willy when she spoke, puzzling still.

When dad broke the news, I stayed silent. I tried not to look at Willy, at the anguish on his face. My parents left us and Willy rested his head on the arms of an armchair, gazing distantly at nothing. He probably wouldn't see his father outside a prison until he was of university age.

"At least… you get to stick around here longer." I said from a nearby couch. He glared at me, and I averted my eyes. "Y'know… if your dad did something wrong… if he broke the law… shouldn't he pay the price?" Willy sat up and turned toward me swiftly.

"How could you say that!? So what if my dad stole stuff in the past? He's not a bad person."

"Yeah, but… to lie about who he was for so long… did you

know about all of it?”

"I knew some. Like how his real name is Manders, and how my real parents died and left everything to him." I stood, shocked at my friend.

"And you were fine with that? He's a criminal!"

"But he's still my dad! Only one I ever knew at least..." It's painful to say, but I left him then. My sense of justice was too strong. I couldn't accept his attitude, even if it was his own father.

"You'll be better off without him." I said at the doorway, then I went up to our room and our relationship was never the same.

Willy stayed as part of our family for over half a year after that, sometimes it was alright, there were even times we were able to laugh together like before, but a constant weight dragged us down in the back of our minds, and as time passed it became more painful, despite our efforts to paper over it. Then my mother died.

I was sitting at the bottom of the stairs, back in our regular house. In the days after she passed, I didn't want to do anything or talk to anyone, like I'd fallen in a dark well and couldn't pull myself out. Willy came down the stairs, walking around me.

"Hey. How do I stop it from hurting so much? What do I do?!" It was perhaps the first time I'd spoken to him in a week. I was desperate for something, some rope to pull me out of the well.

"Figure it out yourself. I haven't had a family for a while now, at least you still have yours." I buried my face in my arms. A sack slung over Willy's shoulder, and he opened the front door.

"Where are you going?"

"I can't stand it here any longer. I belong on the streets. It's the legacy I've inherited after all, right?" He started walking out, but paused and looked back. "Do I have to be alone, Arthur?" I glared at him with spite.

Detective King

"Yes. You know I was right to turn him in. Now go off and become him." I tried to maintain my scowl, I tried to hate him with all my being—but he looked so devastated.

"I wanted to be wrong. But I guess I ended up being right about you." I thought I saw tears in his eyes as he turned away from me and softly shut the door. That was the last I saw of him outside the newspapers until he tried to steal The Blue Carbuncle from the British Museum, about a month before the missing children's case[10].

Elaine and I walked down a marble staircase, where Elaine stared at me, confounded.

"Why did you turn Willy's dad in?"

"I was blinded by justice. By turning him in, I laid the groundwork for my admittance into the detective academy, though it took them almost two years to gather the evidence to arrest him. He's still in prison, but since he pleaded guilty, he'll be out in a couple years."

"Well, if I didn't know better, I'd say Willy was the victim here."

"Maybe so, my father thought so too..."

I didn't realise what had happened at first, it was so sudden and unexpected. I thought he'd be proud, that he'd praise me and make me feel better—instead, my cheek stung from the strike of his palm. An explanation wasn't to be found in his expression—a mix of anger and sadness I couldn't understand.

"Arthur!" He spoke louder and more fiercely than I'd ever heard him speak before. "How could you do such a thing?!"

---

[10] I could've sworn my notes for that case were somewhere...

LionBolt

How could I not? Was all I could think.

"H-he was a criminal, it was justice-"

"Justice? That's not justice! All you did was tear apart a family and hurt your friend!"

"But he was a thief! Sherlock Holmes would've-"

"MY friend would have never done such a thing without purpose. Was Mr. Manders hurting anyone? Did he continue to steal? Did Willy need his father? The law is the law, but the law itself is not necessarily justice. Rather, when the law is applied to help, protect, or comfort victims or innocents, that is justice. Even Sherlock Holmes and myself were sometimes outside of the law, you know. In the case of Charles Augustus Milverton..."

"I'm familiar, and I've always been troubled by it. You burgled and let a man get murdered. The law protects all— even those who don't deserve it—and condemns all wrong-doers, even when it's cruel. That's justice." My father shook his head and sighed.

"At any rate, there's not much to be done now, except to apologise to poor Willy." I could not believe the words coming out of my father's mouth. He had dedicated a life to justice, to the upholding of the law, of social order, for him to defend a criminal!

"N-never. I did the right thing. It should be Willy who apologises for lying to me for so long." My father sighed and sat down in his chair, looking tired.

"How have you gone so astray? Your mother and I taught you to use your talents for good, but somewhere along the way, 'good' became confused. I'm sorry, Arthur." I felt sick.

"You're one to talk about justice." I said, with a dark, angry feeling boiling inside me. "You were so absorbed in your adventures, in reliving your glory days in Afghanistan and Baker Street that you were always away while mum was dying. In the end you're just a bystander, and you stood by and let her die-"

Another slap.

Detective King

"Not another word, boy."

"I saw you." I said. "It was a long time ago, but I saw you, with that woman." At this, he grew silent for a long while.

"What on earth are you talking about?"

"Don't play dumb! You were with some woman with blonde hair! I saw you!"

"N-no, that... I only dreamed that, I'm sure of it." He was more speaking to himself. "I dreamed Mary returned to me, you couldn't possibly have..."

I'd seen enough—I took a sheet of paper out of my pocket and put it on the table in front of him. It was an application to a faraway boarding school (a prerequisite for joining the detective academy early).

"I wasn't sure I wanted to go here, but I don't have any reason to stay anymore. Sign it."

"Arthur..."

"Just sign it, so we never have to speak again." I stormed out, leaving my father a broken man.

—❦—

I sat on the bottom stair with Elaine, the vast lobby of the museum expanded before us.

"And that catches you up. I spent two years at boarding school, then back to London for detective training, the youngest police student ever, at 14."

"Do you still think you did the right thing? With Willy, and your dad?"

"I'll admit I didn't handle things as well as I should've, but I wasn't necessarily wrong either."

"Who was the woman you saw him with?"

"I don't know—he claimed it was a vision of his first wife, Mary Morstan—but at the time I thought it was a ridiculous lie. Now that I know ghosts and such are real, I'm not sure what to make of it."

A shout made us jump, and we rushed to our feet as the shouting continued from inside the reading room. It sounded like Lily and Owen.

CHAPTER 29 — ONE LAST BATTLE

The Reading Room is a large circular library with scores of books and study spaces, all under a grand dome, lined with tall windows along its sides and at its apex. It's quite a sight any day, but even more so when you witness a flurry of books flying about. In the centre of the massive chamber, amid this blizzard of pages, was Willy, sitting most casually with an open book. Owen stood between him and Lily, his cross raised.

"'Bout time you got here! Goodness." Willy said, closing the book.

"You said the museum, not the library." I said.

"Same difference. Both are evidence of the bourgeois poison gripping the w—"

"Oh, shut up already! That's not what this is about, and you know it." He stood up, one hand gripping his book, the other stuffed in his pocket. His smile was so serene.

"Yeah, I know. I wanted to see'ya, Arty. Stealing something is just a part of the fun."

"And what are you stealing?" He held up the book.

"Just this, nothing fancy." Elaine strode past Owen until she was right in front of Willy, her arms crossed.

"Arthur told me about... everything. I understand how

you felt—abandoned. But if you just talk to each other—"

"I tried that. And what do you think Arthur's answer was?" I looked down. Guess I didn't tell her *everything*.

"Th-that's in the past." I said, "You can change, I won't turn my back this time!"

"*I* can change?! You turned me in like you did my dad. You were my only friend, and you betrayed me, over and over again. Now you wanna talk?"

"I was a fool to throw away our friendship. I know that now. But I'm chained by my responsibilities. Now even more so. Still, I can't stand to see you like this, so—"

"It's all about you, huh? You don't think I have responsibilities? I never wanted to get mixed up in all this, but I'm still me—and I'm going to fulfil my responsibilities to myself, even if you don't understand it." Searching for words, I wasn't able to stop Owen from charging forward past Elaine, swinging with his cross with a yell.

"We don't have to understand you! You killed Father Michael and helped turn me into..." Willy blocked it with his arm, then something grabbed him by the robe and flung him backward and high in the air. Scarlett stepped out of OtherLondon and held up a book. When Owen fell back down, the book sucked him in! Lily screamed, and to my horror, she charged at the witch. She sucked Lily into the book too, then closed it.

"What did you do to them!?" I asked before a twinge of chest pain, and that shortness of breath struck. It couldn't be... "Elaine... open the door, would you?" She looked confused, but she did as I asked. Beyond the door was... nothing, just a void. "I thought so... we're in an Otherworld." As I spoke, something wrapped around Elaine's leg and dragged her out into the void. I ran to the door to see that same serpent that attacked us in the park. I felt an icy sting on my cheek as a pale hand slide onto it. A cool breeze blew on my ear as Scarlett put her clutches around me.

"Hello Arthur. Have you figured out who I am, about the

truth of your mother?" I wanted to speak, but I could only gasp. My insides felt like they were on fire. Finally, I was able to muster a response—

"I know you're not human—that you and your horsemen are collecting spirits to stage attacks like today's and take down our country as your 'revenge on God'. You've been at this for a long time, right?"

"I have."

"So then... did you start the flu? Did you kill my mother with a spirit or demon?" She laughed softly, then pushed me into the void. As I fell, I looked back at her—her face so similar to my mother's, and the expression she wore perplexed me—it was of sadness. Her lips in a frown, her eyes sagged, and I thought I saw a tear. The doors began to close, and I heard a roar that I assumed was that of the serpent's spirit. I closed my eyes, the pain was so unbearable, this damned ghost sense or whatever you want to call it—it reminded me of when I fainted at the park, over two months earlier, like I was being swallowed by pain and darkness, nothing I could do to stop it. Then I felt a hand grasp mine. I opened my eyes and saw Willy pulling me into the light, the doors being propped open by a hastily thrown chair. I couldn't hear what he was saying, but he had a smile on his face. Heat permeated nearby— warming me after I feared freezing in the void—the fire came from Willy's hand, his eyes glowing yellow. He was aiming below us, and when I followed his line of fire, I saw the serpent was seconds from snapping down on me before Willy's attack. *Elaine...* I was regaining my consciousness and soon I was floundering about, desperate to catch sight of Elaine.

"I think she's been eaten..." Willy said, though he sounded far away despite being right beside me. He led me closer to the light, but I couldn't leave Elaine. I called out to her, reaching out to the serpent as it struggled against Willy's fire, my other hand was grasped onto Willy, grappling as he tried to get me into the Reading Room—the doors slowly crushing the chair. In our struggle, something popped out of his shirt, something silver and round. I grabbed it by instinct and as soon as I did—the black void turned white, with sparkles of different colours floating around. Willy's fire ceased as the serpent, which I could now see clearly in all its massive glory—was shuddering and contorting (perhaps from the light). Pieces of it started flaking off, and its screech was enough to send even the hardiest running for the hills. It lunged for us in a final attack, its enormous wings flapping as they fell apart and its jaw open wide—when it stopped, before Willy or I could do a thing. It shrivelled and turned grey, and a white light became visible from within its depths. Elaine emerged from its jaws and jumped into my arms. I let go of Willy and we spun around with each other for a long moment.

"You didn't leave me." She said.

"I'd never abandon my assistant."

"I kicked it good from inside! Think that's what stopped it?"

"Might be..." I looked back, and to my astonishment, the world was a black void once again, though the serpent was nowhere to be seen. Willy took my hand again, and we shoved through the door as the propping chair split into splinters. We were sprawled on the floor together, and I couldn't help but laugh, I think from relief more than anything. "Will, thank you." He'd started laughing too.

"Why do you think I've been working so hard, hm? I could easily steal some big-cheese fortune and retire to an island somewhere, but that'd be boring without you by my side! We might not agree on the small stuff yet, but you're still my mate." We smirked at each other, then he helped me up. Scarlett sat reading a book, in much the same fashion Willy was when we first entered this trap.

"Very interesting. You show more and more promise, Arthur." She said.

"Promise in what?!"

Detective King

"Arthur—we don't need to be enemies—I've committed no crime on my own, indeed what authority does an officer of the law have to chase after a denizen of another world, with its own law? I want to create a world without pain, inequality, or even death—you could see your mother again, Arthur. You may be the key to unlocking such a world."

"You're insane. Even if I believed you, I couldn't build such a world using your methods. What's more..." I pointed at her and flashed my badge. "I'm going to arrest you and bring you to justice, no matter the world." She closed her book and stood, giving a curt bow.

"Then I look forward to the chase. I'll make sure our friends at The Yard put in a good word for you, after all—no one gets promoted without some influence." She tossed the book at me, and while I missed it, Elaine caught it. Scarlett flashed a glare at Willy and jerked her head for him to come along.

"Wait, this is my choice." He said, holding up a book. "Answer my question from before—what was so special about Rose?" My mother? He was holding up The Legend of King Arthur. Scarlett turned away.

"She stole something from me that was very precious." What could she have stolen? An object? Like a locket? Or perhaps a person? Scarlett disappeared into OtherLondon and the pressure of the ghost sense eased. Elaine opened the book, and we saw Lily and mouse Owen on the pages—they were in a house that appeared to be flooding in a scene from early in *Alice in Wonderland*.

"Help!" Lily sounded as if she were speaking through a telephone. "Not much space before we hit the ceiling!"

"H-how do we get you out?" I looked around, my eyes landing on Willy's locket. "The locket... it worked before..." Willy looked hesitant, but took it off and handed to me—only for it to do nothing.

"Come on!" Owen's snout was barely above water. I got frustrated and turned the book around in different ways (maybe I could spill them out). No effect—then I turned the page—and they were in a garden, gasping for breath. I shouted in triumph.

"Don't celebrate yet, we're still in here." Lily said. I turned to the last page—where Alice wakes up, and as I did, they sprang out from the page, Lily dressed in a gown reminiscent of the illustrations in the book, while Owen returned as a human wearing his robes as he had been before. The book also spit out his cross, which knocked him on the head. Elaine and I embraced both of them.

"I'm sorry. I put you all in danger."

"Arthur, we chose to come here with you." Lily said.

"I was reckless and charged without thinking." Owen said. Willy turned from us and started walking away, but I called out to him and tossed him his locket.

"Are you sure? It's yours to begin with." He said.

"It's a gift, so long as you promise to give it back if I ever need it again." He grinned and saluted, then he jumped unnaturally high to one of the windows, which he pried open and slipped out from. Perhaps it would prove to be a mistake, giving him the locket back—but it didn't sit right, taking it back like that. I wanted the gold one Scarlett took, and I was only now beginning to realise how valuable it really was.

With that last battle behind us, we met up with Gwen and explained what happened. She apologised for not being there numerous times, but curiously, she kept dodging when asked where she was. I had complete faith in her, of course, but I was reminded of how she lied about the vision from the well. It was a slight doubt in my mind, but one that stuck with me, despite my better judgement.

Detective King

CHAPTER 30 — RECOVERY AND EPILOGUE

I held a newspaper, my leg shaking up and down (as is a habit of mine), as I flipped through the pages.

"Oh, this one's Violet's..." I said to myself. We were in a hallway outside a hospital room (not my favoured venue for an afternoon). Elaine, Lily, and Gwen sat beside me, all looking tired from the previous day's adventures. Owen hopped on my lap (which stopped my leg shaking) and looked at the paper with me.

"Why aren't they mentioning everything that happened yesterday? It's all about the treaty that got signed."

"They must've put a gag order on the media. They don't want people to panic, as if that's going to work." I turned at the sound of footsteps—Hopkins, Gregson, and Rusty approached and stopped at the door before us. They all looked tired, but Rusty seemed on the verge of falling to pieces. He knelt beside Lily and took her hand.

"Thank you. I don't understand everything that happened but... You and your brother saved Tim's life."

"I just did what I could... he must mean a lot to you." He

nodded. Hopkins shook my hand graciously.

"We've heard of your heroics during the incident, Watson."

"Well, it was mostly Gwen here who—" A door opened, and a nurse appeared. She gestured for everyone to enter the room. In the spacious, very white room were two beds—Sam laying closer to the window, Tim in the other. Sam smiled and attempted to wave as everyone gathered in but winced and put his hand down. Tim raised his head slightly and made a weak smile. Rusty and Lily sat by Tim's side.

"Hey, Tim. How're you doing?" Rusty said. "This here is Lily, she saved your life." She smiled and waved meekly.

"Hello. Nice to meet you. All I did was stop the bleeding."

"But they said had he lost much more, he would've..." Rusty's voice croaked and trailed. Tim reached out his remaining hand and touched Lily's.

"You're Watson's sister, right? Heh. Imagine that. I guess I owe you my life." Hopkins and Gregson stood between the beds. Hopkins clapped and brought everyone to attention.

"Alright! I know you all want to extend your well-wishes, but business first. First, you should know that I've been appointed as the late Chief's replacement." That's a big promotion. Gregson clapped sarcastically.

"Yep, not the choice I would've made, of course, but..."

"AHEM. As Chief Inspector of the precinct, I've decided to reward the bravery of you fine boys. Tim, you've been made a full Detective Constable. Congratulations." Rusty looked overjoyed, while Tim gave a weak smile. "Tristan, I've put you on a fast track. You'll be serving under Gregson here alongside Rusty. You two should make DC around the same time next year." Sam nodded, looking pleased.

"Thank you for the opportunity, sir." Then Hopkins handed me a letter.

"And for Second Class Detective Sergeant Arthur Watson." I was dumbstruck. I took the letter, my hand shaking.

Detective King

"Th-thank you, sir." Tim laughed softly, causing everyone to turn to him.

"How long has it been, two months since you made DC? The funny thing of it is you deserve it... unlike me."

"Tim..." Rusty reached out to him, but Tim shrugged him away and turned his head from us.

"I decline the promotion and intend to step down from the force."

"What?! Tim, no—"

"I... I aided the enemy... While I didn't have full control over my actions, I still gave them a map... of the postal tunnels... and they used it to..." The nurse stepped into the room and hurried to Tim's side.

"Perhaps the patient needs some time alone. I'll fetch a wheelchair for mister Tristan." We were ushered out of the room, with Sam wheeled out with us. The door closed on a broken Tim Dartmouth, broken in more ways than one. Rusty looked devastated, and for a moment he turned back to the door like he was going to barge back in there, but Lily took his hand and shook her head. He nodded and followed us to the hospital courtyard, where there was a circle of benches under a tree that could be seen out Sam's window. The sun glinted off the freshly fallen snow, and a freezing gust of wind reminded us that winter had arrived. Hopkins and Gregson tipped their hats as the rest of us sat down.

"We should be going, anyway. We'll talk to Tim when the time is right." Hopkins said.

"And I look forward to working with you from now on, Mr. Tristan." Gregson said, as they departed. Rusty followed them out, taking a last glance at the window of Tim's room. An uneasy silence gripped us as we watched them leave.

"So... how are your injuries, Sam?" Gwen asked, breaking the silence. He winced as he rubbed his shoulder.

"Eh, I'll be okay. They said I'll be out of here in a few days. But damn..." He crossed his arms, wincing more. "I should've been able to beat that bastard. How did he get like that?"

"His choices are his own but, I should've been there for him when he needed me." I said, thinking about the previous night. I owed my life to Willy, as did Elaine, Lily, and Owen. He wasn't evil, or anything close, just on a wrong path.

"H-hey, you never opened the letter." Elaine said, breaking my thoughts. I opened the envelope and drew out the letter, which I dropped with a yelp when I read the first line.

"Um... can someone else read it for me? I-it might be too much for me." Gwen picked it up and read.

"From the Office of the Prime Minister. In light of the incidents of the fifth December, it is my assessment, based on testimony and personal experience, that the actions of William Manders and the group identified as 'horsemen' pose a real and pressing threat to national security. As such, I am commissioning a dedicated Military Intelligence investigation into the matter. Due to his personal connection to Manders, Arthur Watson, DS, Second Class, is to conduct his own investigation on the issue. Any and all resources and personnel he sees necessary are to be afforded to him, and only cases which hold some sort of connection to the investigation are to be assigned to him. Detective Watson shall be expected to give regular reports to Military Intelligence and is to be directly supervised and assisted by Chief Inspector Stanley Hopkins. Assignments will be at Inspector Hopkins' discretion. Signed: Right Honourable David Lloyd George, Prime Minister of the United Kingdom."

Gwen put the letter down, and I slowly grinned as Sam put his arm around me.

"Ow. Congrats, Art! Ow."

"Y-yeah. Heh. Any resources or personnel I want, huh? I guess I'll be ordering you all around a lot more often." In essence, it was exactly what I wanted—respect and acknowledgement. The prime minister himself had honoured me and given me a position of authority and respect. Was this it? Was I on the path to my crown as Detective King? It was a mix of emotions, and it would take a while to process it all. As the others conversed amongst each other, I walked off on my own, thinking over all the strange things that'd happened over the past two months. Elaine tapped my shoulder.

"What'cha thinking about, looking so serious? I thought you'd be happy."

"I am. It's just... there's so much I still need to do. This is just one step. I still have a long road ahead of me."

"Well, I'll be here to help you along. Speaking of which, I heard *he* was at this hospital too."

He was indeed at this hospital—his hair was now a mix of ginger and white, and one hand was handcuffed to the bedpost, but Connor sat there looking cheerful, a book on his lap. His face lit up with a wide grin when he saw us.

"Arthur! Hey, look at this!" I was surprised how warm a welcome I'd got and leaned over his shoulder to see an illustration of a certain two famous Victorian gentlemen. "This is your dad, isn't it? Doctor John Watson?" I groaned.

"Yeah, that's him. Have you taken an interest in British literature, or criminal investigation?"

"No, just in you. So what brings ya here?" I'll never understand this boy. I sat down at his bedside.

"I'd like to ask you a few questions."

"About the horsemen? Or about Fionn? Or are you just concerned about me?" He spoke so rapid-fire, I struggled to keep up.

"All the above, I guess. Who are the horsemen, and what do they aim to accomplish?" He closed the book and grinned with mischief.

"And what do I get in return?" He jangled his handcuff. "My wrist's gettin' sore, and I've got questions of my own. Deal?" I looked to Elaine, who shrugged and nodded.

LionBolt

"Handcuffs come later, but I'll tell you whatever you wanna know... within reason."

Connor was very informative, telling me the mysterious woman who controlled Tim was code named White and another horseman the others witnessed during the Battle of the Treaty (as I termed it), was code named Black. The government had apparently confiscated his key to OtherLondon, and while I could theoretically get it, it would be a long process. He told me alternatively he heard of non-magic users possessing a map to OtherLondon's entrance, a lead I'd investigate thoroughly.

I sat at the dinner table surrounded by my knights—Lily and Owen smiling at each other (they'd got rather friendly as of late—I wondered why), Gwen winking at me, causing a flutter in my heart, Sam was raucous and glad he'd been discharged, and my assistant Elaine, who so rudely barged into my life was there to stay, my ghostly apprentice and dear friend. We still had a long way to go—I wanted to learn more about Otherworlds and OtherLondon, and to expose Scarlett's secrets and bring her to justice. Lastly, I was certain Willy would sit at this table with us someday and complete our round table (it wasn't really round, but you know what I mean).

"Arthur, quit looking all sentimental. Your food's getting cold." Elaine said as she ate off my plate.

"Oh, you're a ghost, how can you eat so much?!"

"It's because I'm a ghost! I don't get hungry, but I don't get full either." She took some more of my food, leading to an (admittedly pathetic) skirmish for a forkful of chicken.

I'm stuck with this girl, aren't I? Well, guess it's better than when I was alone. A meal's much less appetising when you don't have to fight for it.

Thus closes the first chapter in the legend of the Detective King. The next would be ever more strange, supernatural, and fantastic—wrought with wonders and tragedies.

END OF BOOK I

LionBolt

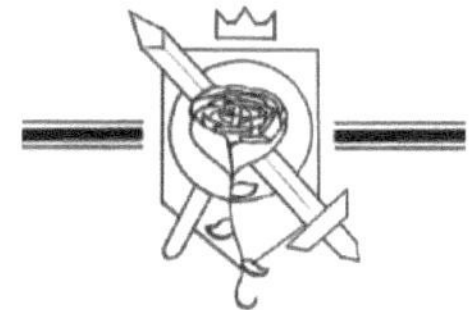

Thank you for reading! I hope you enjoyed it and will continue to support the series. Please consider leaving a **review**—it's the number one way to help the book gain traction!

If you haven't yet, you can get a free prologue short story exclusive to my newsletter at dk.lionboltkingdom.com

You can support me by joining my Patreon or Ko-fi campaigns (new short stories every month and 10% goes to charity, both under the name LionBolt) and subscribing to my YouTube channel—LionBolt Books and Animation.

You can also follow me @LionBolt1921 on Twitter and Instagram.

More books coming soon, Audiobook version too! Spread the word, ask your library to carry the book, tell your friends. Thanks again!

—LionBolt

9 780578 359816